A LADY'S AGREEMENT

UNEXPECTED HEIRS  OF SCOTLAND

Also available from
Terri Brisbin

UNEXPECTED HEIRS OF SCOTLAND series:
The Lady Takes It All
A Lady's Agreement

A HIGHLAND FEUDING Series:
Stolen by the Highlander
The Highlander's Runaway Bride
Kidnapped by the Highland Rogue
Claiming His Highland Bride
A Healer for the Highlander
The Highlander's Inconvenient Bride – crossover with
the CLAN MACLERIE series
Her Highlander for One Night

The MACKENDIMEN CLAN Series:
A Love Through Time
Once Forbidden
A Highlander's Hope (novella)
A Matter of Time

WARRIORS OF THE STONE CIRCLES Series:
Rising Fire
Raging Sea
Blazing Earth

The STORM Series:
A Storm of Passion
A Storm of Love (novella)
A Storm of Pleasure
Mistress of the Storm

The DUMONT Series:
The Dumont Bride
The Norman's Bride
The Countess Bride
Love at First Step (novella)
The King's Mistress
The Claiming of Lady Joanna (novella)

The CLAN MACLERIE Series:
Taming the Highlander
Surrender to the Highlander
Possessed by the Highlander
Taming The Highland Rogue
The Highlander's Stolen Touch
The Forbidden Highlander (novella)
At The Highlander's Mercy
The Highlander's Dangerous Temptation
Yield to The Highlander
The Highlander's Inconvenient Bride – crossover with A
Highland Feuding series!
Related stories (same clan 500 years later)
The Earl's Secret
Blame It On The Mistletoe in ONE CANDLELIT
CHRISTMAS

STAND-ALONE STORIES:
The Queen's Man
The Duchess's Next Husband
The Maid of Lorne
Kidnapping the Laird (short story)
What The Duchess Wants – for newsletter
subscribers only!
Upon A Misty Skye
Across A Windswept Isle
A Traitor's Heart in BRANDYWINE BRIDES
The Storyteller – A Ghosts of Culloden Moor (novella)
An Outlaw's Honor ~ A Midsummer Knights romance
Tempted by Her Viking Enemy
The Highlander's Substitute Wife (HIGHLAND
ALLIANCES series)

The KNIGHTS of BRITTANY Series:
A Night for Her Pleasure (short story)
The Conqueror's Lady
The Mercenary's Bride
His Enemy's Daughter

A LADY'S AGREEMENT

A Lady's Agreement

Copyright © 2025 Theresa S. Brisbin

This story was previously published by Dragonblade Publishing and is now republished by the author through Luckenbooth Press.

Cover Design by Dar Albert
WickedSmartDesigns.com

Formatting by Nina Pierce
Nina@NinaPierce.com

ISBN: 978-1-949425-17-8

This one is for my friend, wonderful writer and travel mate Madeline Hunter. We spent three weeks driving and sightseeing and visiting museums and castles and ruins all over Scotland and we're still friends – that says a lot! (Especially since I did the driving!)

This one is for you, Madeline

ACKNOWLEDGEMENTS

I am embarrassed to say that I left out some very important people in the acknowledgement section when this book and THE LADY TAKES IT ALL were originally published by Dragonblade Publishing.

When I was trying to come up with titles for the books in their series, I turned to my Maine-NJ-TX romance writers group and they came through for me! In addition to the titles, they also helped me hone the conflicts in the stories, too.

So – HUGE thanks to Cara Carnes, Delsora Lowe, Michelle Libby, Mo Boylan, Luanna Stewart, and Kathy McVicars for all of your help and support, not just with this series but with the many ups and downs in my writing life.

PROLOGUE

Glasgow, Scotland
1788 AD

"I gave ye a simple task t' do and ye failed."

The blow that took him to his knees was not a surprise, for he watched the hand fist and then felt the blow on his head. Freddie understood the rules of the street and knew who was the boss here. And he knew his own position, too. But that second punch, the one that landed him face-first against the slimy cobblestones, was unexpected. "Not once, but 'twa times."

The taste of the mud and filth of the street never changed. It certainly never improved—no matter the amount of rain that washed down from the clouds—and, thank the Almighty for a small favor, it never got worse. As he spat out a mouthful and pushed up to his feet, Freddie wiped the back of his hand across his face to clear it away.

The tang of horse shite, cow dung, piss, and a mixture of discarded filthy, used water and refuse yet filled his mouth so he spat again. This one was aimed at the foot of the hulking yet stupid man who'd knocked him down the first two times. Old Baxter did the boss's dirty work and now he raised his fists and took a step towards Freddie, as the man who ran the gang that controlled this part of the Glasgow streets, bawdy houses, and cutpurses stood in the shadows watching. Albert Sanders stared out of those dead black eyes and nodded. His cronies encircled Baxter and Freddie.

He'd seen this before. Hell, he'd done this before.

It would not end well for him.

"I amno' a bairn-killer," he said quietly.

It had taken Freddie the successful completion of hundreds and hundreds of sordid, questionable, illegal, dangerous acts on Sanders' orders over the last five years since the man grabbed him off the street and took him in to discover he actually did have a limit.

And he'd reached it with this latest order.

A whispered order from Sanders stopped Old Baxter in place, but that gave Freddie no sense of comfort, for the glint of fury that filled the bigger man's eyes screamed out the danger. He'd seen men lose control of their bodies and shite themselves when Old Baxter gave them that look. Freddie must still have some sense of self-protection within himself for he felt like doing just that right now. His stomach clenched and his mouth went dry.

"Ye are what I make ye to be, Freddie. Ye should not forget that," Sanders said. "I think ye need a reminder of just who ye are and who ye work for." He nodded at Old Baxter who clenched his fists as he moved one step closer. "If I tell ye to lift a purse or pilfer a house or a gent, ye do as yer told."

Another step as tension grew around him. Not just tension, but excitement in those watching and waiting. Blood lust that smelled just like arousal filled the damp, close air around him.

"If I tell ye to bugger someone or be buggered, ye will be buggered." Freddie tried to swallow but could not. Old Baxter took another step. "If I tell ye to kill anyone, ye kill them."

The punisher was within an arm's reach now and Freddie tried to prepare for what was coming. But he really could not. He'd seen the man's work before and did not believe for a moment that he could withstand the pain coming his way.

"Take him down a peg, boys. Remind him of his place."

His dogs unleashed, Sanders stepped away from the gang, as he usually did, to watch with his cold eyes.

Sometime later, the strangest thought occurred to Freddie as he lay face down again in the muck of the Glasgow street. Unable to see, his eyes swollen shut from the blows, he tried to lift his mouth out of the puddle where he'd landed. Certain that his nose, his jaw, several ribs, and his left arm were broken, the laugh that escaped him at the momentary realization sounded like the cackling of a raving lunatic. And mayhap he was out of his mind from the pain.

It was different now.

The taste of the sludge was different now.

Blood, his blood, had changed it. Another laugh turned into a gurgling choke as his mouth filled with it all.

And, on that dark night, as Freddie lay in the street, bleeding out from the vicious beating, he swore that no one would ever lay a hand on him again. That he would answer to no one. That he would be the one giving the orders. He would choose who to kill or bugger or steal from.

All he needed to do was to survive this. And to escape Sanders.

For that, Freddie Dubh would have to die.

And so he did just that.

ONE

Leith, Scotland
September 1815 AD

"Lady Clare! Lady Clare!"

Clare turned towards the excited young voice and smile. A boy of about six approached, holding out his small board for her inspection.

"What is this, Robbie?" she asked, positioning the boy's chalk-covered piece of slate so she could more easily see it.

"'Tis a perfect letter B, Lady Clare!" The boy beamed at his declaration. "Even Mr. MacLaurin said it is!"

Clare Logan, formerly Lady Clare Napier, eldest daughter of the Earl of Heath, straightened up and nodded at the boy. She'd tried, unsuccessfully at that, to have them call her by her married, now widowed, name. She stopped objecting because here it did not matter a bit. Glancing across the small sea of faces in the classroom, she smiled.

"Well, if Mr. MacLaurin said that it is, then it must be so, Robbie." She patted the boy on the shoulder and gave him a small push towards the seat in the second row. "Excellent work, I see." She slowly walked the aisles, examining each boy's attempts to master writing their alphabet. Considering their circumstances and their late arrival into education, they were making so much progress.

"I shall have Mrs. Inglis send along a small treat to reward you all for these excellent efforts," she said. The boys cheered, for the cook's treats were well-known. "If that is allowed, Mr. MacLaurin?" The young man teaching the boys here at the Logan School for Orphans and Unfortunates was a kind man and she did not doubt his answer for a moment.

"Oh, aye, my lady," he said with a slight bow. "Cook's treats would be a wonderful reward."

Clare walked to the teacher's side and spoke in a low voice to him on the matter she'd come to discuss.

"Thomas has not returned to class?" She glanced quickly around the room and saw the empty seat.

"Nay, my lady. Three days now."

Clare glanced briefly at the empty seat before stepping away from the boys' teacher. "Advise me if he returns?"

"Of course, my lady."

She made her way out of the small classroom, one which would be replaced by two larger ones soon and drew her notebook from the pocket of her apron. As she'd remembered, Thomas was not the first boy this month to disappear from her school. Indeed, he was the third. The fifth when she added in Molly and Rebecca.

You cannot save them all, my dear.

Jonathan's warning echoed in her thoughts each time another child did not show up for lessons. And it usually was those who yet lived with relatives or family, children dragged back to the realities of living in poverty or working for their keep. Even so, she would ask Mr. Chalmers to seek out more information about the children. He had contacts that her other solicitor and advisors did not, ones who could ferret out what she wanted to know. A shiver passed through her at the thought of the fate facing those missing.

"My lady?" Clare had not realized she'd stopped in the middle of the corridor and in front of the door of what used to be Jonathan's office. Her headmistress watched her with a guarded expression in her usually-kind blue eyes. "Have ye forgotten yer appointment with Mr. Garvine? He is in yer office." A meaningful glance at the closed door before her was a reminder Clare truly did not need.

"I am on my way there now, Mrs. Dunbar," she said, smoothing her hands over the apron that protected her day gown in her work at the school.

She paused for less than a breath before leaving the doorway of Jonathan's office but got no farther than the end of the hallway. As she passed by the window, with its shutters opened to let the sunlight in, Clare saw her reflection there and stopped.

This woman was not one she would have recognized even a few years ago. Gone was the carefree daughter of a powerful earl, destined for a good marriage, children, and a place in society. The young noblewoman referred to in glowing terms, one known for her wit and beauty and for being the perfect daughter and all that entailed.

Lifting her chin, Clare saw flashes of that woman but gone was the naïveté of the young woman she'd been just, what, eight years before? Tucking a loosened lock of hair back in place, she allowed herself an honest appraisal and did not find herself lacking.

Meeting Jonathan had changed her life, her world, even her soul. Defying her father and relinquishing the life she'd known had been the best thing she'd ever done. And loving Jonathan had given her the strength to do it and she'd looked back in regret only rarely.

Clare Napier Logan would not begin to now in spite of the temptation to do so. The loss of a child saved by her efforts was as hard to face as the bairns she'd lost in attempts to give Jonathan one of their own. Indeed, it was her inability to bear him children that had inspired their work here among the poor of Leith.

So, she smiled at her reflection, content with her life and accepting of her losses, and turned away, ready to carry on with the next steps of Jonathan's legacy. The door leading to her office burst open and Duncan called to her as she approached. Alarm filled the man's voice and since he'd been Jonathan's choice to manage their business affairs because of his calm, deliberate manner, it unsettled her. Clare battled to control the worry until she knew the situation they faced.

Had Thomas or one of the others died? Was it possible? She forced her fisted hands into the pockets of the sturdy apron and rushed inside, surprised and alarmed to find Andrew Lamb, the solicitor who handled most legal actions for the businesses, waiting for her.

"Andrew?" She waited until Duncan closed the door. "Is there some problem?"

"My lady," the older man said, standing as she entered and made her way to her desk. Once she was seated, she waited as he took a deep breath before speaking.

"Is there some disaster brewing, Andrew? You know I prefer plain speaking to dissembling or vague words."

"No disaster, my lady," Andrew said. He glanced at

Duncan several times. "More an unexpected business move."

"Gentlemen, pray sit." Well, at the least, danger was not at their door. She trusted these two men most among those who advised her on the wide range of matters about the various business accounts and interests. They had not given her faulty or less than thorough information in the past and Clare expected that this situation would be no different. "And tell me what has you both so agitated."

"My lady, you might remember the offer we received for the land near the dry docks?" At her nod, Andrew continued, "Since you were adamant about the property and your intentions for it, we drew up a response."

"And?"

"Two more offers were received."

"Two? So, the first offer has stirred more interest then?"

The properties involved would be the cornerstone of Jonathan's, and her, plans to enlarge the school and orphanage to accommodate so many more desperate children. And, truly, no amount of money would change her mind on that. Too many dreams were tied to those particular blocks of land, their location and the buildings that would be renovated to house children in need.

"Actually, my lady, the two additional offers were from the same company." Well then, that was unusual.

"Is there some misunderstanding then, Andrew?" She blinked against the tears that inexplicably threatened. "What is their interest? What company is doing this?"

A loud knock at the front door prevented the solicitor from explaining and the second banging on the door, a louder and somehow angrier sound, made her gasp and rise to stand. Such an intrusion made no sense. She had the support of the surrounding community in her presence and her work. And in return she helped the businesses and tradesmen and women in Leith. Though this neighborhood was not the best, it was filled with hardworking people who valued family and honor and loyalty.

Another loud knock on the door shook her from her thoughts and spurred both Andrew and Duncan into action. Both men left the chamber and headed for the voices in the foyer beyond. Clare recognized her footman's, but not the deeper one, the one that conveyed anger and impatience and privilege and expectation. A shiver rushed through her, from the top of her head to the bottoms of her feet, and she stepped away from the desk intent on discovering the reason for this interruption.

It was not fear that filled her body and soul at the sound and tenor of that voice. Nay, the fear did not begin until the door opened so quickly that it bounced loudly off the wall behind it. A man entered before anyone could stop him. *A man entered* was such a tepid term for the person who invaded her office and his manner of doing so.

Tall, he stood taller than anyone there, even when he removed his top hat and tossed it to the footman trailing his every step. William backed from the chamber after her slight nod.

The man crossed the expanse of the chamber in but three strides. His black greatcoat floated around him and when he turned, seeking something or someone, she imagined him as some dark angel seeking his enemy. He noticed her, standing at the edge of the desk and strode over to her. His hard breaths stole the air from the room and his intensity chased all thoughts of resistance from her mind.

"Well?" he said, glancing at her with little interest. "Seek out your master and bring him here now."

He was a man used to giving orders and being obeyed. When she did not run, he stepped closer forcing her to tilt her head back to meet his gaze. Her stomach tensed when she did.

His fierce dark blue eyes, his short hair worn back, his heavy, expensive coat, his lacquered walking stick and all his clothes—from shoes to neckcloth—were relentlessly black. And everything he wore or carried was extremely expensive in cut and quality. Clare's breath caught in her throat at the strength in his expression.

"I said go and bring your master back. I will not be kept waiting."

So shocked by his arrival, his appearance, his behavior and his orders, Clare could not move or react. But both Duncan and Andrew did, rushing to her side and trying to form a barrier. In spite of their intent and efforts, nothing moved the man away from her.

"Mr. Buchanan, I must insist you—" Andrew sputtered out the words.

"Sir." The man corrected him without breaking his gaze from hers.

"Sir Iain, you must step—" Duncan was no longer calm. His voice shook with anger, the first time she'd ever heard such a thing. It was in her defense and yet it shocked her.

"I know the owner of the properties I want to purchase works here on Mondays, gentlemen. I wish to speak to him about the terms of my offer." Clare noticed for the first time that he'd never raised his voice, even while giving orders.

"Sir Iain, if you wish to schedule an appointment, I can arrange one," Duncan offered.

"I am here. The owner is here. Somewhere. There is no need for another delay. You." He nodded once more at her. "Seek out your master and tell him I am here." He tapped his walking stick on the polished wooden floor of her study as if it would hurry her along. The sharp sound echoed through the astonished silence.

It was clear she could avoid this no longer. This man, this Sir Iain Buchanan, would accept no excuses or be put off in his intentions. She'd not kept her ownership a secret, but it had not been bandied about by her solicitors in their efficient handling of the matters after Jonathan's death. Indeed, Jonathan's will had been filed and was on record with her listed as his heir. The ruse of using her initials would discourage only the least of any attempts to discover the truth.

C. N. Logan could be anyone and she suspected most would think it was Jonathan's brother or other male relative and not his wife. All his business interests, all the properties he'd accumulated during his short but very successful career were now hers—wholly and completely and undisputedly hers.

This intruder could be forgiven, she supposed, for mistaking her for a housemaid, what with her apron and plain day dress. With her ever-unruly hair falling about her face. And especially with his misinterpretation of her reaction to his presence and orders. Gathering her wits, she stood up straight, clasped her hands before her and nodded at Duncan without moving her eyes from this Sir Iain's gaze.

"Sir Iain, may I present Lady Clare Napier Logan."

The man did startle then. Just for a moment, and it was

so slight she would have missed it if not for her intent stare. Good. She'd surprised him as much as he'd done her and from that little tell in his gaze, she knew for certain that did not happen often to this man. Not to this force of nature used to making his own path.

Sir Iain did step back then, only a few paces, but he put enough space between them that he had room to execute a bow to her. It was a pretty one at that.

"My lady," he said, as he rose. "I apologize for mistaking you for a servant." His gaze, imperious on arrival, now filled with surprise and then something that looked like… appreciation took its place there. "I beg your pardon."

She replied with only a nod of her head, accepting his bow. The steely glint was back in those intense eyes and Clare was certain this man never begged for anything. A shiver raced down her spine at that realization.

Clare could not trust her own reaction, that of being overwhelmed by his mere presence, so she did not speak at that moment. Instead, she walked around the desk, sliding her hand along its sturdy surface to regain her control. Duncan walked behind her and held the chair as she sat. Andrew sat in the chair closest to the desk, remaining seated as Sir Iain stood there, walking stick in hand, waiting for her to speak first.

"Sir Iain, tell me why you will not take nay as an answer to your offer?"

Two

God Almighty, she was magnificent!

His blood, and cock, rose in response to the passion his very flesh recognized in her. He shifted to allow his prick to find a better position within the cut of his breeches. Thankfully, his greatcoat covered the weakness of his physical reaction to her.

Iain had made an error, something he rarely did, in not knowing that a woman owned the properties he wanted. Granted, his haste and need to firm up his expansion plans had led him to go around his own man of business and seek out the present owner. Hell, Ned and Ben would be insufferable over this when they learned of it.

But, that owner being Lady Clare Logan was completely unexpected and he could not be faulted for his misstep as he'd entered this chamber. At first, she'd nearly melted into the polished wood of the wall where she stood when he walked in. He should have looked at her closely before assuming her position in the household. His anger at being put off and denied what he was determined to attain had allowed a simple apron and a bland gown in a washed-out shade that nearly matched the color of her hair to mislead him.

Now, getting a better look, nay, paying heed as he

took a closer one, he noticed the graceful arch of her neck and the intelligence in those eyes that were the color of the sea off the western isles. Wild, loose tendrils of mahogany hair framed a heart-shaped face. Iain shook himself free of her enticing features, shocked that anything, anyone, had come before his business.

"To be honest, my lady, I rarely hear that word," he admitted. The swift indrawn breath spoke of her surprise. "Especially not when I make a more than generous offer and then increase it twice over."

His words were not the whole truth. Actually, he could count on one hand the times that anyone refused his offer and lived to tell of it. Old ways were sometimes the best, but now with his higher presence in society, destroying any object, or person, in the way he used to could not be his first choice. The ways of honorable society must be tried first. Then…

"Well," she said, as she rose from her chair, "Sir Iain, I will not be accepting either your first, second or third offer." She nodded to someone behind him, and he heard the door being opened for his departure. "But I do thank you for taking the time personally to clarify the matter. William will see you to the door."

Iain was tempted to stay as he was, standing in the middle of her office making everyone very uncomfortable. As he placed his free hand on top of the one that rested on his walking stick, the very fact he was indeed tempted to stay here made him move.

"My lady." He nodded and accepted his hat from the footman now at his side. "Gentlemen. My man will be in touch with you shortly." He saw the nervous smile on her secretary's face and noticed the way her solicitor's mouth firmed into a tight line. They understood the reality and the accompanying danger of her refusal.

He adjusted his hat and stepped outside, pausing and seeking the clarity of mind that sometimes only the cold Edinburgh air could give. After several slow, deep breaths, Iain headed to his waiting vehicle. His own footman opened the door of his coach and Iain climbed in, seeking the corner he preferred. As the coachman guided the horses into the street and to his next destination, he considered his options and made a mental list of matters to discuss with his own secretary and solicitors.

The first, of course, would be how they could have missed the not-so-insignificant detail that C.N. Logan was actually the Earl of Heath's daughter. The disgraced one. The one who married without her father's approval and who gave up most of the privileges enjoyed by daughters of the nobility. Oh, he studied the Scots peerage and knew who her father was—a ruthless bastard of a man not too unlike himself. He tucked those connections away for now.

Secondly, he thought just as the coach hit a rut in the cobblestones and forced him to slide to the edge of the bench seat before he could control himself and push back. Secondly, he thought again, his own men would have to answer to the lack of knowledge over the extent and control of Jonathan Logan's businesses. Iain rubbed his forehead at the first sign of an oncoming headache. Jonathan Logan had managed to forestall Iain's attention from the properties he wanted from the man for months after he'd been the one to initiate the discussions. Unacceptable delays and then the shocking occurrence— Logan died suddenly.

Another rut caused the carriage to jostle him once more and he let out an old epithet he'd not spoken in a long time.

And that concerned him, too. His legendary control—over his temper, his voice, his manners, his past—did not slip often, if at all. Yet it had just now. Two lapses in self-control within just minutes of meeting Lady Clare Logan.

The carriage slowed as it climbed the incline of the eastern road back into Edinburgh proper and he leaned back against the thickly-padded seat, as the unfamiliar feeling of dread filled him. Forcing his way into that building, into her building, he'd had no idea that his entire world would shift on its axis. He could not blame the unevenness of the road's surface or the gap in the information provided to him for the anger that filled the empty place deep inside him in this moment. Oh, making an error in front of his adversaries was not something he could accept gracefully. That was not the source of the seething inside him.

Nay, the truth hit him as he only just now remembered the words on the small sign at the door. He'd seen it and yet he'd not taken notice of it as he knocked and pushed his way in. He had not even truly read it, but the words apparently reached his mind without any effort and lay waiting for him to realize their presence.

The Logan School for the Orphans and Unfortunates.

Orphans.

Unfortunates.

Black filled his vision and his gut clenched sending bile into his mouth as he fought to force the memories back into the abyss in his soul where they existed. He could not this time and the rage they caused filled him.

His belly gave him warning and he hit the roof of the carriage with his walking stick. He could not and did not wait for it to stop before he opened the door and jumped to the street. Emptying his belly along the side of the road did not end the shaking tremors passing through him. When his footman approached, Iain waved him back. The spasms in his stomach finally calmed enough for him to stand. Accepting the flask offered in silence, he swished the first mouthful and spat it onto the stones.

The second swig burned its way down as Iain gathered the frayed shards of self-control and tried through force of will to reinforce the wall within him that kept his past… in the past. He held the flask out to Boyd with a nod. Glancing around and determining where they'd stopped, he called up to the coachman.

"Ewan, take the coach back to the house." He heard the whispers and saw the expressions being exchanged among Ewan and Boyd. "I want to walk a bit, but I have a stop to make first."

"Sir?" Ewan asked. "Boyd will accompany ye."

"Boyd will return with you to the house." Iain tugged his pocket watch free and opened it. "Come back for me in three hours."

"Here, sir?" Iain reached inside the coach and retrieved his walking stick. After testing the release for the blade within it, he nodded.

"Our usual place." Ewan shifted on top of the coach, his body indicating his plan to object. "Our. Usual. Place."

"Very good, sir."

The coachman watched as Boyd closed the door and climbed to his place on the back of the coach. He urged the horses on, and Iain waited as the coach proceeded for several blocks before turning towards the New Town and home. Then he turned himself in the opposite direction, towards the Old Town and its unsavory people and places.

When the rage bubbled inside him like this there was no way to completely tame it other than drinking and fighting. Fucking sometimes helped, but this rage was a dangerous one and he could not rely on or risk that physical release would even take the edge off of it. So, the establishment tucked into a close near the bottom of the High Street was the perfect place for him right now.

Between its sordid, wild pub on the street, the dark private chambers below where the fights happened or the cramped spaces above stairs where other physical tussles happened, the Cock's Spur was nothing to look at from the outside. But the magic happened once you entered it and, as Iain pushed open the door, he knew he'd made the correct decision. A cup was waiting for him by the time he reached the worn wooden bar.

Iain slammed it back, not caring what it was, because George, or *King* as he was called here, gave him what he needed. Iain tapped his fingers on the counter and the cup was filled. He took it in one mouthful, ignoring the terrible burn of the rotgut tearing its way down. Two more followed without pause.

Sometimes the excellent whiskies or brandies or wines that he could afford now just did not do what he needed. Sometimes though only gin, or this rough whisky—distilled God knew where, by God knew whom—fit the bill. His next signal was ignored.

"Tess above or the fights below first?" King asked as he took the cup, gave it a quick wipe with a dirty cloth and placed it on the shelf behind him. At his raised brow,

King continued. "Ye hiv that look aboot ye, Iain. The one that says ye need to fuck or fight yer way to oblivion." Another man would never have said such a thing aloud, but then not many others had known Iain as long as King had. "She saw ye come in."

The bartender nodded over Iain's shoulder. Glancing back, he found Tess watching him. Her body arched under his scrutiny, pushing her large nipples against the flimsy fabric of the dress she wore. Tess was known to like a bit of the rough fun and was usually his choice when he needed that. She pushed her long, auburn locks over one shoulder giving him a better view of her voluptuous body. Her hand stroked over her breast, across her belly and stopped when it reached the cleft of her thighs. He imagined the curls there that did not quite match the shade of the hair on her head and smiled. Her fingers played there as he watched, understanding her purpose and her need.

"Fights," he said to King. He tossed a rather large gold coin to her as he passed.

"Mayhap later?" he whispered as he passed her. The pout made Tess's lips tighten, reminding him of the many talents of her mouth and the relentless pursuit of pleasure they'd always enjoyed. It would be a distraction now, but…

"Definitely later." He gave her a rough kiss and spoke the promise against that mouth before walking through the door in the corner that led down to the fighting pits.

Day or night, there were fights here. And betting on outcomes or injuries. Iain unbuttoned and let his greatcoat slip off his shoulders. A servant trailing him gathered it up and waited on the rest. Walking stick, neckcloth, waistcoat, shirt and even the daggers he kept inside his boots followed until he wore nothing but breeches. Those were the rules here—and they were hard and fast. Breaking them resulted in a brutal punishment, swift and worse than any beating in the fights, which deterred many men from trying to keep an advantage other than their wits and their fists and their feet. He tipped the lad enough to ensure his belongings would be kept safe. Iain did it in spite of knowing his would always be here.

But with each bit of refined and expensive clothing he removed, a piece of this façade he wore and lived fell away, too. He stripped down to his core—the part of him that knew only kill or be killed. The feral part that understood the ways of predators and that was on watch for any attack. The uncivilized center that lived and breathed every moment of every day, just waiting to be needed.

Iain knew his way and followed the noise of the crowd to the current bout. These chambers were below the street, in old, long-buried buildings and spaces in the oldest parts of the city. As Edinburgh expanded over the years, before they aimed north and built the New Town, buildings were built on top of others. Even built on top of streets and closes. That resulted in these hidden places, some long forgotten, where activities best done out of sight could be accomplished. A roar told him a challenge had been decided. Pulling the final door open, whispers became shouts as people noticed him and his readiness to fight.

The roar echoed through him, his heart pounding in anticipation of the coming fight. Everything around him blurred into a strange silence and the only thing he heard now was the sound of his breathing. His hands tightened into fists and his body began changing the way he moved, spreading out his feet to gain a better-balanced stance. When he reached the cleared circle at the center of the crowd, Iain was ready. Pausing only to have his hands wrapped in strips of cloth, he nodded his readiness to the man deemed the referee, while never looking at his opponent. It mattered not at all to him. One was much like another when the fight began.

Kill or be killed. The fury within him fueled his senses, preparing him to attack.

Oh, he would get as good as he gave and his body would suffer, but it was the only thing that allowed the anger to ease.

The fight was called and Iain remembered nothing until he woke in the fair Tess's chamber, a private one used by the owner when he visited. The taste of blood coated his tongue. His ribs ached. His jaw felt swollen. When he moved his hands, to reach for the glass being held out to him, they were stiff and would not do as he wished.

"Here now, love," the lovely Tess whispered. "Let me help ye."

Emptied of the burning rage, he lay back and allowed her tender ministrations to ease the aches and pains that were making themselves known. A swallow from the glass brought a smile to Tess's face, one side of her mouth curved up as she held the glass at his lips. "Yer eyebrow wi' need some stitching."

He reached up with fingers finally loosening up and tipped the glass until the contents poured into his mouth. Though she was quite skilled with needle and thread, it was going to hurt.

"What time is it?" he asked as she took the glass away.

"Nigh on half-past three."

"Well, then, get to it," he said, patting her hip and sliding his hand around her shapely flesh and lovely arse. "I fear I can stay no longer." Tess turned and stared at him, as though he'd startled her in some way.

"The gent is back in place then?" She lifted her leg, exposing her bare thighs and the glistening flesh between them to his view. Playing her game of temptation, she straddled his legs and traced her fingers along the bruised flesh of his belly to tease his nipples. They tightened, as they always did when she applied her skills to a sensitive place. "Is there something I could do to change his mind?" He recognized the humor and the arousal in her gaze.

"I fear not, lovely Tess." Struggling against the pain, he lifted her free of him. "He has several people who are not as accommodating as you are with their time. So, with apologies, no."

She did not argue then. Instead, she closed the silken robe over her beckoning breasts and cleft and tied the belt around her waist. It took but a few moments to bring the supplies she needed closer. Good girl that she was, Tess had gathered everything before he came back to himself. They'd been through this before, and would be again, he had no doubt.

His head spun, the room spun and his vision went dark. And when he looked up at her, he did not see Tess with her curves and luscious softness. He no longer looked into blue eyes or noticed the curling locks of auburn tossed over one shoulder as was her wont to do.

Emerald green eyes stared back at him. The voluptuous body, fed well on his coin, disappeared and a slim, petite woman replaced it. Long, mahogany hair lay loose around that delicate face. And the hint of a smile tempted him to touch her lips.

Lady Clare Napier Logan.

Everything genteel and graceful that was expected in a woman of the cream of society. A woman meant only for the best and highest of men.

Everything in a woman he wanted as much as he wanted anything else in his life.

Everything he'd craved from that single moment as he lay dying in that filthy street in Glasgow and rebelled against it to reclaim his life.

"Are ye ready, love?" His vision cleared and he watched as Tess leaned in to repair his torn flesh.

Thoughts of the lady, an example of everything he could destroy in but a moment or two, dissipated as he allowed the pain back in.

"Aye, Tess. Have your way with me."

It was more than an hour later, but still by his three-hour deadline, that Sir Iain Buchanan climbed into his waiting carriage and drove back to the life he'd created. The life he'd earned through blood and flesh and loss and struggle. The life he was not finished building.

He settled back against the cushions and came to a realization.

No matter the lady's beauty. No matter the intelligence he saw staring back at him as he insulted her or the way she accepted an apology they both knew he did not mean.

No matter the primitive desire he'd felt for her when she challenged him—a need to take her and claim her in every way possible and make her bend to his will.

No one would stand in his way. He would find a way to get what he wanted, as he always did.

And nothing and no one would change that.

Not even the headstrong, vulnerable, stunning noblewoman who made his flesh harden and his appetite soar.

Not even her.

Three

"You have a guest, my lady." Poogan closed the door behind her and stood waiting there for her coat. "The Marchioness of Nairn is in your sitting room." A glance at the clock in the hallway told her she was fifteen minutes late.

"Tea?" she asked, though her thorough butler would have seen to it as soon as her sister had been welcomed into the house.

"Just now, my lady." Clare turned to see Emily, the younger of the housemaids, entering the sitting room carrying a tray.

She thought to remove her bonnet, but she was already later than was polite. Not matter that Caro would absolve her of the infraction. Rarely had a day gone by in their years growing up together that Caro had not had to rush her along because Clare never could finish preparing for anything when expected. Her mother berated her endlessly, her father complained and her sister... well, Caro just accepted her.

Still, impolite was impolite. Taking a moment to gather her thoughts, Clare followed the maid into the comfortable room where she hosted only family or friends. Her throat grew tight, and the lump would not ease. No family members came here to her house. Well, none but her sister.

"Caro," Clare said, taking her sister's hand and sitting at her side. "I have made you wait again."

"Shorter than most times, but more than others," her younger sister replied. "You look well, Sister."

Caro always had a smile for her, no matter the turmoil surrounding them. Her deep green dress suited her sister's coloring and made her eyes simply glimmer. Of the highest quality and designed by the most expensive modiste in Edinburgh, the gown accentuated both Caro's height and curves. Clare almost covered her bosom in envy of her sister's more bountiful one.

"And are you well, Caro?" A quick inspection noted good coloring in her sister's lovely face. Every hair was perfectly in place, her posture was perfect, her smile was... perfect.

"I am well," Caro said. "I have come in person so that a written invitation would not be misplaced or not delivered."

Her slanted gaze and raised eyebrow reminded Clare of some of the excuses she'd used to avoid attending Caro's soirees and gatherings and noted her sister's disbelief in them. The only one to ignore their father's command that Clare was no longer part of the family, Caro carried on inviting Clare and visiting her. It had not skipped Clare's notice that a marchioness had precedence over an earl and Caro wielded that superior statue like an expert swordsman over their father.

And Clare loved her even more for that. Tears burned in her eyes.

"I would not have you suggest that Poogan does not do his duty, Caro. The man would be devastated to know you did such a thing." She teased her way out of the threatening emotions.

"Oh, you! I know exactly where the blame falls, which brings me to you now." Caro turned herself to face Clare. "I expect, nay demand, your presence at a small dinner I am holding tonight."

"Tonight? I could not possib—" Clare found his sister's hand covering her mouth and preventing her from speaking.

"You can. You will. I have already checked your schedule with your secretary, your other secretary and Poogan. I confess Poogan was the most difficult to get an answer from on the matter, but he did acquiesce to my demands." Caro dropped her hands from Clare's mouth only to take hold of her hands. "I expect you to arrive promptly at eight of the clock."

"Samantha returns this evening, I believe. I would like to greet—"

"Clare. Mrs. Hunter is quite able to return from visiting her relatives in Inverness without you waiting at the door for her arrival."

Jonathan's distant cousin had moved in with them when her own husband had died and had remained a part of Clare's household, and friend, after Jonathan passed. So, when her argument was rebutted like that, Clare knew it was a weak excuse at best. She crossed her arms over her chest and met her sister's steely gaze. If one of them was to surrender, it must be Caro.

"Caro. I cannot," she said without elaborating more.

"A few friends, Clare. Some of Nairn's and a few associates. The focus will not be on balls and assemblies and the latest who said what where and when that you detest so. Perfect for you."

The last thing Clare wanted to do was disappoint the only family she still had. Nay, that wasn't true. The last thing she wanted to do was attend some society gathering where she would be the pariah. All of Edinburgh society knew of her father's declaration and her situation—disgraced, married against her father's wishes, married to a commoner, a man in trade no less, and then widowed. She detested walking into rooms and meeting with groups of people who gaped and stared and then turned their backs as her parents had.

But Caro had not.

"You must accept, Clare. I need you there." Clare let out a sigh.

"Very well."

Caro was on her feet and almost to the door before Clare could say anything else. Her sister turned back to her and waved one judgmental finger in the space between them, directed at Clare's attire.

"And not… this." A shake of her head made her command clear.

"Very well," Clare said. Caro turned the knob and Poogan completed the task of opening the door. He truly was a model butler, no matter that she teased her sister over his manner.

"Poogan?" Caro barely paused. "Your lady has agreed to attend my small dinner this evening, promptly at eight."

"I will see to it, my lady," Poogan said. He bowed as Caro walked by him, but he never took his gaze from Clare's.

"Traitor," she whispered.

"My lady," he replied, with another bow, to her this time. As she passed him, he continued. "What is a servant to do in the face of a marchioness's demands?"

He'd been with her through it all—from the time when she and Jonathan set up their first household until this day—and he'd seen it all. He understood that this had nothing to do with a marchioness's position and all to do with it being Caro making the demands. She did not need to comment after his rhetorical question.

"Archer has a bath ready for you, my lady."

So, it was a conspiracy then.

No matter that she preferred to remain home, she had agreed to go and would do so in good cheer. She could not diminish her sister's efforts or be so rude to her to give less than her best. With a bit of prodding and help from her maid, her butler and her coachman, Clare stepped out of her carriage in front of her sister's, or rather the Marquess of Nairn's luxurious townhouse on St. Andrew's Square at precisely four minutes before eight.

And found that Sir Iain Buchanan had as well.

Even dressed in full evening attire, he moved with an uncanny grace. She had seen a lion in the Tower of London's famed Menagerie on a trip there with her family and she recognized the same feral movement of that predator in this man. His eyes shifted across the area, strategically surveying everything around him as he closed the gap between them. Though he walked at a leisurely pace, his body seemed tense to her, at the ready, expecting something unexpected to approach at any moment. Waiting for an attack, even while in one of the safest areas of the city.

As he stopped between her and the door to her sister's house, Clare's instincts screamed to jump back in her coach, slam the door and ride for the safety of her own home. Why did this man affect her so? They were strangers. He was a gentleman, existing within society and its expectations of behavior. But she knew he was more and different from any man she'd ever met. Dangerous to her in so many ways she already knew, and others could not yet fathom or identify. Attractive, too, and charming when he wished to be. Confident. Aggressive.

All of that made her body prepare to flee. And she may have except that the front door opened now, awaiting her, clearly their, entrance.

"My lady, what a pleasure to see you here," he said, holding out his hand to her.

His glove was spotless and his manners impeccable, but her skin tightened and her heart pounded as she placed her hand in his. He lifted hers to his mouth and touched it ever so slightly, but his heated breath permeated the fabric of her glove, warming her hand. When his gaze met hers, she could not draw in air.

Though it was growing dark as the sun set behind the castle rock, she could see his eyes and a flow of emotions in them. He wanted… he wanted so much. She'd never witnessed so much desire and need and pure feral hunger in a man's gaze before. Clare lost her balance as she tried to lift her hand from his.

"Here, my lady," he said as he stepped back, not relinquishing his hold on her hand. Instead he slid his other hand under her elbow to steady her wobbly stance. The glint in his eyes and the way one of his dark eyebrows lifted told her he knew she wanted to pull away. "Allow me to escort you."

To do otherwise would bring attention. The footman at the door heard every word and saw everything. No doubt other servants stood out of sight but would witness her actions. They knew the gossip—her status and her situation with the rest of her family. And good, loyal servants of the marquess or not, they talked.

"I thank you, Sir Iain."

Clare walked at his side as he shortened his longer strides to fit hers. Once through the door, he let her hand free but kept his other one under her elbow. Through several layers of gloves and the fabric of her sleeve and pelisse, the heat of his touch warmed her skin. He did not guide or support her now—he simply touched her.

"Clare!"

Her sister stood in the expansive foyer at her husband's side, smiling and motioning to Clare to come to her. If her voice was raised a bit too loudly, her husband never reacted. The Marquess of Nairn unreservedly loved Caro and never tried to change her sometimes lively manner of talking or behaving. Clare watched as her sister's gaze slid over to the man at Clare's side before meeting Clare's once again. She could see the question waiting there in her sister's ever-inquisitive stare.

There was a possessiveness in the way Sir Iain kept his hand in place under her elbow, even as she walked away from him to her sister. He kept pace until they stood before their hosts. She had no choice but to introduce him to—

"Buchanan! I am glad you accepted my invitation," her brother-in-law said, clapping the man on his shoulder.

"Nairn." Sir Iain bowed his head for a scant moment. He was closely enough known by the marquess to address him so? "I could not refuse when it promises to be a delicious meal among such pleasant company."

They were acquainted? Caro's expression said quite clearly that she had never met the man.

"My dear, may I introduce Sir Iain Buchanan?" James drew Caro's attention to their guest. "Sir Iain, my wife, Lady Nairn."

"Sir Iain, welcome to our gathering," Caro said as Sir Iain bowed over her hand. Only then did Clare realize the warmth of his hand was gone from her arm.

"Lady Nairn, thank you for including me this evening," he said. His voice was deep and smooth as he spoke to her sister. Not the threatening tones of their own conversation, but a masculine one. When he laughed at something her sister said, Clare felt her blood race and the heat of a blush rise in her cheeks. "I can absolutely see the resemblance, my lady."

Clare blinked several times, realizing her thoughts had drifted and she'd not paid heed to the topic under discussion.

"And how do you know each other, Sir Iain?"

"We do not," Clare blurted out, taking a step away from him and shaking her head.

"To my regret, we have only met once before arriving at the same time here, my lady. And it was a brief one at that, as I mistook her—" Clare drew in a gasp. Would he reveal his own rude behavior now? "For someone else," he finished. What game did he play here?

"Well, I am glad for both of you accepting my invitation," Caro said.

"My dear, if you and Lady Clare do not mind, I would speak to Sir Iain on a matter before we go in for dinner?"

Caro agreed quickly, but Clare knew the truth—her sister wanted to interrogate her about the truth of what had happened between Sir Iain and her. After the men excused themselves and walked to a private corner for their discussion, Caro grabbed her hand and led her to sit on one of the couches nearby. Since they awaited the last guests, Clare could not hope for help to avoid this so she spoke first.

"He wanted to buy some of Jonathan's property in the Leith docks and arrived at the school to plead his case."

"Pleading," Caro said. Then leaning in closer, she lowered her voice. "I would not mind seeing that man plead for something he wanted." Clare blinked, realizing her sister's innuendo. "Well, come now, be honest, Sister. He is one of the most attractive men we've ever met."

"Caro!" She had no idea her sister even noticed other men. The deep love between Caro and Nairn was quite public ever since the marquess had made his declaration at a ball in the Assembly Rooms. Caro would never…

"Oh, Clare! There is no question of my love and faithfulness to Nairn, but a woman has eyes and he certainly is a man to see." Caro released her hand and leaned away. "There is something very primal, almost intoxicating, about him."

Clare couldn't believe her sister was reacting as she had to his completely overwhelming presence. And his appearance. If she was being honest with herself, Clare understood her sister's response having lost her wits and words when the man directed his attention at her. And somehow, the masculine attractiveness was not diminished even by the bruising under his eye or the cut healing on the edge of his mouth took away from it. That purplish-green area that spread across the angle of his cheek was new. As was that gash still evident on his lower lip.

"Clare?" Caro touched her hand, gaining her attention. "Are you concerned? Worried about something?" Clare shook herself free of thoughts of his face.

"Nay." The frown on Caro's brow deepened. "Truly, nothing. But why is he here? Why did you not tell me he was coming?"

"Nairn asked if he could invite a new business associate since this is an informal gathering. Should I have refused him?"

"As if you could refuse him anything!"

Clare let out a very ungenteel snort. A pang of longing shot through her and she tamped down the very inappropriate jealousy that burned her stomach. Silence surrounded them and Clare welcomed it and dreaded its discomfort.

"Forgive me, Caro." Clare let out a sigh. "I find your expressions of affection for each other adorable."

"And, I admit, Nairn and I are obnoxious in our affections."

"Never stop! Never let a day go by without being ridiculous in your affections." A pang of loss pierced her heart as regret over all the wasted moments of her own marriage surfaced.

The butler announced the last of the arriving guests—Lord and Lady Marlowe—they stood to greet them. Clare was grateful for the interruption for it gave her a moment to put aside the maudlin emotion that sometimes dampened her spirits. It happened fewer times and much less often now that two full years had passed, but there were times when the sad weakness made her regrets over past actions and decisions rise, too. Caro's gentle squeeze of her hand signaled her sister's support as she walked to greet the new, and last to arrive, guests.

The marquess entered the drawing room and held out his arm to his wife to escort her to the dining room. Another breach of proper protocol for he should have escorted Lady Marlowe, leaving Caro to walk with Lord Marlowe. But, as he'd said many times—his house, his guests, his rules—and no one would argue with his clear determination on it. Whether he'd followed correct etiquette or not, Clare would have found herself on Sir Iain's arm.

"My lady?" The uninjured corner of his lip curved just a bit as he held out his arm to her. "May I have the honor of seeing you to your seat?"

Clare knew she could not feel his skin on hers, but even with the intervening layers of her glove and the thick, well-made sleeve of his coat, the heat of his body warmed her. As they walked into the dining room and reached the table, he stopped a bit abruptly as the others found their places. A mix of surprise and confusion filled his dark gaze. Glancing at the table she understood.

"Ah, you wonder over the seating arrangements?"

"Should they not be apart?" he said in a lowered voice as he leaned closer to her. "Shouldn't they?"

A few words but they were filled with the same confusion and surprise that she'd seen in his eyes. As someone only recently granted a knighthood and the movement in the higher levels of society, he clearly knew that the host and hostess should sit at opposite ends of the table. Somehow, this less than complete confident moment made him seem more human. As though he was out of place and unfamiliar with being less than perfectly in control.

"Lord and Lady Nairn are quite known for their

unconventional and unseemly displays of affection. This is what comes of it," she said. If her words sounded sarcastic, she had not meant it that way.

A sound halfway between a huff and a breath was his only response as he led her to the chairs indicated by the butler. Though she suspected he would be seated next to her, he was instead across from her, at her sister's right, as she sat at Nairn's left. And not even the tall candelabras blocked their view of each other across the finely set table.

A thrum of anticipation filled her as the meal commenced both from the intimacy of the gathering to the presence of Sir Iain. In this setting, they did not follow the prescribed process of speaking only to the guest on their left and then switching to the other when the hostess did. Conversation flowed smoothly around the table, on a variety of topics and news of the day. A polite society dinner it was not and Clare was glad of it.

Or it did until her sister decided to take it in hand and interfere as only Caroline Margaret Napier Murray, the Marchioness of Nairn, could.

"Sir Iain, I would love to hear how you and Lady Clare met?"

FOUR

When they were just lasses and growing up together, there had been times when she and Caro fought. Not just with words or insults, but also with hands and a fist once or twice. For years now, feeling the responsibility to be a lady and to behave as one, she had not engaged in such behavior.

For the first time in years, she wanted to slug her beloved sister.

"Lady Nairn! Please." Clare could not help the tinge of discomfort in her tone.

"Lady Clare," Sir Iain said, his voice deeper than usual as though he was going to chastise her. "If the marchioness wants to hear it, how can a simple knight refuse her request?"

A shiver tracked down her spine as he met her gaze with his own and only his left eyebrow and the left corner of his mouth lifted the tiniest of bits. Was he teasing her? Where did this charming, flirting version of the angry, overbearing, insulting man who'd stormed her office come from? Her true dilemma was how could she continue to protest and not look unhospitable in her sister's home? A tilt of her head signaled her acquiescence.

"As Lord Nairn knows I am expanding my facilities

near the waterfront in Leith and buying unused warehouses and the like," he said, glancing at Caro's husband before turning his attention to Caro herself. "Lady Nairn, I am not known to be a patient man when it comes to my businesses and I fear I was not the day I met Lady Clare."

"That sounds interesting," Caro said. Clare would have to wait to let her sister know exactly what she thought of Caro's clear and plain and unseemly curiosity about a matter better left private. But when Sir Iain laughed at her sister's comment, Clare lost her breath.

The laugh came from the depths of his being and changed his entire countenance and bearing. She'd seen overbearing. She'd witnessed charming. But this laugh, it was something so authentic and real that Clare knew she was seeing a part of this enigmatic man that few saw. Her blood heated at the sound of it. It was the sound of pure passion and her body ached at both the memory of such feelings and their absence in so long.

"Forgive me, Lady Clare," he said with a nod. "I laugh at my own behavior and not yours that day."

"Which was what, Sir Iain?" Caro asked with the focused attention of a dog with a juicy bone. Truly, there was nothing to be discovered but for an embarrassing moment or two of mistaken identity. He waited as the footmen removed the serving plates and replaced them with the next dishes and she could see Caro's interest grow in those moments.

"I have been trying for months and months to get an answer about my offer for two properties previously owned by the late Mr. Logan. I'd been stymied in another business arrangement and let my impatience overrule my usual method of handling such matters."

What or who else had said no to this man? She suspected that he was not accustomed to refusal.

"Over my man of business and my secretaries' recommendations, I discovered the location of the new owner and went there to… negotiate." He winked at her then.

He winked at her.

That small expression made her insides feel like warm treacle. Clare waited on the rest of his explanation and description of the chaos that ensued in their tumultuous first encounter.

"I burst in and did not allow anyone to stop me," he said as he turned his gaze to her sister. "Pushing into the office there, demanding to see the owner and encountering a woman I assumed was a maidservant."

"Oh, Clare!" Caro said. "Pray tell me you were not wearing that apron."

"I'm afraid Lady Clare was indeed wearing an apron."

The heat of a blush crept up her neck and filled her cheeks at his declaration. Clare grabbed her glass of wine and drank some, hoping to cool her embarrassment.

"And one of those frilly, white caps that most household servants wear." Though he turned his dark gaze to her, she did not see any sign of mockery or derision in his eyes. Instead, humor shone there, sending a shiver down her spine.

"I was working, Sir Iain," she said in her defense.

"Oh, Lady Clare, 'twas my mistake. I expected to find the one I wanted to speak to about my interest and found someone completely different. Then, compounding my error and being so single-minded on my own matters, I did not see the woman before me." He lifted his glass in salute to her, shocking Clare into silence. "I hope you can forgive my rash actions?"

No one had ever taken her feelings into account and yet this enigmatic, attractive, somehow dangerous stranger did. And as brash and overbearing as he'd been in that first encounter, here he was admitting his fault before her sister and her brother-by-marriage with whom he was in some business endeavor.

Iain Buchanan was *not* the man she expected him to be.

Clare smiled and nodded. "Apology accepted, Sir Iain."

"To Lady Clare," he said as he lifted his glass higher and nodded at her. The others repeated his words, leaving Clare unable to breathe.

Seeing Caro's smile and meeting the marquess's gaze warmed her heart. No matter that her father and mother had shunned her, Caro and Nairn had never joined in their cruelty. Her parents' deletion of their eldest daughter from their lives and family had been complete and utterly clear to their extended relatives and acquaintances and friends in society. Early in her marriage Jonathan had been enough to see her through, but in the few years since losing him, they had been the one link to her past that had not been severed.

The kind act of this man had unnerved her. She could eat and drink only by rote after that. Her wits had fled at his words and his gesture, and it took some time to gather her thoughts. How she managed to say the correct words when needed to reply to a question or how she continued to function at all was a mystery to her. But she did.

Until Nairn's butler entered the room as the table was being cleared.

His usually impeccable manners faltered when he allowed his gaze to meet hers for just a moment. Placing her cutlery on her plate, Clare waited as the footman removed it before studying the whispered exchange. The butler left and Clare held her breath, knowing somehow that she was directly involved.

"Lord Heath is joining us for our final course this evening," Nairn announced.

A glance at Caro revealed she was surprised in this as well. The only one who did not tense at such a declaration, she noticed, was Sir Iain. But then why or how would he know the situation in her family?

'Twas not something openly, or even frequently, discussed. It was a matter of fact and even society did not question it. In her rare appearances at events at Caro's behest or demand or for her charities, those who associated with or needed her father's favor ignored her presence. Others simply accepted it. And, she never knowingly attended gatherings when she knew that her parents would attend. Simpler to avoid the ugliness than to walk into it.

But now? How did she handle this without alienating or insulting the two people dearest to her?

"Nairn?" she whispered, leaning closer to him. "I should leave." She began to stand, pushing the chair back before a footman could reach her. The touch of her brother-by-marriage's hand on hers stopped her.

"He knows you are here, Sister." He patted her hand. "He is here to renew his acquaintance with you."

Her body dropped without grace to the chair behind her. Nairn's words stirred both shock and turmoil within her. Tears burned and no amount of blinking would keep them controlled. She clutched at the handkerchief placed in her hand and then dabbed, hopefully with some modicum of calm.

"Why?" She asked it of him only when she could speak.

"I want Caro to be happy. And the continued shunning by the earl and countess distressed her. I am only sorry I did not press the issue prior to this," he explained.

"But how? He has always refused?" Clare asked. Nairn's maneuver had not been the first attempt by her sister, and even other interested parties, to reconcile the earl's eldest with her parents. But one thing or another, usually the earl's outrageous and insulting demands regarding her behavior or decisions, stymied their attempts. The slightest tilt of Nairn's head in the direction of his guest gave her the answer.

She should not have feared the end of the world was near, as her father had always sworn would be needed for him to approach her again. Instead, as always, his business interests had tamped down whatever scruples he held onto and allowed him to come here this night.

To meet… him. Not her.

Never her.

"My lord, the Earl of Heath," the butler announced as he opened the door to allow her father entrance.

Did he never age? His countenance was that of a younger man and barely any gray touched his hair. His bearing spoke of his continued practice of walking and exercise. She stood as the others did but remained in her place as Nairn and Caro went to greet him. After a private word, they turned back to the table and her father's gaze met hers for the first time in years. Then he looked away as Nairn escorted him towards his true target.

Jealousy froze the blood in her veins as she watched

her father greet him warmly. Anger melted that ice and turned her stomach to a block of burning acid. Finally, as she met the deep blue gaze of Sir Iain Buchanan, grief stabbed deep into her heart once more as the truth of the matter struck her once more—her father never had cared a whit about her.

She was now, as she'd always been, a means to his ends.

In spite of the pain she felt, Clare found it impossible to look away from Sir Iain and relief filled her when he did so first. His attention was engaged in being introduced by Nairn and making a first impression on a man, an earl, who could help him in many matters when she held no sway over anything at all.

Glancing around the room, she wondered if she could slip out unnoticed as the men continued to speak as they returned to their chairs. The efficient footmen quickly adjusted the settings and seating to place her father in between Sir Iain and Lady Marlowe, who looked thrilled at the addition to their group and her proximity to the earl.

Once settled, bowls of fruit, a small cake, a plate of cheeses and a pudding were brought out. A selection of beverages was offered—another of Nairn's eccentricities of not separating from the women to enjoy their port or other drinks.

"Clare, you look well," her father said.

Surprised by the first words spoken to her in years by her father, Clare was overwhelmed by unexpected feelings. Waves of longing. Pulses of betrayal. Stabbings of heartbreak and loss. And anger. Anger was always there and never revealed.

Her throat tightened and words would not come out.

In that moment, she could not, for the life of her, choose a way to address him. My lord? Father? Sir? Each of those would have been appropriate at one time or another in her life, but now?

Finally, she forced a reply free.

"I am well."

So, the first words spoken to her father in years were a lie and yet, she could think of nothing else to say.

Iain watched as a myriad of emotions flickered through her emerald eyes in those few moments and it took his breath away. He'd underestimated her several times and he wondered how her father's arrival would affect her. Nairn had been eager to see the invitation extended to his wife's father as a gesture of peace in their family. When Iain had suggested the meeting to further discussions on matters of mutual interest, in other words the pursuit of more wealth, Nairn had grabbed at it. Since Iain's major goal in life matched that of most other men—more wealth, more power, simply more—drawing others into his plans to help him succeed made sense.

Should he feel badly about using the lady's family against her to secure the properties he wanted? Oh, aye, he should. Any decent human being would. But scruples and regrets had been burned out of his soul long ago. His only priority, his only aim, was to satisfy his needs and appetite for… more.

The lady would survive without two blocks, two large warehouses, near the Leith waterfront. Indeed, with the amount he would pay her, she could not only survive but flourish and pay for more of her special projects. And, if this gathering resulted in her regaining her ties to her father, then she benefitted even more.

When he considered his new position with its access to the higher levels of society and, sadly, the scrutiny that came with it, he would rather ease his way into the ownership of what he wanted than to call too much attention to his bid to control it. As a simple businessman and merchant from Glasgow with ties to certain elements that operated outside the view of most, he could apply the force needed. But now, having received the king's favor and being accepted in genteel company with the sought-after alliances, he must step carefully.

Hence, keeping his ownership of The Cock's Spur a secret from the upper echelons of polite society of Edinburgh. As well as his other less polished enterprises.

Hence, taking this approach to gain the lady's properties.

Iain sat silently, partaking in some of the dessert and in some of the marquess's fine port, and all the while watching and evaluating the interesting family dynamics play out around him.

The marquess had a good head for business and Iain knew he could make money with him. Though what effect Iain's dismantling of Lady Clare's holdings would play on the upright noble, Iain could only guess.

The earl, not known for his forgiving nature, would most likely cry with glee if he could prosper while putting his eldest in her proper place. Penniless and at his mercy would be Heath's preference. So, with enough bribing to keep him pliant, Charles Napier would be no impediment to Iain's success.

The other guest, Lord Marlowe, was a baron and invited more as a distraction at his suggestion to Lord

Nairn. He had interesting prospects and properties but not even close in wealth or connections as the other two men.

The talk did not focus on business. Like most conversations at polite meals, the topics included the weather, their estates, their horses, the news from the continent about various subjects and a smattering of casually mentioning any and all-powerful people they knew. The latter to convince him of their standing. Nobles tended to underestimate those not raised as they were and to assume they would be impressed by such antics. But, this puffing of chests and demonstrating their connections kept things sociable at the table.

Finally, the usual topics exhausted, the earl attempted to turn the talk to his concerns, but it would not benefit Iain to speak of such before he sensed it would be the most advantageous time. As her father raised his voice, Lady Clare stood.

"My lord, my lady, if you would have my carriage brought around? I must take my leave."

A deep furrow between her brows showed her consternation. She worried her lower lip with her teeth as she waited for Nairn's response. That lip grew red and puffy from the action and his body reacted swiftly to the sight.

"Of course, Clare," he said, as he nodded to his butler before holding his hand out to his wife. "Are you certain you will not stay? We will move to the Drawing Room shortly which is more comfortable than here."

Though her father took his seat once more, the baron and his wife remained standing. Out of respect for those of higher standing. Of which her father had none. Even with his lower title, he did not give the marquess the courtesy of standing when Nairn did.

"Nay, my lord, I thank you for your kind invitation, but I must go," she said. "My lords, my ladies—" When he thought she would ignore him, she faced him. "And Sir Iain. It was lovely to see you all."

"Lady Clare," he said as he tilted his head down. "As unexpected as it was, I was pleased to see you again."

The lady turned to leave, and Iain was struck by the need to… do something. To call out to her and make her come back. To rush to her and hold her against the pain she felt. To tear her apart for the threat, the real danger, she presented to him and his plans.

Mostly though, his blood rampaged through his body, heating it, feeding the primal hunger he felt for her. To take her from here and take her. Take her, make her his and mark his claim in some fierce, animalistic way. So that everyone looking at her, every man gazing at her, knew she was his.

Mine.

Iain shook himself free of the hold of such emotions and regained his control. The beast within him pushed for freedom from time to time and the only thing Iain could do was recognize the strong passions that existed deep inside him and move on with his well-thought-out plans.

He sat down as soon as it was polite to do so, planning to remain there and not do anything as rash or impulsive as following her outside.

Until he did just that.

FIVE

Excusing himself with some vague reason, he followed her out across the exquisite, marbled foyer and onto the landing outside the door. Her carriage, brought by the efficient servants of the marquess's household, already approached. He moved quickly down and around her, arriving on the sidewalk before she did and blocking her last step.

"Sir Iain?" The lady tugged on the fingers of her glove, adjusting its fit over her fingers when she stopped. "Do you need something?"

The coachman said… something, but Iain waved him back. The footman ready to assist the lady into the carriage took his meaning and shifted his position to give them a moment of privacy. Lady Clare stood two steps above him and it brought her face level with his. Iain stared at her mouth and his watered in anticipation of discovering the taste and heat of hers.

As quickly as he'd moved to intercept her, he stepped away, feeling his control slip and the need to taste her grow. He could not endanger the longer plan with this short-term attraction. Too much was at stake. But the lady had reached out for him and grabbed at the empty air where he had been, losing her balance and missing the step beneath where she stood. Stumbling, she landed with a cry as soon as her foot landed hard on the sidewalk.

Iain scooped her up into his arms, holding her too close. He knew it. He knew the danger of feeling her body against his, but it did not stop him.

"My ankle!" she moaned out as he gained his balance. "I twisted it."

He could place her in her carriage. That was what he should have done. Send her home and allow her people to see to her injury. When the footmen opened the front door and the butler stepped out, Iain called out instructions.

"Lady Clare is injured," he said as he carried her up the stone steps. "Summmon Lady Nairn and show me where I can make her comfortable." The footman and butler went off and soon the dinner's company appeared in the foyer.

"Here now," Lady Clare whispered to him. "I am perfectly well and can return to my home." When their hostess arrived, Iain observed some silent and secret dialogue between the two sisters.

"What happened, Clare?" Lady Nairn asked, breaking their wordless exchange and eschewing the formalities in the emergency. "Did you fall?" Nairn, Heath and the Marlowes stood behind her, watching the scene without comment.

"I stumbled on the steps and Sir Iain kindly caught me. Please put me down now, Sir Iain. Truly, Sister, 'twas more of a startle than an injury."

The lady still clutched his shoulders, but as he lowered her to her feet, she allowed her hands to slide down his arms. As her feet touched and settled on the floor, she hissed and grabbed hold more firmly.

"Apparently not," he muttered under his breath as he lifted her once more. "Where can I take Lady Clare so she might be comfortable?"

The quickness in which Lady Nairn's servants answered the call for action made him envious. Moments later, he was climbing the stairs to the second floor and a well-appointed guest room. The resistance in her body—she held herself stiff and separate—softened only for a moment just before he placed her on the bed there. The soft curves he'd only witnessed through the layers of clothing ladies wore pressed against him and made him want to glide his hands over them. To see if her breasts would be a handful or a mouthful. To taste…

Lady Nairn's clearing of her throat reminded him that others were present. And, from her knowing expression, he'd allowed his lust to show in his expression. A foolish mistake on his part. He stepped away from Lady Clare who settled herself there on the edge of the bed. The sensation of having her in his arms dissipated with every pace back and his hands itched to have her back once more.

"Thank you, Sir Iain. Quite gallant of you to see to my sister's safety."

"If you wrap it tightly and use cold compresses, the swelling should not be too bad, my lady," he said to Lady Clare. With pain evident in the tightness of her mouth, she nodded at him.

Iain left. He did not miss the brief and quizzical expressions of the other two men in the chamber. Both Nairn and Heath gazed at him in a different way now than before. He recognized it, for he'd studied people and situations with the same intensity, the same intention, himself. He could even name it—avarice. Not for wealth but for what he could do for them.

His rash reaction to the lady's distress had now placed him in a dangerous situation—that of being a target. The exact elements of his life that he'd worked and given up everything to accomplish his aims—wealth, property, honored by the king—now made others covetous of those things. Bloody hell!

At a pace nearing haste, Iain walked down the stairs and out the door, leaving word to send his carriage after him with the footman.

The always cool Edinburgh night air did not soothe his concerns as it usually did. Walking around the small park in the center of the exclusive square, Iain could not believe his slip. He wanted and needed to do business with the marquess and his extended family but did not wish to get personally involved. Business needed to be handled with a cool, distanced approach and not be bogged down by a pretty woman with a title and wealth.

Not even one who, he would only admit under duress, felt so right in his arms that it terrified him.

So, he walked and walked and walked more, almost until dawn, to escape that realization. He was aware enough of himself to understand that walking, without a destination, alone, usually in the middle of the night, was the other way he dealt with questions or challenges he faced. He fought or fucked or walked. Now, with his new position and success, he tried to avoid the outcomes of those fights in his previous life.

Instead, many of his battles were done with money and power rather than fists but somehow physical blows rained down on an opponent were extremely more satisfying. Which served only to confirm his belief that the brutal, ruthless person he was deep inside would never actually change. It would just find other ways to continue his path to getting whatever he wanted and especially whatever he needed.

As he reached his own townhouse, located on the other and more prestigious square and easily twice the size of Lord Nairn's, with its luxury, comfort and efficient, and its own well-trained staff, Iain's control was back in place. As was his certainty in his plan to get the property he wanted. The brief note of thanks from her that arrived in his office just after he did gave him the opportunity to move ahead.

Surely, that was a sign of coming success?

He'd no sooner settled himself behind his desk in the large chamber he used as a private office before he was set upon by Ned and Ben.

"You have meetings that begin—" Edward Pemberton, his secretary, paused to withdraw and glance at his pocket watch. "In thirty minutes."

"I have the new contract for the holdings in Glasgow for your signature," Ebeneezer Gilchrist, his man of business and all-around manager of details of all sorts, said. "And, by Christ, you look like you have been ridden hard and put away wet, Iain." Silence controlled the room for two long moments before Ned joined in.

"Those toffs play hard, do they not?" Ned asked. Well, not asked, because he tapped Ben's arm with his elbow declaring his sarcasm. Both men knew of his plans for the previous night.

"I have seen you just after you spend hours at the—" Ben stopped. The two worlds in which Iain lived could not overlap. Not aloud. Not publicly. Not even in a jest. Ben cleared his throat and moved on to business. As expected, none present acknowledged the change in subject. "If you sign those now, I can have them delivered to Black in Glasgow by tomorrow."

Iain took the pile of papers from him and laid them on the desk. Meetings in half an hour. Contracts to sign. Other commitments on the day. Yet, the small, folded square of parchment on top—one not mentioned by his secretary or man of business—caught his attention more firmly than any other demand.

They noticed, for the two men let out matching sighs before shaking their heads at him. Ned and Ben were perhaps the only two, with the probable addition of King, who could speak and act so boldly with him. At least privately. Though this morn, he would brook no challenges even here. Without meeting their gazes, he turned the letter over and broke the seal. Unfolding the sheet, he discovered its sender, as he'd suspected, was Lady Clare Logan.

Entranced by the neat style of her handwriting, it was a personal note of thanks for his help the night before. To him, holding her in his arms had felt like only minutes ago and yet hours had passed. Rather than sit under the staring eyes of his employees, Iain stood and walked to the window and enjoyed the surprising sunshine as he read the rest.

I am in your debt...

Practically, he knew those words were just a throw-away ending, the polite thing to say in a note expressing gratitude for a kindness or other help, but it gave him an opportunity to use it to speak directly to her about the property he wanted, he faced the others.

"I'm writing a reply to Lady Clare, and I want it delivered directly to her at the Marquess of Nairn's residence. Immediately." Lady Clare was not the lay-abed kind of person and would leave her sister's as soon as was possible to return to her home or the school.

Lay-abed? A vision of her naked but for the silken sheets tangled about her struck and his cock hardened in an instant. Her hair down, spread on the pillow. Her mouth reddened from his attentions to it and her attentions to his…

"Sir?" Iain shook off the shockingly graphic image and looked at his secretary.

"I will reply immediately and want it delivered personally to the lady. Is there a problem with that, Pemberton?" At the man's acquiescence, he continued. "Clear any scheduled meetings or other business from my diary at midday on next Monday, Tuesday and Wednesday. I will give the lady a choice."

"What happened last night to change her mind, Iain?" Ben asked. "We have worked for months and have nothing to show but absolute refusals, even to meet about it."

"As has happened before, I was in the correct place at a fortunate time." His own handwriting was rougher than hers but legible, of that he made certain. He signed it and handed it to Ned to finish sanding and folding and sealing. Iain's raised eyebrow provoked a response.

"Immediately, sir," Ned said, heading out of the office to make it so.

Only when the front door closed could Iain turn his attention to the business remaining on his desk. His secretary returned as he shuffled through the contracts he needed to sign.

"The changes I asked for?" Iain waited for the report.

The original contract offered was not as advantageous to him as he'd demanded.

"Aye, sir," Ben said. "After the unfortunate incident, the owner has decided the quicker things are settled the better." Iain found the end, having glanced over each sentence quickly, and signed it.

"Just so," he said as he handed it back. "Sometimes, those unfortunate incidents have a way of clarifying issues." Ben met his knowing gaze for a moment before taking the papers.

They sorted out what was left to be done this day and word came that his scheduled appointment had arrived. Once his business was accomplished, Iain could turn his attention to preparing for his meeting with Lady Clare. His men had gathered most of what he needed, but there was more he wanted to know. Witnessing her family's interactions and speaking with the marquess had yielded so much.

Now, he must learn more about this woman.

In his past dealings with women, highborn or low, it always came down to the price. Throwing more money at them usually worked. But he'd done that, twice over, and had not gotten what he'd wanted. So, he must discover the true reason she held fast to those properties and the price needed for her to relinquish them to him.

"Will you meet with her three times?" Ned asked. He opened the appointment diary to the correct place and began to make notes.

"Nay, once."

"But you want three times on different dates held open for her?" Iain leaned back in his chair and stared across the chamber to the window. "Does that not give her the control over this?"

"The perception of control, aye. But she played into my plans with her note," he said, with a nod to the note laying there on his desk. "Let her believe it is her decision." Iain stood and tugged down the cuffs of his shirt within the sleeves of his coat. "At least this way, we will begin the discussions amicably."

"And end that way?"

Iain smiled at his ever-hopeful secretary. In spite of the man's background and years working for Iain, Ned still had a way of looking for the good in people and situations. That urge had been beaten out of Iain long ago and he preferred to have a cold eye when looking at business dealings in particular and people in general. Never expect the best and the worst will not surprise you. And many times, it had kept him alive, too.

"One can hope." His sarcasm was not missed by either of his employees. "We have four days left until Lady Clare arrives at the office, so—"

"You did not invite her here?" Ben asked.

"Nay, I want her to see what's at stake for me. Why those blocks of Leith properties are the ones I need. Why no others in the area will work. Why she must sell them to me." He shrugged. "All nice and honest. All in plain sight. And I am certain that the lady will see it my way."

Neither asked the obvious question, so Iain let it lie.

He got what he wanted. Now, his position and recognition by the king forced him to work a bit differently than in his past, but it mattered not. The end result was the same—he got what he wanted. The strange thing in this matter was that he did find himself hoping— hoping that the lady gave in quickly.

For once in his life—in either life he'd lived—he hoped that his target would see the futility in resisting his efforts and give up swiftly. Lady Clare was dangerous for so many reasons and he'd rather be done with her and on to other endeavors quickly and cleanly. Every dealing he had with nobles endangered his reputation for success and created a desire within him for… something else.

For he'd faced the truth a long time before—his would never be the life of a usual man. His past held too many secrets and his soul too many black marks for him to gain the life of a decent man at the end. And, Iain had few regrets over his past. He understood it though and understood what it meant to his future.

So, he would continue to increase his holdings to satisfy his need for… more. He would rid himself of those who resisted his plans. And he would continue to repeat those actions until he was satisfied.

"Four days, gentlemen. I need all the information, scraps and bits about the lady that you have missed so far. What will work to soften her opposition to selling to me? What would make up for the loss of those particular properties? Which of her employees will cooperate with us? How much and what will it take to ensure that the earl works to my advantage?"

Iain needed a bath and a shave badly. His clothes were now thoroughly rumpled, and he needed to change before he left for the evening.

"All that and more, gentlemen. All that and more."

Iain strode out into the hallway and up the stairs to his private chambers. Exhaustion rode him hard now and he was ready to give in to it. His valet appeared behind him and followed him into the bedchamber. About to order a bath, a meal and whisky, Iain smiled as Paul handed him the crystal goblet filled with an indecent amount of his best whisky.

"Your bath is nearly ready, sir. I will have a small meal ready for you when you finish."

Iain swallowed a large amount of the smooth, smoky liquor before his valet refilled it. He must look much worse if the servant did not argue or raise a brow at how much he consumed. Two mouthfuls more emptied the glass. Paul silently took the glass from Iain and then opened the door to the bathing chamber. His body surrendered as the escaping steam swirled across the room in welcome.

If Paul or his other servants thought the frequency of his bathing was unusual, they did not mention it. And he paid them enough to keep their mouths shut so his habit went unremarked upon. He did not need the advice of some physician of the body or counselor of the mind to understand his need to wash often. Too long in the filth and dirt made his skin itch if he did not bathe daily.

Though his body found relief as he sank into the specially-designed large tub, his mind began racing to the meeting coming four days in the future. He considered each offer he would make, the expected response and his counteroffer. By the time he rose from the cooling water and accepted the drying cloth held out to him, he had his plan in place.

Four days and he would have what he wanted.

And, in four days, you will see her again.

The traitorous temptation whispered inside his thoughts, followed by another one.

In four days, you begin to take what's hers now.

Iain rubbed the cloth down his body, encountering his hardened cock. His flesh understood his base needs. He did not just want the acres or buildings, he wanted the woman who owned them. After refusing him, he wanted her capitulation. He wanted her mouth where his hand now touched. He wanted to…

The cough at the door behind him brought him back to himself. Using the cloth to cover his aroused flesh, he walked into the bedchamber and climbed into the freshly-made bed, dropping the linen on the floor next to it.

Once alone, it took little effort or time to bring about satisfaction, but that did not quiet his thoughts or the growing hunger within him.

Four days. For better or worse, just four days.

SIX

The thing she missed most about Jonathan, if there was only one, was his friendship.

He had opened up the world to her, nay he'd created a new one for her. One in which she was his partner. One in which her worth was measured by love, not the marriage settlement she brought. One in which they shared a vision of their future together—in business, in life, in love.

And they talked for hours, planning and plotting their expansion.

Though her advisors and staff gave her the benefit of their knowledge and experience, all trod carefully around her and would never argue too strongly against her decisions. And, if she was honest with herself, she'd not faced a choice like the one that challenged her now. She wished she had someone with whom she could discuss the whole matter of Sir Iain and his offer. Someone not her employee. Not her sister. Someone…

Clare watched out the window as the children ran about the yard next to the school without actually seeing any of them. She tucked away a reminder to ask Mr. Chalmers if he'd discovered anything about the missing children and then went back to staring.

One of the three days he'd given her to visit him to speak of his offer had passed. She wanted to say her ankle had pained her and prevented her from walking much, but part of her wanted to see him again. Though she'd not changed her decision about his offer, she was curious about it.

And him.

Another reason for her to avoid him.

"Lady Clare?" She turned away from the window as Mrs. Baird approached. Philomena kept the children who lived here housed, fed and well. And she tried to keep them safe when they did not. "Mrs. Hunter has arrived and asked to speak to you."

"She is here?" Clare glanced down the hallway and found it empty.

"William has shown her to the small parlor."

"Did she say what this is about?" Clare asked.

She headed towards the parlor opposite of the office that was a less formal and more comfortable place to greet guests. She'd not spoken to Samantha since the day after her return from Inverness. That was not unusual in itself for, between Clare's commitments here and overseeing other business matters, there were times when the two women lived in the same household without seeing each other. It must be important if Samantha sought her out.

Clare almost stopped at the realization that Sam might be the very person she needed most right now. Mrs. Baird was close on her heels, so Clare moved along and entered the parlor to find it... empty. The chattering of the children outside the window drew her attention and that was where she spied Samantha.

Outside.

Speaking with Mr. MacLaurin.

Laughing with Mr. MacLaurin.

Clare heard Mrs. Baird's indrawn breath at the same moment she did the same. The encounter they were witnessing was not just a casual or accidental one for the two were clearly comfortable as they stood laughing together.

"Samantha and Peter?" she whispered even while not expecting a response.

"I do not ken how I missed it all this time," Mrs. Baird said. "I am usually better at seeing these things." A regretful tone filled her words.

"You are?" Clare faced the school's housekeeper. This was not a particularly good place for the blooming of romantic relationships.

"My family considers me quite a matchmaker, Lady Clare. I have had many successes at introducing couples, but I am doubting my own abilities having missed this one." Mrs. Baird nodded at the two as they leaned their heads closer, exchanging some sort of private conversation.

Samantha had lost her much older husband several years before moving in with Clare. Though worn down from being her husband's caretaker for the last years of his life, she'd bloomed once she was widowed. With a reasonable fortune, she did not depend on Clare or anyone for her living. She contributed generously to Clare's special projects, this school included, as well as belonging to several societies for educational and artistic studies.

Now, watching as she and Mr. MacLaurin spoke, oblivious to even the boisterous play of the children kicking a ball around them, Clare could see that this had been happening without her noticing for some time. In her own attempts to ignore what she missed the most in life, she'd missed this happening even within her own household.

"Well, well."

So caught up in their thoughts, neither noticed that the couple had stopped talking to each other and were staring in their direction. Clare quickly turned away and Mrs. Baird stepped away just as quickly. Making her way to one of the high-back chairs, she sat and smoothed her gown and ever-present apron over her lap, waiting for Samantha's arrival… and comments. Mrs. Baird retreated from the parlor, passing Samantha in the doorway and calling the maid for tea.

A blush filled Samantha's cheeks as she entered and sat across from Clare. Between that and the glint in her eyes, she appeared younger than her more than one-score-and-ten years.

Which was some years old than Mr. MacLaurin.

"I did not mean to keep you waiting, Clare. But I remembered something to tell… Mr. MacLaurin and thought to do it while I waited."

The excuse seemed polite enough and reasonable enough. The two had been introduced before and had even worked together on several events held here at the school. But the blush deepened and Samantha glanced away as she spoke, belying her casual words.

"I had no idea." Clare spoke honestly. When Samantha met her gaze, she could see her friend struggling with the decision whether to continue the ruse or admit the truth.

"He is quite appealing," she said. A smile flitted across her face, and it tugged at Clare's heart. To find joy after such unhappiness was a good thing.

"Mrs. Hunter! He is younger than you."

"Mrs. Logan!" Samantha's smile widened and her blue eyes filled with a mischievous expression. "He is younger indeed."

They both laughed aloud at all the inferences and innuendos of her words, for her tone spoke of the more carnal implications of a younger, enthusiastic man.

"I wish you happy, Sam," she said.

"You are not angry then? I so worried about telling you or not. Peter… Mr. MacLaurin wanted to ask your permission to court me."

The maid arrived just then, forestalling any other admissions for several minutes as Clare served the tea. When the door closed, Clare shook her head.

"I cannot believe I missed it."

"Well, you have been busy lately," Sam said. "Which is why I should not take up more of your time." She lifted her cup and drank from it as though hesitating to get to her purpose here.

"So, you did not visit for a *tête-à-tête* then?" She could not help but tease now, for this now-shared secret gave her great joy. Sam placed her cup on the tray and straightened in her seat.

"I come with an offer for you." Sam cleared her throat and looked extremely uncomfortable now. That only happened when Sam was pressed to do something—

"What did Caro ask you to do?" Her teacup found its place on the tray, too. "Do not dissemble—tell me plainly." Too many years and too much meddling made it easy to spot when Caro decided to step in the middle of Clare's life.

"Caro suggested I might accompany you when you meet with Sir Iain. She thought it might be more

supportive to have another woman in a chamber full of—
" She paused. "A chamber full of argumentative and controlling men who think they know what a woman should do."

"Her exact words?" Clare asked.

"Aye. Exactly. I have her note if you would like to see the rest of it, but that explains it." Sam reached for her reticule and retrieved a folded paper.

"No need. It sounded just as if she spoke the words herself." And as much as Clare would like to refuse, she could not argue that it might be the best thing to do.

She'd planned to bring along both her man of business and her solicitor; having Samantha would give her a silent ally in the room. Worse, her sister was not wrong about how men generally behaved while dealing with business matters with a woman. They usually got caught up in discussing details with the other men present and would seem to forget her presence and involvement. If nothing else, Samantha could be an impartial observer of the discussions.

"Are you at ease with such a task?"

"It might prove interesting at the least," Sam said.

"And at the worst?" Clare asked.

"A few wasted hours." Sam stood. "Speaking of which, I should not waste anymore of yours."

"I am planning to send word in the morning that we will arrive at Sir Iain's office at the docks at two. Will that be acceptable?" They walked to the door. "Or is there a more convenient time for you, since this is for my benefit?"

"That is fine."

"We can sort these details out at dinner," Clare said. Sam shook her head and smiled.

"I will not be joining you for dinner this evening," she said. Sam blushed again. "If you send the carriage for me at half-one, I will be ready." Just before Sam left, she turned back to Clare. "I do have one question for you."

"Of course."

"Is he as devastatingly handsome as Caro says?"

Clare choked as both a laugh and a gasp tried to escape at the same moment. By the time, she could respond, Sam was out the door, leaving only the echoing sound of her laughter in her wake.

God help her now that Caro had the bit between her teeth over the matter, and appearance, of Sir Iain Buchanan.

Clare called her advisors together in her office well before noon so they might make final preparations for the meeting. Over the weeks since his invasion of her office, she'd learned more about the whirlwind called Sir Iain Buchanan.

Or as much as her men could discover.

The man came from Glasgow where his first business success had been in the processing and transport of sea kelp, of all things. His fortunes soared since other sources of the valuable chemicals in the kelp were blocked for years by the war on the continent. From there and with the money he'd stockpiled, he expanded, building his fleet of transport ships that eventually helped in the efforts to supply the British troops in that very war. Hence, the king's knighting and his entry into society.

From what Duncan had explained, the investments Sir Iain made always seemed to reap wealth and so he became sought-after by anyone looking to increase their own coffers. Hence, her father's and brother-by-marriage's interest in him.

Now, as his business empire thrived, he wanted to capitalize on the advantageous harbor in Leith. With its location on the North Sea, it was accessible from Nordic and continental countries and even farther afield. Hence his desire for her properties.

Hence… hence… hence. So many logical reasons for his attempts to buy it. Clare understood those, but understanding did not necessitate acceptance or acquiescence. Just because he had reasons for wanting her property did not mean he should get it.

But something else bothered her when she considered the last several months since Sir Iain's first offer.

"Duncan, when did you begin the process of approvals for converting the warehouses?" she asked, looking up from a document that had long since blurred from staring at it too long. Her man of business sorted through a pile of documents searching for the correct information and handed some paper to Mr. Chalmers as well.

"Early in October of last year, my lady." He shuffled around a few more pages. "The sixth of October."

"And when did we receive the first offer?" she asked. A suspicion, based on nothing more or less than a strong feeling about the man involved, tickled at her thoughts.

"The seventh of October, my lady."

Clare slid her hand along the edge of the desk, feeling the smooth, polished wood under her fingertips. Moving them back and forth, she considered her next questions.

"How long did it take to get initial approval?"

"Well, my lady, as you ken, there was some issue with the original forms—"

"And how long did it take to sort that out?" she interrupted as she remembered the details of the problem.

"Almost four months, my lady. In the end, there was no actual deficiency in our application." Just as she remembered. She began to ask her next question when Chalmers spoke first.

"The approval came in on the twenty-eighth of February, my lady, and the second offer on the first of March."

His gaze narrowed as he met hers. He was a canny one, born on the streets but through a turn of luck raised and educated well. But James Chalmers had a streak of his origins that ran strong within him, allowing him to consider means and methods outside the customary ones. He had contacts that none of her other business advisors or employees had and those had benefitted her in the past. Sometimes, one had to look outside the usual to find the answers… or the child.

"I apologize for missing that, my lady," Chalmers said.

Duncan glanced from her to Chalmers and back again, just realizing the connections she was making.

"'Tis not your fault," she said. "I have asked you to focus on other matters."

"Do you think he could have been the architect of our delays?" Duncan asked.

"Do you, Mr. Chalmers?" she asked. He did not have to say a word for his expression said it all.

So, the charming, wildly attractive knight had a darker side? He was playing his own game while trying to manipulate her.

He was not the first man who'd tried such maneuverings since she took over control of the Logan estate. But he was the most devious to date. Most did not expect her to understand what they were doing in the pursuit of their goals. Clare had discovered they were bested by simply playing the role they'd assigned her.

But not this one.

Though he most likely underestimated her, he was attacking using all possible elements—business, family, society and even governmental approval processes. Nothing too public. Nothing too gauche that would be noticeable.

"Since he's made a third offer, we can assume our application has suffered some kind of setback that we have not learned about yet?"

Duncan jolted from his seat and left the chamber in a rush. From that sudden exit, Clare knew the answer already. Her secretary returned holding out a thick envelope in his hand.

"It was marked two weeks ago but delivered to your home, Lady Clare. Timothy only discovered it and brought it over earlier today."

Her fingers returned to sliding over the surface of the desk as Duncan took some time to examine the documents. Circles felt more soothing than zigzag lines, so she continued until Duncan was ready. The intensity in his eyes did not bode well for their efforts.

"He must ken someone influential enough to be interfering with our applications," Duncan said. "I cannot believe we did not see it."

"Or paid them off," Mr. Chalmers said.

Money paved a smooth path in every journey, and this was no different. Actually, the stakes and rewards were higher, so Buchanan must have spent large amounts to steer decisions to his benefit. Clare huffed out a breath and shook her head. Pushing her chair back to stand, she looked at each of the men there.

"James, I want you working on this project along with the other. Please," she said. "Duncan, give him what he needs to bring him up to date."

They had a meeting in a few hours, but she was now better prepared than before, in spite of the surprising revelations. And that would work to her advantage.

"Does this change your decision, my lady?"

"How so, Duncan?"

"Will you accept his offer knowing what he is willing to do to attain this?" He held up the deed and documents.

"My decision has not and will not change."

Clare walked to the door, needing a few moments alone to gather her thoughts and her resolve. The knowledge of his zeal to purchase her property and the methods he might use to encourage her to sell to him revealed a whole aspect of Sir Iain Buchanan. One that, she was surprised to admit, did not immediately turn her opinion of him.

"My carriage will leave my residence at half-past one with my cousin, who will accompany us. I will see you then," she said.

Clare opened the door to dismiss them. Once alone, she sat on one of the chairs she had in a somewhat cozy arrangement off in the corner and allowed herself to take a breath.

The upcoming appointment would be so much more than a simple business meeting—clearly buying what was hers was of some importance to him. Then, Clare remembered a small detail that Chalmers had mentioned in passing during his review of what he knew of Sir Iain Buchanan and his empire.

The man does not fail in his efforts. He is relentless in his pursuits.

Her body shivered then, remembering his strength as he lifted her effortlessly into his arms and carried her up all those stairs—into Caro's house and up to the guest room. Though Chalmers had been referring to his methods of carrying on his businesses, her body flooded with waves of searing heat in reaction to the words.

Their encounters so far had shown his relentlessness in different ways. Between trying to intimidate her with his height and muscular build and aggressive entrance the first time or the sparkle in his intense gaze when he stared at her across the dinner table, that trait was obvious. The dangerous thing was that it called to something deep within her. Whether to accept his challenge or to capitulate, she knew not. But, instead of dreading the coming meeting and the difficulties of such, she was excited by it. Excited to pit her skills and knowledge—and preparation—against his.

Oh, the plans she had for the property were too important to her, too connected to Jonathan and their dreams of helping the less fortunate, especially children, to relinquish them. It involved not only memories but also the future and the legacy of his name.

So, no matter the amount of money offered nor the obstacles placed in her path, she would see the new school and orphanage built and flourish.

No matter what. No matter who.

SEVEN

Iain watched out the window of his office for a sign of the approaching coach. And even as he did, he chided himself for showing such an obvious amount of anticipation of her arrival. Her note to inform him of her arrival time had been short, almost curt, but he laughed when he read it. Chairs scraping on the floor behind him made him turn.

Douglas, the young man who did menial tasks around the offices for Ben, dragged a heavy wooden chair across the space. He left it in front of Iain's desk but only for a moment. As soon as Douglas positioned it, Ned disagreed with its placement and ordered it elsewhere. As amusing as the trio was to watch, it was his own escalating tension about the coming meeting that was spreading to the others. His temper would have snapped after the third move, but Douglas had as much patience as he did brawn and continued, following each of Ben's directions without a word or a pause. It did at least until the rattle of carriage wheels on the cobblestones outside drew his attention back.

Lady Clare was here.

"Put three in a row, one slightly closer to my desk than the others, Douglas," he said over his shoulder. "Ned, see to her." He did not look to see if his orders were obeyed, for they would be. Iain dropped the curtain and watched through the openings in the pattern of the lace. Once she alighted and Ned presented himself, Iain turned to take his position as he waited for her to arrive.

As the sound of the group echoed up the staircase, he tugged his shirt cuffs down within the sleeves of his coat and adjusted his neckcloth. Paul had outdone himself today in dressing Iain, so much so that Ned and Ben had taken great pleasure in making jokes about his attention to his appearance this morn. They would pay for their mocking.

But not now.

Lady Clare led her entourage into his office and the woman with them surprised him. If he was not mistaken, she was Mrs. Hunter, a cousin of a sort who lived with the lady. Lady Clare had not mentioned bringing along a companion.

"My lady, thank you for meeting me," he said as he bowed then took her hand. "You have met my secretary, Edward Pemberton—" He nodded to Ned. "May I present my solicitor, Mr. Robert Cairns?" Iain waited for Lady Clare's acknowledgement of Cairns before moving on to the others on his staff. "Mr. Ebeneezer Gilchrist, my man of business."

He watched as she greeted them with all the politeness expected of a lady and waited on her introductions. She wore a pelisse in a shade of dark green, bottle green he thought they called it, over a gown of lighter green and both colors enhanced the color of her eyes. The pelisse, accentuated with military-style epaulets on the shoulders and gold braid ties, was cut to accentuate the fullness of her breasts. The way it draped down to the unadorned lower edge allowed it to move over her legs as she walked closer. Her ensemble was finished with a smart bonnet topped in several feathers that swayed with her every movement. Her strides as she crossed his office were smooth, with no sign of her injury in each step.

"Sir Iain, you have met Mr. Duncan Shaw, and this is Mr. David Balfour, my private secretary." Iain nodded at both men. "Previously you met Mr. Andrew Lamb, my solicitor, but he was unable to attend today. Allow me to introduce my other solicitor, Mr. James Chalmers."

A sound emanated from Cairns who stood at Iain's back that would usually raise his defenses. Though no overt threat existed, Cairns' growl could mean nothing good.

"Chalmers," he grumbled.

"Sir Iain," the newly-introduced Mr. Chalmers said in the expected polite tone to him before the man stared over at the solicitor. "Cairns," he growled back in the same deep tone that Cairns had used to address him.

The lady's startled expression told him she'd not known of a past connection between their solicitors. He thought he was going to have to ask about her companion when she blinked several times and met his gaze.

"And this is Mrs. Hugh Hunter." He waited for more, but she said nothing else.

"Please be seated," Iain said. "Will you have tea or coffee, Lady Clare?" He nodded at Douglas.

"I am fine, Sir Iain. I would rather get down to business."

The show was on. *Fine*.

He expected her to sit in one of the chairs and motioned to Douglas to bring another forward for Mrs. Hunter. As soon as it was placed, Lady Clare spoke.

"Please place those two over there and place this one just there," she said.

Douglas looked at her and then at Iain, clearly uncertain about who to obey. He tilted his head, and the servant followed her instructions. Then, the lady sat, slightly closer to his desk, with her companion at her side, just inches away from her. Her advisors took places a few feet away from her side and her secretary—with notepad in hand—stood in the corner behind everyone while his own secretary sat next to Iain at a small desk. Looking over those assembled, now in their places for the coming battle, Iain almost laughed as he noticed the result of positioning her staff so—Iain could not look at them and her at the same time.

Lady Clare Logan was the center of this gathering and would not be ignored.

Interesting.

Surprising again.

Something within him felt the challenge of it—the lady giving orders in his own office—and his blood raced from it. He relished a good fight and, until now, until she purposely tasked him in front of his own staff, he was willing to consider her title, her sex, and her relative inexperience to his as excuses for her refusals.

Now?

His nostrils flared as he inhaled the scent she wore— something fresh and flowery without being too frilly. Nay, Mrs. Hunter's perfume was that obnoxious mix of spring flowers and something else that displeased his senses. Lady Clare sat to all appearances at ease waiting for him to open the discussion.

For the first time in… forever, Iain lost track of the opening he'd planned. Looking into her eyes, he simply and completely lost his wits. Ben saved his arse by handing out copies of the report they'd prepared for this meeting.

"This is simply a review of the most recent offer, my lady," Ben said.

She took the document and read it over, the list of numbers and definitions and such did not intimidate her or slow her down. As he gave her solicitor and man of business copies of the same, Ben continued his explanation. And as Iain had directed, the man who managed did not lessen the number of details shared, the financial terms or the expected timing of the contracts.

Having done this before, Iain watched and allowed his men to do what they did best, not needing to add more than a comment or two or to answer a question along the way. And he fought the growing admiration for her with every word she spoke. This was no reticent lady of society. Nay, she was quite knowledgeable in many aspects of planning, architecture, raising funds to finance the building and the like. And Lady Clare even answered a few questions he had no response to.

His cock hardened more with her every word, every question and especially every bloody time she looked at him. Iain clutched the edge of the desk and prayed he would not humiliate himself when she slid her lower lip out into a pout as she read one of the pages.

Had she any idea of her effect on him and his ability to attend to his business matter? Did she know that he was aroused now or had been the last time they'd been together? Iain shifted now, praying his cock did not bang on the bottom of the desk and bring attention to his lack of control over her!

Listening to Ben's answer to this last question from

Lady Clare's solicitor, Iain knew he needed to walk, or he would do something incredibly stupid. He caught Douglas' eye, nodded and then waited for Ben to finish. When he had, Iain spoke.

"Thank you, Gilchrist. You have given Lady Clare much to consider." Iain faced the lady and her companion. "This went on much longer than I expected, so I've sent for tea and refreshments." Lady Clare stood and everyone else in the chamber did as well.

"May we speak privately, Sir Iain?"

"My lady?"

"Perhaps you could show me around your facilities?"

He glanced at her business advisors, and none raised even the slightest objection or suggestion about how it might be ill-advised to be alone with him during this critical time. Not that she was in danger of harm, but because the negotiations were at a delicate place. She was, after all, a widow and did not require the same level of circumspection that society required of an unmarried woman. Still, Iain gave Mrs. Hunter one last chance to tag along in case Lady Clare wanted a companion before gesturing for the lady to precede him from the office. He turned back for a moment and noticed that Cairns and Chalmers stood on opposite sides of the room but in the same exact stance—one he'd taken many times, so he recognized it immediately. Feet apart, arms crossed over chests, shoulders back, chins out.

The two solicitors were sizing up their enemies.

Well, in this situation it might be more about opponents than actual enemies. Or so he thought as he stepped out to let Douglas pass with a tea cart. One last glance told him his first impression had been the correct one—the two men were enemies on some level. That was interesting. Now though, Lady Clare Logan drew his attention, and he would sort out the two men in private.

"My lady," he said as he guided her through a door at the end of the hallway. It led to the edge of this part of the second floor which was more a loft or balcony as it projected over the warehouse's main floor below. "This is the center of my—"

"Empire?" she asked. From the tone of their discussions and the depth of her questions, it was clear she'd learned more about him since their first encounter.

"But that would make me an emperor instead of a mere knight," he said. He liked jesting with her this way. It cost him nothing and gave him pleasure. His body reminded him though not enough pleasure. "A conglomeration of businesses is all."

"A far-flung, profit-making, ever-expanding conglomeration at that." She walked to the railing and looked over the people working and rushing around below them.

"Is there a better kind, my lady?" As he watched and waited on her reply, she examined the way the huge space was laid out. Her eyes were bright and a blush filled her cheeks. What could she be thinking? Finally, he just asked his question. "You have been refreshingly direct today so I will be as well." Her left eyebrow lifted at his words. She placed her hands, one on top of the other, on the railing and waited for him to speak. "What did you want to speak to me about… in private that could not be spoken before others?"

The tip of her tongue slipped out and moistened her lips and Iain nearly dropped to his knees. Between the blush in her cheeks and the sight of her tongue, heat raced through his body until sweat beaded on his forehead. Her breaths now came out as shallow panting and he wanted to take hold of her, tear the pert little bonnet from her head, loosen her hair and then kiss her to within an inch of her life.

Until she was his.

"Will my next refusal come with the same reaction from you, Sir Iain?"

For a moment, the words made no sense and yet they might. Would she refuse his advances? He'd had no complaints from women, from lovers, in the past so he was certain he would…

Make an utter fool out of himself.

Lady Clare spoke of business while he and his body wanted possession. He pulled the lust that threatened everything he'd worked for back under control and realized the accusation in her words. She knew.

She knew the actions he'd taken to secure her properties. At the very least, she knew about the interference in the application process even if she had no idea about the other efforts in his plan. Bloody hell, she was splendid! Nervous about speaking to him about it, but unlike any woman, or competitor, he'd faced before. Bloody hell.

"I will not offer insult, my lady, by pretending I know not to what you refer. Aye, I will continue to slow down the process of converting those warehouses, those spaces, until they're mine."

The shallow panting continued, and it made her breasts quiver beneath the layers of her clothing and her body tense. Although she had not moved or released her hands from their tight clutch, he sensed her first response—if she allowed herself the freedom of it— would be to punch him. That she clasped her hands together to prevent herself from swinging madly at his head made him want to smile. A lady would never do such a thing as strike out, but Iain felt the waves of anger pouring out of her.

"Why would you do such a thing?" Her voice trembled but he did not mistake the fury for fear.

"Because I want those properties. I have learned to do what's necessary—"

"To get what you want?"

"Why else?" he asked.

"No matter what? No matter who is harmed?"

He had not harmed anyone. He'd spread a huge amount of his money around to accomplish what he wanted done. And maybe a few heads had been knocked about or a few threats made, but no harm. His delay in denying her accusation gave her the opportunity to continue.

"My answer remains the same, Sir Iain. Those properties are not for sale."

She lifted her hands from the railing she'd been clinging to and walked past him. He reached out to stop her, for there was much he wanted to say to her. Taking hold of her upper arm, he used her momentum to guide her through another door and into a small chamber off the balcony. Once there, she tugged until free of him and stared at him. From her expression, his touch shocked her. Her mouth formed a perfect 'O' and her eyes widened and flashed like green fire.

He'd forgotten all the proper manners of a gentleman in society—lessons studied hard and practiced long and yet clearly misplaced when need and desire arose. All gone in a momentary lapse of reason because of her.

"My lady," he said, lifting his hand from her. "Forgive me."

"For that?" She glanced where his hand had been. "Forgiven." Now she met his gaze, and he knew the rest. "But for what you tried to do? Only if you cease these nefarious means and negotiate in good faith."

Any other man would have taken her demands as an affront to his pride. Iain found himself more aroused by her spirit and courage. He did not understand her resistance to selling, for that was one thing his efforts had not uncovered yet, but he relished this battle.

"If you wanted something, something you needed, would you not use whatever means necessary?" he asked. Leaning closer to her, he fought the urge to inhale her scent. "What lines would you cross to succeed?"

The lady startled then, at his words or his closeness he knew not, and she tilted her head back and met his gaze. Everything, every noise, every other thing around them disappeared and there was only her.

Iain took hold of her shoulders and lifted her closer to him. Her breath heated his cheek and desire shuddered through his body. Only an inch separated their mouths and when she did not object, he kissed her the way he'd wanted, nay, the way he'd dreamt about taking her mouth.

Deeply.

Completely.

It was not the kiss a gentleman should place on a lady's lips. This was meant to expose his desire and mark her with himself. His lips covered hers and he kissed the breath from her. Lifting to cant his head, he tasted her, filling her mouth with his tongue. Seeking hers. Tasting her mouth. Teasing her tongue to touch his. He felt the moment she capitulated to the passion.

Her body leaned against his and the feel of her breasts

heaving against his chest aroused him more. Sliding his hands down onto her arms, he eased her closer until their hips were touching. Then, he rubbed to allow her to feel what she did to him—his erection between them could not be mistaken.

Had she found pleasure with Jonathan Logan?

The strange thought did not dampen his ardor. Instead, it made him want to show her the pleasure they could share together. To free the strong, passionate woman he could see within her to take what she wanted from a lover. To take what a lover had to give. Iain was determined to be that lover who would pleasure her as relentlessly as his desire and his body was demanding now.

Lady Clare leaned her head back, lifting her mouth from his as she stared at him. Her gaze moved over his face, meeting his eyes for a moment and then settled on his mouth. Her own lips were swollen from his kisses and he was pleased by that. There was a place just above her breast that he wanted to suckle and mark with his mouth, but that would have to wait. Now, when he expected her to end this, to pull away since she was tugging her arms free, she once more surprised the bloody hell out of him.

When she reached up and wrapped her arms around his neck, he stopped breathing. When she pulled him down closer, he could not but hope. But when she kissed him, he lost his wits and his control completely. At the first touch of her tongue exploring his mouth, he pressed her against the wall and thrust his hips. Rather than frightening her off, it seemed to encourage her own actions. Her tongue swept into his mouth as she tightened her hold on him. Then, she pressed her breasts against him and shifted her legs a half-step apart that allowed him to step between them and position his cock even more intimately. He kept his hands on the wall just above her head to keep himself from taking a step too far, but the next sound she made made his body shake from the need to.

"Iain," she whispered against his mouth.

Iain lifted his mouth from hers and saw the passion in her gaze. Her lips were unmistakably swollen from passionate kissing. Her breathing was shallow and erratic, and her body still pressed against his hard flesh. The choice of how to carry this to its conclusion—a willing one from the look of things—gave him pause. And that pause was just enough time for him to hear the raised voices from his office down the hall.

The lady's arms dropped slowly from his neck and, for a moment, she closed her eyes and leaned her head back on the very wall against which he'd pressed her. He swore to himself that when he finally had her, he *would* take her against a wall. His cock throbbed at that thought and the image it shot into his mind.

The sounds of their excited breaths filled the chamber and a few moments passed before she opened her eyes. Slowly, movement by movement, the lady returned and straightened, shook out her gown and pelisse, pulled her gloves back into place over each finger and made a few other adjustments to her appearance.

The fire in his blood urged him not to end this so easily. If any other woman, he would… Bloody hell, this was not just any woman. He stepped back and ran his hands through his hair, and she slipped around him. For a moment he wanted to bash his head against the wall where she'd stood. If taking her by the arm just minutes ago had shocked her, what must she be thinking now?

As she reached for the door and sanity returned, Iain saw his entire plan falling apart because he could not control his cock. So much for the preparation, the targeting, the bribes, the threats, the investigations and collection of information for the past two years. The sheer extent of his efforts to get the properties that her husband had promised him in a gentleman's agreement were at risk.

A rare mistake in those early days of bargaining, for Iain had slipped up and accepted without getting a written contract. In the thrill of the king's honor and patronage, Iain had made a mistake. And now, all his efforts to finally acquire those properties might be for naught. All of it gone, wasted, fruitless, because he allowed his lust to run free instead of staying with his well-planned scheme?

"Bloody, bloody hell," he whispered on a rough exhale.

Nay. He would not allow that to happen. There was a way to use this to further his plans, not stop them. The lady had enjoyed their encounter as much as he had. He could feel the way her body softened as he aroused her with his mouth. She opened to his kisses, and he had no doubt that, if there'd been more uninterrupted time, he could have taken them much, much farther in their mutual pleasure.

He would salvage this and not allow it to stop him. But still…

What had he been thinking?

EIGHT

What had she been thinking?

A moment more and she would have begged him to toss her skirts up and have his way with her!

Shocked at her actions, and his, Clare put some distance between them in the small chamber. Now glancing around it, she found it was some sort of closet for storing boxes of a sort. No furniture other than a few shelves on one wall. Empty. Smaller than an office and bigger and more private than an alcove, it had been useful for this assignation.

Did he use it for that purpose often? A man like him must have women by the dozens who allowed him to kiss them and… more. The blush at such thoughts tingled up to fill her cheeks. When he spoke her name softly, she faced him to find a usually-calm, controlled man wearing a very befuddled expression. He appeared as dazed and confused as she felt.

"Sir—"

"Lady—"

"I must go first, my lady," he said. "I… took liberties and I apologize for my actions." He sounded genuine in his words. She wanted to believe him and yet, having been the first time a man had ever lost himself in passion towards her, she did not want his regret.

Her body throbbed and her mouth both ached and hungered for the touch and taste of his. This encounter was not truly a surprise, for each of their previous ones had left her thrilled in some way. Either the mental challenge of confronting and engaging him or the physical awareness of him and his every move, she walked away feeling alive and energized in ways she'd not felt, well, not felt in years if ever.

Her relationship with Jonathan was even-keeled, respectful, loving. They did not confront or refuse—they cooperated and supported each other.

Any dealings with this man would never come close to what she'd experienced before. And that realization did not frighten her as it should.

Nay, it made her want to clash with him.

To oppose him.

To say nay so that he would make her say aye.

From the passion and desire in those kisses, ones that bordered on him claiming possession of her, she would be easily convinced. David's arrival prevented her from admitting that or anything of a personal nature.

"My lady?" her secretary said as he opened the door slowly after a soft knock. "Is all well?" Sir Iain let out a noise that partly sounded like a laugh and a cough behind her.

"We were just finishing our… discussion," she said. "We will rejoin you all in a moment." From the incredulous look he gave her, David was well aware of what the *discussion* was about. He did not argue—he never would—and he even closed the door as he left with a nod at them.

Now, she must say something to the man who stood just behind her, heat yet pouring off his body now. He'd apologized and she was required to accept or deny it. Since Clare had encouraged his bold actions by grabbing the man and pulling him closer, and then kissing him back, she must accept responsibility. She must tell him it could never be allowed again.

"Do you regret it?" she asked instead.

He did not reply immediately but his gaze moved over her almost like a caress as he studied her from the toes of her leather half-boots to the bonnet she wore. He paused several times and her body heated as she realized just where he was staring when he did.

"I do not regret it, my lady." The corner of his mouth lifted in the slightest of smiles, but she felt it. As he stepped past her to open the door, he leaned in and whispered in her ear. "And if you permit me, I plan on repeating it." His breath warmed her sensitive skin there as he continued. "Again and again." She shivered against the rush of heat. Just when she thought him done, he whispered again. "And again." He opened the door and became the consummate businessman he'd been in his office during the talks. "With your permission, my lady." He extended his hand towards the hallway.

Ice and heat vied for control over her body. His words were both polite and an invitation to wickedness at the same time. Though she knew that any experience with him would be unlike anything she'd had in the past, even the danger of this man excited her. Clare could not meet his gaze as she passed him by to lead them back to his office.

Nor could she meet the gaze of anyone in the room as she took her seat again. A cup of tea appeared before her, and she accepted it with a murmured word of thanks. Her cheeks must be absolutely aflame since not a single person among those assembled there were stupid enough not to realize what had happened between her and Sir Iain. Her lips throbbed from his kisses as a reminder. Clare tilted her head up as she took a sip of tea and noticed that it was a woman who'd handed her the cup and not the servant from before. With the tightening in her stomach, now or later, she would have to face Samantha and her knowing gaze.

It would be later.

Samantha waited a moment more before moving aside. She would make things uncomfortable later but would not do so now, in front of Clare's staff.

"Thank you for clarifying some issues, my lady," the dangerous, wicked man said as he walked behind his desk. Their staffs all took their previous places and waited for him to continue. She tried to calm her racing heart and to be ready for whatever he said. "Gentlemen, lady," he said to the others present, "I have agreed to forego any efforts to impede Lady Clare's application process."

"You what?" she said sharply. A bit too that and too loud as the others erupted with questions and statements.

"I agreed to your request, my lady." The others were arguing with each other and amongst themselves and missed the wink. She did not. "In exchange for not interfering with your company's approval process, you agreed to continue negotiations in good faith."

In good faith? Those words could cover all manner of sins—both of commission and of omission as well. She could stop this right now by denying his words. If she did that, more expensive obstacles would be placed before her efforts, possibly preventing her from completing the project and costing her an enormous amount of money.

Considering their heated moments and intimate kissing, Clare understood his meaning of negotiations. Clearly. Shockingly for her, she was contemplating something that had never entered her thoughts until he barged into her office and sent her senses reeling.

Somehow, her quiet purpose-filled life was changing, and he was the catalyst. She could not attain what she wanted, do what she must do, build what she must build with this man as an obstacle. Though in the end she would never sell those precious blocks of Leith property to him, the idea of allowing him to try to entice her into doing that intrigued her. In spite of her sister's urgings, she was existing in a well-worn rut, living only to carry out Jonathan's last dream. When this project was completed and the day-to-day workings turned over to more qualified and experienced people, what would she live for then?

Mayhap it was this uncertainty that spurred her to want more? Even Sir Iain bringing her father back into her life recently—though surely for his reasons and not hers—had forced her to see the emptiness within her. Worse, how much she needed more. The isolation from her parents and initially from her sister had been the saddest part of the life she made with Jonathan. In so many ways, she'd gained more than she'd dreamt was possible.

But the losses had weighed on her more heavily these last two years. Now…

"I would never refuse negotiations, Sir Iain. Your service to the king and your earlier offers prove your seriousness."

"My lady!" Duncan whispered rather furiously. The three men with her probably thought she'd lost her wits completely by now. They had been the ones carrying out the plans that were hers, and Jonathan's, and understood her full commitment to the project. So this turn-about in willingness to negotiate with Sir Iain was a shock to them. To her as well.

"I have given Sir Iain no expectation of success, Duncan." Her man of business' incredulous glance matched the one on the faces of Chalmers, David and even Sir Iain's men. "But he can certainly try his best."

She heard the swift intake of breaths, but she was watching *him*. His eyes narrowed and he smiled, a movement of his mouth that was just enough to be called one. Then he tilted his head in a semblance of a bow that was really just an acceptance of her challenge. With that, she stood, handed the cup back to the attendant and nodded back.

"Mrs. Hunter. Gentlemen. Let us not waste anymore of Sir Iain's valuable time."

She did not wait for them to gather their satchels, Clare made her way around the chairs and walked to the door. The attendant quickly opened it for her.

"You will hear from me shortly, my lady."

"I would expect nothing less from you, Sir Iain."

Clare glanced over her shoulder and met his gaze and smiled back. She did not stop until she was seated in her carriage. Samantha was dying to ask questions, but she wisely held off as the others climbed in. Only Chalmers was missing.

"He said he would meet back at your office in the residence," David explained. As they drove away, she could see her solicitor in an intense conversation with Sir Iain's solicitor.

"Chalmers knows the man?"

"'Twould seem so, my lady," said Duncan.

"Did you know of a previous association between them?" she asked, tugging her gloves into place.

"I did not, my lady. But then there are many things I do not know about Chalmers." And better left in the dark, if she knew anything about him.

They'd all heard the growls of the men when introduced earlier. There was no doubt that the two men had some connection. Her question which she would not voice aloud was which man would win in a fight. A street fight. A no holds barred, bare-knuckle one.

As the carriage returned them to her residence in Edinburgh, she hoped it would be Chalmers. But between the look of Cairns and what she knew about Iain Buchanan, she worried he would not.

It took some time after they arrived back home for her to put off talking with Samantha and to calm the waters with her own advisors. By the time the butler interrupted them, her staff had their assignments to review their notes about the meeting and any new information that might have been slipped in with what they already knew. Chalmers had returned, though was quite close-mouthed about Cairns, and she decided she would speak to him privately about that and other matters.

When Poogan opened the door, he directed Richard to see the men out as he held out a silver tray to her. As he left, she saw Samantha in the foyer.

"Please ask Mrs. Hunter to join me, Poogan," she said.

She put the letter on her desk and walked to the more comfortable seating nearer the fireplace. Clare had no sooner sat than Samantha rushed in. Instead of speaking, she paused and walked in a more sedate pace over to where Clare was and sat in the other chair.

"Should I call for tea?" Clare asked.

Samantha stood and walked to the cabinet in the corner. Tugging open the glass door, she reached inside and lifted out the crystal decanter of whisky kept there. Placing it on the table next to the cabinet, she turned to Clare and raised an eyebrow.

"Certainly."

"Whisky or brandy?"

"Whisky."

After this whole day, a wee dram might calm her nerves. She did not imbibe spirits as a practice; however, she would make an exception. Samantha poured two servings and brought them over to Clare, tucking the decanter handily under one arm. Now it was Clare's turn to raise a brow.

"I've a feeling we may need more to fortify ourselves for the coming discussion." Clare could not disagree.

They sat in companionable silence until they'd each swallowed several sips of the aged and potent drink.

"You are a widow," Samantha said. Clare felt as though her friend had begun in the middle of some private conversation heard only by her. "And so, there is some leniency when it comes to relationships."

"Relationships?" Clare nearly choked.

"Well, you are contemplating entering into one with that man, are you not?" Clare was going to object, but Samantha was not ready to stop. "From the way that man looked at you, as though he was waiting to devour you, and the way you looked at him, well..." Samantha put her glass down and waved her hand over her face as though trying to cool her skin. "And that doesn't even take into account whatever happened between you two when you went off to *discuss* some matter or another."

Clare could not say anything. She wanted to argue, to explain, to say something. No words came. It was too soon. Too much had happened that she needed to think about before saying too much. Or saying the wrong thing. So many depended on her for their very lives for her to make a mistake in dealing with this man.

"Clare?"

"I beg your pardon, Samantha. It has been a very long day and—"

"And you do not want to talk about the thrill and excitement and terror and feelings of being attracted to a man like him?" Samantha took her hand. "It would be terrifying even if it were not as complicated as your life is. But, Clare, any moment of joy, and aye, pleasure, you can grab in the life is worth the chance you take."

"Is that why you are with Peter?"

Samantha consumed the rest of her whisky in one mouthful and poured more into her glass, all without a word in reply. Only when she replaced the stopper in the crystal bottle did she speak.

"I am with Peter because he makes me happy," she said. "And I believe I make him happy as well."

"You deserve to be happy, Cousin. After—" Samantha waved off what Clare was about to say.

"Aye, my life… before… was a horrid existence. Aye, he was a miserable man intent on breaking me. Aye, I was relieved at his death," she explained. "But, just because I suffered through that and now seek my own brighter future with a lovely young man." She paused and took a breath. "That does not mean you cannot seek happiness now because you were happy."

"I was happy with Jonathan," she said.

"Aye, you were. Incandescently happy. And fulfilled. And busy. You two were good for each other," Samantha said, her fervor growing as she spoke. "But, Clare, dearest Clare, Jonathan is gone. Through no fault of yours or his. Gone."

"I know that." Clare emptied the last bit of whisky into her mouth and swallowed against the tightness in her throat.

"I fear that, if you go on as you have been, I will see you dawdling around the square alone in twenty years. All in black, still mourning the loss of him."

"Samantha," she said. She stood and winced at the sound of her glass hitting the table's surface as she placed it there. "You go too far now."

"And you think too much, Clare." Clare gasped at her cousin's words. "Perhaps this man is not the one who will steal your heart after your great loss, but he may be enough."

"Enough?" When she thought of Iain Buchanan, she would never think of him in such a minimalistic way. If anything, he was too much—too powerful, too physical, too dangerous, too wicked.

"Enough for now." Samantha slid to the edge of her chair and turned to face Clare. "You had the extraordinary experience of marrying for love. Not many of us had the courage to do what you did, Clare. And now, I think, you are afraid to move on. Afraid that either you will never find such a love again, or that you will."

"It has only been—"

"You have been his widow as long as you'd been his wife."

That truth knocked her back. How could that be? Jonathan had been the center of her world since the moment they'd met. She'd been shopping along Princes Street and had dropped her reticule in the street. Jonathan had been meeting with several proprietors of the larger emporiums about contributing to his educational charity when he spied her trying to retrieve it.

He was gallant and handsome, tall with curly blond hair he wore a bit long. His clothing belied his wealth, everything from boots to his neckcloths always looked a bit worn. From the first words they exchanged, he spoke to her not as her parents or other male acquaintances did but as though she knew her own mind and she mattered. They met for tea, the first time to thank him for his help, and then contrived to meet at other gatherings or salons or even balls. Each time they were together, she fell a bit more in love with him.

By the time he asked for her hand in marriage, she would have stood against the Emperor Napoleon's whole army to be his wife. And, with her parents' reaction and opposition to his proposal, she did feel as though she had just might have. The one thing she never doubted was that he was the love of her life. And she'd walked away from her family and friends and her very way of life to follow him.

Now, surprised at Samantha's words, a quick counting confirmed it—he'd died two years and six months ago, and they'd married two years and six months before that.

Clare stood and walked to her desk, her hand trailing along the smooth wooden surface until she reached the chair. Unsettled by the exchange, she shook her head.

"I did not think of it in that way." She smiled even as

tears gathered. "I have been so caught up in completing his work that I never took notice."

Samantha walked over and wrapped her arms around Clare from behind. Her cousin always was an affectionate person. At least she was more recently and now Clare thought she understood what had changed Samantha's demeanor and outlook.

"Well, if nothing else, this man has shaken you from your reverie of grief." Samantha released her and stepped away. "He may or may not be a man with whom you wish to have a relationship, Clare," she said with a knowing smile. "But Lord above, he is as devastating as Caro described and you should give him a chance."

A knock interrupted the laughter that followed Samantha's words and Poogan entered.

"Yes, Poogan?" Clare sat down.

"The footman is awaiting your reply, my lady."

"The footman? A reply?"

"Sir Iain's footman waiting on a reply to the message there, my lady." Poogan nodded at her desk.

Clare looked down at the letter Poogan had given her just as Samantha entered. Lifting it, she broke the seal and unfolded the sheet of paper. She wanted to read the words slowly to give herself time to think but raced over them instead. He said she would hear from him soon and he had certainly done that.

"Clare?" Samantha said. "Whatever did you read to cause that expression of pure confusion to settle on your face?"

Clare looked from the words, the invitation, to her friend and back again.

"Is it something rude or daring then?" She moved closer to Clare trying to see the contents, so Clare handed the letter to her. "A ball at the Assembly Rooms this evening?" They both glanced at the clock.

"In five hours." Clare glanced back at the message. "Three if I would like to join him for supper before the ball."

This was a game to him, Clare understood that. He could not allow her challenge to him—and her refusal to sell to him—to go unanswered. Was this simply to gain some information to use as leverage against her or as some kind of bribe to encourage her?

Of course it was. Even knowing that, even knowing he was doing this for his own reasons and none of them had to do with her personally, she would accept. She must. For she must play the game and find out more about him.

Without a word, she sat and took a sheet of paper from the stationery stand. She quickly penned a short reply, folded it, sealed it, and held it out to Poogan.

"Please apologize to the footman for the delay, Poogan. It is never necessary to be rude or ignorant of another's time."

Poogan disagreed with her over this *eccentricity* of hers for he'd told her so. When she'd asked him about his reaction the first time, she offered an apology. Waiting was part of a footman's or house maid's or other servant's job, he'd explained, and they expected it when carrying out their duties—to literally and figuratively wait on their betters.

She, however, did not live or treat those who worked for her as her parents and society and even those like Poogan did. A little kindness went far in keeping a loyal and respectful staff in both her house and her school. And that would never change.

Poogan bowed and took the letter, placing it on the tray he held. He nodded as he left.

"So, will you go?"

Clare entwined her fingers together and rested her hands on the desk in front of her. The sound of Samantha's tapping foot echoed in the silence of the room.

"I must." Samantha let out the breath she'd been holding. Clare allowed a smile to break. "Weakness is one thing he seeks out in an opponent. Refusing now would expose my fear to him." Clare shrugged as she stood. "So, aye, I will accept his invitation to dinner."

Samantha went to the door and opened it. "Dinner only?" Clare nodded. "I will help you choose a dress if you'd like?"

"That would be helpful. I am sorely out of practice at such things."

"Clare." Samantha stopped before entering the foyer and took hold of her hands. "If you do not wish to. If you are opposed to taking this step. I do not want my earlier words to force you to do something you are not ready to do."

She appreciated Samantha's support and nodded at her.

"I am not being forced to this by anything but my decision to find out more about him."

"You hire employees to do that."

"But, Samantha, I may succeed in learning more about the man this way. I may discover *his* weaknesses. *His* fears. And more."

Clare wrapped her arm around Samantha's and led her to the stairs. They were halfway up the first flight when she leaned over and whispered.

"But I will do this on my own terms."

NINE

Lady Clare would meet him for supper.

He laughed aloud drawing the servants' notice. Iain read the reply again and laughed… again. From their reserved but yet obvious glances, his household was questioning his sanity.

The lady declined, however, to accompany him to the ball.

So be it.

From what he'd learned, she'd not attended a society function since she married Logan. Better that than to be constantly snubbed by family and friends and even strangers. Iain understood that feeling having lived it most of his life. Even after he'd taken over Old Buchanan's factory and inherited the rest, a fortune by any standards, he was still not enough for society.

Oh, they profited from him and with him and he was soon too successful to ignore, but they interacted with him as though the stench of the street yet hung about him. No matter that he had forced the cant from his speech and learned to present himself as a gentleman, it did not make them welcome him into their private affairs and gatherings.

Iain folded her reply and placed it on the table next to

his bed. He nodded to Paul that he was ready to be shaved. His valet waved the other servants from the room and held out a chair to Iain. Seated, with his face and neck wrapped in a steaming towel, he felt a wave of sympathy for the widow. A moan escaped him.

"Too hot, sir?" Paul asked.

"Nay, Paul. Continue."

He simply could not allow softer feelings into this matter of the properties. He could not. He would not. He needed to keep her in perspective—an opponent who wanted something he wanted, nay needed, and who stood in his way of one of the greatest accomplishments since his rising from the dead.

The expansion of his businesses, aye his empire, would not be stopped because a maudlin widow wished to hold onto the properties of her dead husband two years after his passing. It would not be stopped because they'd share the same shaming by society and the same position as outsiders staring in and wanting to be accepted.

Nay. The companies that spread around the kingdom, the continent and even in the previous colonies, now a united country, gave him as much solace as he needed to soothe his hurts over the insults. Almost unlimited wealth that he could use to acquire anything he wished softened the blows of his earlier life. And the accumulated power to make men do what he wished eased his now shiny path amongst those who had shunned him before.

He would allow himself the fury and excitement of lust that she aroused in his flesh, even if it made him want her in a way he'd never felt before. That need could be satisfied with the lovely Tess when he decided he needed her attentions. Iain would allow himself to admire the lady and even respect her. But pity would not change his mind or his plans. A knock on his chamber interrupted his thoughts of her and he was glad for it.

"Come." Paul removed the towels as Puggles entered. Nodding, he waited by the door until called forward. "What is it, Puggles?" It was a ridiculous name, even while his butler insisted it was his true, or at least preferred, name.

"The arrangements for your supper are set, sir," Puggles said. The man's deep voice belied his skinny stature. "The meal you requested will be ready at the appointed time. The table you requested is already reserved."

"Excellent."

"Will there be anything else, sir?"

"Nothing else, Puggles."

The scene was set. The players at the ready. By the end of this night he would discover what was truly at the center of her refusal to sell to him. He'd suspected it involved her late husband, but why would she refuse twice or triple the worth of the lands in addition to other concessions he'd offered? She was too… smart, too… savvy to rely on sentimentality, was she not?

Paul finished his work and Iain washed and dressed. They would meet at the Royal Waterloo Hotel, the newly opened and already renamed hotel at the end of Princes Street. The dining rooms were popular and open to the public—if they could afford the prices. Far above the variety and selection of any pub or eatery in the city, even above most private clubs he'd visited here, so it seemed the perfect place.

He did not miss the absolute irony of the situation— as the owner of one of the most disreputable pubs in

Edinburgh, his tastes did not deserve the food they would dine on this evening. But certainly the lady's more refined tastes would be satisfied.

A quick look in the mirror as Paul completed tying his neckcloth reminded him just how far from the gutters of Glasgow he'd come. To him though, after the shock of that first glance, all he saw was how much more the man in that mirror still wanted.

And tonight, he would take the next steps to get what he wanted.

As he turned away, a shadow flickered in his reflection and all he could see was the memory of her face and the expression of sheer panic and desperate need the exact moment when her father's presence had been announced. The vulnerability glimmering in her green eyes made him want to wrap her in layers of blankets and protect her from all that was bad in the world.

Unfortunately, he did not delude himself and understood that he was one of the bad things that threatened her.

He left his bedchamber and his house and was at the hotel at least twenty minutes earlier than when he expected Lady Clare to arrive. Everything was indeed prepared as he'd ordered, and he sipped on a glass of a very excellent brandy as he waited for her. Until he spotted her entering the dining room, he suspected she might beg off at any moment. And then…

She was here.

He stood and watched as the manager helped her off with her coat in the entry. A footman motioned her in Iain's direction, and she looked past the man and noticed him. In spite of his plans to wait for her at the table, he found himself walking to meet her. Searching for any sign of reticence or fear, instead he found her gaze bright and curious as she glanced off to one side and then the other of the aisle through the other seating areas before he reached her.

"Lady Clare," he said with a bow. "I am glad you accepted my invitation." He stepped back and waited for her to follow the footman who waited to guide them back to their table. "Even if only part of my invitation."

She waited until seated before saying anything at all, but the scent of her perfume wafted back to him with every step. Unsurprisingly, his body was a tense mess when he finally took his seat across from her.

"I have wanted to see the hotel since it opened," she said, openly studying the dining room and those around them. "A bit nicer than the tavern down the street."

"Do not tell me that Lady Clare Logan frequents the local taverns in New Town?" Nothing should surprise him about her. At least he was certain she did not show her noble face in *his* pub, though watching her, he thought she might even find it entertaining. Their food might not be the same as the fare served here, but it was not pig's feed.

"More often the ones near the school in Leith," she admitted in a low voice. "Though if you share that knowledge with Lady Nairn, I will never speak to you."

Iain laughed. A waiter approached with an expectant expression and Iain asked her about wine.

"What are you drinking, Sir Iain?"

"Brandy, my lady."

"The same, please."

"My lady, we have a lovely—"

Iain interrupted. "Lady Clare will join me in a brandy." How many glasses of brandy would it take to loosen her tongue? How many after that would it take before her inhibitions slipped? Her gaze narrowed at him, and Iain prayed he'd not spoken aloud.

"Unexpected, my lady."

"I have been told that, Sir Iain." One corner of her mouth, the left one, curved in a smile he could only describe as wicked and proud. "It is known that I have flouted expectations in my life. Having a brandy is a minor infraction after what I have done."

The lady's drink and a new one for him arrived and he held his up in the space between them. "To flouting expectations, Lady Clare."

When she sipped the brandy, she did so without artifice or hesitation. It was a very good one, one he would like in his own collection, and he would ask Puggles to contact the manager in charge of their cellar for the details later.

The waiter returned and, with her permission, he ordered their meal—servings of roasted quail, beef, and ham, along with several accompaniments. The mention of several special sweets made her eyes sparkle and Iain knew he'd discovered a weakness of hers. Not exactly valuable in his quest, but he never knew when information would prove helpful or not. If nothing else, it was a personal detail he now knew and could use when he needed it.

"Can we dispense with the false frivolity, Sir Iain? I would rather just enjoy a very good supper in these beautiful surroundings than try to prepare for your attempts to negotiate my property away from me."

"Aye, let's," he said. It would be a change, for him, for them. "I should apologize in advance, since I confess I am not certain I can leave business out this evening." A lovely lilting laugh escaped her, and Iain knew he would play the fool just to hear her laugh. She nodded and then smiled—a genuine, friendly one that made him do the same thing. The things he was tempted to do to her mouth as he gazed on it made it a dangerous smile as well.

"We can start by speaking about the weather, if you'd like? That should make it easier to stay on task."

"Lovely weather indeed."

He lifted his glass to his mouth and tipped it back, swallowing the last bit before nodding. As if the fates had been listening, flashes of lightning lit up the sky outside the hotel followed by a growing then waning thunder. Storms had been brewing the whole day and they broke now only to mock him. With the topic of the weather exhausted, Iain came up with another topic though he doubted it was an innocuous one.

"I have heard bits about how the marquess and Lady Nairn married, but I would like to know the whole of it." The couple were relentlessly in love and there had been talk about how it had come to pass. And they allowed their love to govern their lives instead of controlling them. "If it is a safe topic of polite conversation?"

"'Tis hardly a secret considering that their courtship and proposal was all done right in front of society," she said. "And I have no doubt that you have received a full report on the matter if you are already in business with the marquess."

Lady Clare was correct—he would never have offered Nairn any deal without a thorough investigation of his background. He knew most of the details—including the name and present location of the marquess's former mistress who'd caused many of the problems for him, and yet he wanted to hear it from the lady. To see which details she would trust with him. Or if she would.

"Humor me, Lady Clare, if you would?"

"Very well." She paused and took a sip of the brandy. "This is very good."

"I plan on finding out more about it and obtaining some," he said. Lifting the glass just placed before him by the efficient staff, Iain swallowed a mouthful and waited.

"They were madly in love," she said. "Anyone with eyes could see it. But pride and anger and a woman who thought she'd been wronged got in the way of the usual courtship of an heir to a marquessate and the daughter of an earl." Lady Clare stared off for a few moments and then smiled. "Father was horrified. Mother as well. Especially when it seemed as though things were broken beyond repair."

"The earl and countess were opposed?"

"They were over the moon to get a marquess by marriage after I... ."

"Ah. After your marriage and defection from the ranks of society." He said it that way to provoke an answer. But then most people he dealt with saw only the benefits in a society marriage and life while he saw it as the tangle of deceit and requirements and pretense it was. So, walking away as she had seemed more a liberation, especially with everything she'd been able to accomplish since she turned her back.

"My defection?"

"You chose to marry Logan even while knowing the consequences. That sounds like you made the choice to leave them behind."

Her gaze narrowed and he glanced away. A miscalculation on his part. He admired her decision though he did not discount the cost of it to her. The pain in her eyes when the earl arrived at Nairn's dinner demonstrated that.

"I have steered into an impolite topic now and expressed an unwanted opinion. Your pardon, my lady."

Two waiters brought their first course, and it stopped all conversation. A large tureen of soup was presented and a cloud of steam escaped when the lid was lifted, allowing the delicious aroma to spread over the table. With great show, they ladled it into a bowl for the lady and then for him. The head waiter announced the name of the soup, but as always, the French language confused him. Considering he was known here and the number of meals he'd bought, the head waiter realized the situation and discreetly repeated the name in English as he turned away.

The some-kind-of-beef soup was plain on first look, but the flavors—beef and spices—were surprisingly complex and delicious. Halfway through his, the lady spoke.

"Some of James and Caro's antics made my parents shudder in spite of his expected title and wealth." She lifted the large spoon to her lips and tilted the soup into her mouth. After another mouthful, she continued her explanation. "Then Caro fell ill, nigh to dying, or so it seemed to everyone."

"Pardon me? Are you intimating that it was not true? She was not in danger of dying?" He sat up straighter now for this bit he'd not known.

"My sister could take the stage at any moment, Sir Iain. Her penchant for drama would put the most popular actors to shame. Nay, not intimating. She was not sick."

His spoon clattered to the table, just missing the edge of the fine porcelain bowl. How had his men missed such a critical detail?

"Does Nairn know? How could a man marry a woman who had purposely embarrassed him like that?" Word was that he made a huge gesture in front of most of society at the biggest event of the Edinburgh season. And, if for naught but a foolish young woman's pride, how could he have forgiven her such a thing?

Clare placed her spoon next to her now-empty bowl and nodded. For a cynical man who had no time for anything but acquiring more, his disbelief and lack of understanding in the possibility that men, and women, made decisions based on love should not have surprised her. How sad.

"He does. In spite of the theatrics of her actions, my sister has a core of honesty within her. Before she accepted his offer, and in the privacy of my father's drawing room, she revealed what she'd done and why." She was not going to do this half-measure. Lowering her voice, she leaned closer and was pleased when he did the same. "They married within days of leaving that drawing room and many counted on their fingers and waited to see the results."

"Bloody hell," he said.

She had shocked him as much as his rude language shocked her. In a way, though, she was pleased. Pleased that he did not know *something*. A wave of satisfaction followed by a twinge of guilt passed through her. Dabbing her mouth with her napkin and placing it back on her lap. The next course arrived, forestalling any discussion at that moment.

Several choices of pies—beef, fowl, chicken and

fish—along with three different casseroles and sauces to complement each dish were offered for their selection. If the soup was an indication of the rest of the meal, Clare knew she needed to be prudent in what she requested. She studied each one but before she could speak, Sir Iain did.

"Please give the lady some of each," he said. The waiters jumped to do as he'd said quickly. "You will regret it later if you do not have a taste of each," he said, his voice low and smooth like melting treacle. From the shiver that passed through her, she knew he could tempt angels to sin with that voice. And most likely had.

They ate in a comfortable silence and he was right—each of the dishes was delicious. When the waiters returned to remove the dishes and plates, she realized something. A small detail but interesting.

"You do not speak French." She did not say it as an accusation, rather an observation.

Sir Iain nodded. "I do not." He held up his glass and the observant waiter brought the decanter to him within moments.

"And they know it?"

Just as she uttered the words, she realized the truth of the situation. Glancing around the stylish dining room of the new and very large and expensive hotel at the foot of Princes Street, she smiled and shook her head.

"You own the hotel. They know your preferences because they work for you."

"Aye." He raised his glass to her. "Very observant, Lady Clare."

"How was that kept out of the reports—" The words slipped out. The reports of his companies, wealth and positions on various boards and investments had been extensive. There had been no mention of this being his property.

"Amazing what money can do," he said. He winked at her and she laughed.

"But why keep it secret?"

He did not answer her immediately. Instead, he sipped the brandy and stared into its depths as though the answer lay there. When his gaze over the edge of the crystal glass met hers, it glimmered with the lights reflected off the amber liquid. Now it was her turn to worry if she'd asked an impolite question.

"I do apologize, Sir Iain," she said.

"Iain." He placed the brandy down. "I wish you would call me Iain."

"'Tis not polite to discuss financial matters at dinner." She wished she could flout the rules as easily as he thought she did. But if she had any chance of regaining her place in her family, she must adhere to the greater expectations of class and society. "Sir Iain."

"So, we will set up a meeting that does not involve a meal and I can explain the reason," he said. It sounded reasonable until he smiled at her and tempted her to break a few rules. "Or we can discuss whatever the bloody hell we wish to here and now?" He stared at her, daring her to do that. And she wanted to, damn her! At her delay, he shrugged. "Very well, my lady. We shall adhere to all the polite rules."

Disappointment filled his deep voice and something made her want to not only break some of the rules but to sin, and sin wickedly, with him. A small indiscretion could not matter in this game of theirs if it built some measure of trust between them, could it?

"Iain," she said. His blue eyes flashed as she spoke his

name. "I am curious about your ownership of the hotel. And, I find myself abominably curious about how you managed to reach the position you have without at least a minimum knowledge of French. Will you tell me?"

Had she truly just asked those questions and used his given name? The dining room and all its fixtures, furniture and people seemed to fade around them as something shifted between them. Aye, she had done that and, in doing so, she had crossed a line she feared could never be undone.

The waiters' approach and voices at that very moment broke whatever moment was happening as they carried trays of food to the table. Once the silent moment was broken, reality intruded and Clare watched and waited as the servers quickly replaced the used plates and cutlery with new or additional silverware and plates. Their efficiency was second to none, not unlike any noble household in which she'd eaten dinner. They were attentive, careful, precise and skilled as they presented the joints of beef and lamb, roasted quail and even a fish dish she did not recognize.

As before, the head waiter named each dish before slicing and serving it to her. This time, with the food so identifiable, except for the fish, Iain waved them off. Once everything was arranged to their satisfaction, she and Iain were alone, Clare spoke the words in French and then repeated them in English. His gaze sharpened and he seemed unmoving and not breathing as she pronounced the words in that language that twisted her tongue and resembled soft puffs of air as she said them. She nearly made up words to keep his intense gaze and attention on her. Finally, she shrugged.

"No French?" she asked.

"Only the bad words." He was tempting her on purpose. He wanted her to ask the obvious, but she'd overstepped too much this evening.

"Somehow, I am not surprised."

The temptation to ask him nearly overwhelmed her, so she tilted her head down and cut up the lovely slices of roasted beef on her plate.

"I am the majority owner of the hotel," he said without any other indication he would explain. "There is a small group of investors who I represent—and with whom I invest as well—who own it."

"Is this one of the profit-making ventures you offer to advantageous people to encourage them to invest with you?"

A pang of jealousy rippled through her as she realized, he'd not offered her such an opportunity. Her father? Aye. Her brother-by-marriage? Aye. She was as wealthy as each of them, though they knew it not, and could have come up with the funds necessary... if invited. Several blinks were necessary to rid her eyes of the unexpected burning that resulted from the realization. Though why it bothered her, she could not explain.

"Not this one. I have found the strategy works well with most m—" He'd scooped a bit of the fish in pastry onto his fork and lifted it to his mouth before pausing midway.

"Men. It works well with the men involved."

His fork clattered on his plate as he dropped it. His expression changed several times in succession as she tried to identify each one. Astonishment or disbelief was easy for she'd seen it recently. Chagrin was appealing in a way she'd never thought possible on such a bold, focused man like him. Then, a mysterious glint filled his gaze and he looked from her to another woman sitting across the dining room. And then another in another section. And then he found the final woman in the far corner.

"My thanks, Lady Clare. I had never even considered approaching women who run companies or who have inherited and control their fortunes. New possibilities all around me and I had been too blind to see them." He smiled and she lost her breath at his masculine beauty. "I shall pay you a finder's fee for each one I do business with in the future since you gave me the idea." He leaned over and his smile disappeared. "Make no mistake, my lady, I understand my error in not considering the ladies as possible business partners. Considering my up—" He stopped abruptly and stared off for a moment. "Considering the extent of my own businesses, I should have taken them seriously long before this."

"Men rarely do."

TEN

The words slipped out against her nature. It sounded bitter, even while the truth. Clare had dealt with the infuriating behavior against her since she inherited Jonathan's estate. No one took her seriously. No one wanted to do business with her. It took a long time and so much money to establish accounts with stores and suppliers. And, with some of the businesses she owned, so much effort to convince them of the stability of a company directed by a woman.

Again, any further conversation was halted as the waiters cleared the table. Iain's blue gaze narrowed as he watched her instead of the activity around them.

He *had* taken her seriously. In spite of their being on opposite sides of their own negotiations and after the first incident of mistaken identity, Iain Buchanan had spoken to her, not around her. He had prepared and conducted a meeting that addressed her directly.

"Perhaps after we sort out our present negotiations you would consider investing in one or another of my ongoing projects?" he asked. Had he seen inside her thoughts?

"I suspect that we will be finished once we conclude our talks." Better not to give him hope or tempt her to continue any connection between them. Silence met her statement, and she waited through several uncomfortable seconds until he finally broke into it.

"Alas, Lady Clare, if that is true, you tempt me to drag out our negotiations so that I can continue in your company."

His tone was light and teasing and yet his words sounded as though he spoke the truth. Heat filled her once more at just the thought of seeing him again. Of doing battle with him with words. Of watching the way his eyes glinted with desire or jest.

Of kissing him and touching him.

Then, a piercing stab of loss filled her at the thought that she would not do those things.

How? How had this happened? Confused over her warring emotions, Clare decided she needed to escape his presence. She grabbed her reticule and stood, only then realizing panic was driving her actions and she had nowhere to go.

"Are you well, my lady?" he asked, standing since she did. His voice deepened with concern.

"I need… I need to…"

Mistaking her need, he motioned to one of the footmen stationed around the large dining room. When the man approached, Iain leaned over and said something she could not hear. With a nod, the footman approached her and guided her out of the dining room and through the exquisitely decorated lobby. Was the similarity to the luxury hotels she'd seen in London of his own choosing, or did some designer make the decisions here?

With the traveling he did and the places he'd seen and visited, it was probably a mix of the best designs of palaces and noble houses and other splendid buildings.

She fought the smile that threatened. Sir Iain Buchanan did nothing by half-measure. This hotel matched his opinion of himself and his worth.

As she followed the footman up the gilded staircase covered in thick, beautiful carpeting, Clare noticed the paintings that were hung between large windows. Three crystal chandeliers that held dozens if not hundreds of candles burned brightly, spreading light through the huge lobby and up the stairs. The light from them reflected off and through the crystals and the gold decorations around the lobby and gave it a magical appearance.

Not even the recently redesigned Assembly Rooms or the exquisite Signet Library could compete with the beauty and grace of this hotel. When they reached the landing at the top, the footman led her along a wide corridor and turned into a narrower one.

"Here is the retiring room, my lady," the young man said, bowing and stepping back as he opened the door. "A maid will help you within." She thanked him and walked into the chamber.

It was a parlor-like room, decorated in a Grecian theme and in colors of pale turquoise, cream and gold. A few small couches were scattered around the main area and the carpeting used the same color scheme as did the cushions of the furnishings and the draperies. On seeing it, Clare decided she loved the palette chosen here and might even use it for her bedchamber.

"My lady?" So caught up in studying the décor, she'd not noticed the maid enter from a door in the corner. "Ye can see to yer needs here."

Since she'd made it this far, Clare decided to take her time, regain her balance, and use the accommodations for her comfort. After a short time and several slow, deep breaths, she felt ready to return and bring this evening's encounter to an end before she did anything truly stupid.

She'd learned a few things about the man and so she counted the night a success. And that did not even consider the delicious food and drink and visit to this lovely new establishment. Now, she knew he did not speak French and that he had more holdings than they'd known before. Clare would tell her solicitors to look into that immediately.

In the meantime, she would avoid being alone with Iain Buchanan, an easy thing to accomplish because he would be leaving for the ball, and she would be going home. And no matter the temptation he was becoming with his wicked smiles and appealing glances. No matter that every time she looked at him or when he spoke, she could think only of his mouth on hers. Opening the door back into the parlor, she found the maid waiting for her.

"My lady, if ye'll come this way."

Clare followed after the young woman and entered the room through the doorway. And stopped two steps into it.

If the lobby and the staircase and even the retiring room had been stylish and luxurious, this chamber or suite of rooms took her breath away.

As soft as the colors of the retiring room were, this was completely the opposite—darker, more masculine tones and shades. The tables, chairs and trim along the walls and the doors were all intricately carved mahogany. Deep burgundies, dark golds and forest greens filled the upholstery, draperies and cushions around the room. Several hearths were set into the longer wall and braces of candles set between those added to the light and warmth in the chamber.

Two seating areas covered the space between where she stood and the beautiful dining table where at least ten people would be able to eat together. In spite of the sheer rudeness of wandering through someone else's rooms, Clare could not stop herself from exploring it. Or from walking further now to have a closer look at such a beautiful place. Only as she reached the dining area did she notice two settings along with plates filled with what could only be the desserts and sweets described by the waiter before they ordered. Pots of what must be coffee and tea, a small bowl of some fruit and a plate of biscuits finished out the table.

"I thought we might finish our meal here."

Clare gasped and turned, finding Iain standing only a few paces from her near another door. The maid left, fled really, at his nod and they were alone. Torn between following the maid out of the suite or remaining here, with him, alone, she wanted to do both.

"I did not mean to startle you, my lady," he said. He walked around her and pulled the chair out for her to sit. "Welcome to the owner's suite."

"How convenient then that you are one of the owners here."

"Aye, convenient and expensive," he said with a laugh. "I use it for guests or dignitaries or important visitors to the city. Or for private meetings and such."

"And such?" Only then did look past him and notice the open double doors that exposed a large, four-poster bed and chamber. "And such," she repeated. Meetings that included a bed? She did not ask.

"The true reason is that I saw your reaction to the waiter's description of the sweets and did not want you to miss trying them. The dining room was getting crowded, so I thought we might enjoy the privacy of this suite in which to try all the delights the highly paid French pastry chef has made."

"You are trying to turn me into a hedonist," she said. His smile, tempting and wicked and somehow innocent all at once, confirmed it to her.

"Epicurean might be the better word for you, considering the rest of your life's endeavors, my lady." He nodded down at the chair he yet held waiting for her to sit. "And I am too busy a man to devote all my time to pleasure." A retort and an obvious question sat side by side on the tip of her tongue—about pleasure, about how much—but she refused to allow them out.

Should she remain here with him? Nay. Clearly nay.

Could she allow herself to, was the more accurate question.

"Will you not be late for the ball if you tarry here with me?" she asked. Her feet moved towards the chair, but she did not accept his offer of it.

"Let me think," he said. He glanced at the clock in the corner of the room, an ornately carved one of the best quality, and shrugged. "To stay here with you, continuing our informative discussions, or go to a pretentious gathering of supplicants begging for favors while I drink tepid punch and fend off those not too offended by my wealth to offer their daughters? Hmmmm."

"It sounds like the same challenges faced by noblemen every day," she said, laughing softly. His expression filled with hunger as she did. Hunger, but not for food.

"'Tis half-past nine, my lady. Plenty of time to indulge here with you and still make an appearance there well before it becomes both impolite and impolitic to the hosts." He leaned towards the table and lifted a glass filled with layers of what looked like cream mixed with fruit and bits of nuts. Studying it, he dipped his finger into it and licked the concoction off in long, slow strokes of his tongue.

Clare forgot how to breathe. Her nipples tightened instantly, and her thighs clenched against the arousal she felt.

"Cream." Lick. "Raspberries." Lick. Her mouth went dry. "Oats." Another lick. A trickle of sweat traced a path down her back. "Whisky." The final stroke of his tongue removed the last of it from his finger. "And honey."

So why did she ache to lick it, to taste the flavor of it? Her body wanted to taste the sweetness of the dessert and his mouth. Clare recognized the reaction of her body. She was no blushing virgin who did not understand the pleasure he offered or whose body did not remember how passion could be enjoyed.

"A taste?" he asked, lifting his hand provocatively towards her. Her mouth dropped open, shocking her, but his mouth on hers surprised her more. He moved quickly, pulling her closer and touching his lips to hers. After a brief touch there, he leaned up and smiled. "Taste," he said, in a tone that was nothing less than an order.

His tongue thrust into her mouth, and she did what he'd demanded, stroking his with hers and savoring all the flavors of the sweet decadence he'd sampled. Sucking his tongue, she could indeed taste the cream, the berries, the whisky and oats and honey… and him. He lifted his head from hers and only the sounds of the shallow breaths could be heard.

And, damn her weakness, she wanted more. She wanted him.

She would swear he'd heard her thoughts before and when he leaned over and dipped his fingers into the creamy layers, Clare decided it must be a secret power of his. She clutched the front of his evening jacket to stave off falling to her knees as they gave out at the sight of his cream-covered fingers.

"Close your eyes, Clare. And open your mouth." The words were uttered so softly, but they were yet another order given. Her body shuddered, aroused and aching, as she did exactly what he'd said, unable or unwilling to resist him.

His fingers slid inside her mouth, moving, thrusting, slipping in and out as her tongue hungrily licked and sucked the delicious cream from them. His other hand moved up her spine and his fingers invaded her hair, rubbing and tugging her scalp in time with the fingers in her mouth.

"Open your eyes and clean off the rest."

His other hand gently but irresistibly held her head in place as he eased the cream-coated fingers apart and held them against her mouth, awaiting her compliance. Her gaze fell on his eyes as she licked each long finger clean. Heat poured off his body and he pressed his hips against hers as she continued her ministrations. Hard male flesh rose between them, and he pumped against her as she finished the task. They panted as their gazes met and she saw desire burning in his.

"I want to taste you, Clare." His voice was deep and rough, and it made the tension twisting deep within her tighten even more. "Sit," he said. His hand on her head guided her to the chair he'd pulled away from the table.

He took hold of the chair's arms and shifted it, and her, before kneeling in front of her. "Lift your gown."

"Iain?" Instead of an answer, he reached for her hips and tugged her to the edge of the chair. He could not mean to…

"Lift your gown, Clare. Now."

Though she could not explain why she obeyed, her trembling hands gathered the layers of petticoats and gown and slowly drew them up, exposing her legs to his sight. His hand encircled her ankles and slid higher, caressing her silk stockings as he followed the gown moving up her legs. Her breaths caught with every inch of her that he uncovered but she did not stop. For some reason, she dared not.

"Steady on," he whispered, his eyes staring at her legs. "Higher." She did not move, overwhelmed by how arousing this felt. He squeezed her thighs at the place where her garters lay. "Higher."

Her thighs clenched, her core heated and grew damp as she could feel the air on her naked flesh. Clare let her head fall back against the chair as his hands spread her thighs open.

"Beautiful, Clare. So bloody beautiful."

The admiration in his voice stunned her. No one had ever done anything like this to her before. No one, not even she, had ever looked on that private place. Suddenly embarrassed, she turned her face away.

"Do not look away, Clare. Watch me."

Her gaze drawn back by the command of his voice, she watched as he leaned forward towards her intimate flesh. The heat of his breath on the sensitive folds shocked her, but the touch of his tongue made her body arch.

"Watch me!" he said sharply. Leaning up, she stared as he licked her the same way he'd licked the cream from his fingers.

Wave after wave of pleasure rushed through her body. She just wanted to fall back and feel every stroke, but his gaze would not allow her to escape. He lifted his face from between her thighs, but only long enough to guide her legs over his shoulders. The position made her thighs fall open to him even more. His gaze lit on the table, and he reached over and dipped his fingers into the creamy dessert once more. She gasped as he carried it to her body and spread it over the feminine flesh—the heat of his hand and the cold of the cream in such a place made her moan. A loud gasp escaped when he touched the bud hidden within the folds.

"I like the sound of that, Clare, but I want you silent. Hold onto the chair and do not make a sound."

It was some kind of sensual game now—he ordered and she obeyed. Her body did not want her to risk that he would stop if she disobeyed him. She held onto the wooden arms tightly. Did he know how it excited her? Did he understand that these shocking caresses and kisses were surprising and new to her? She gasped when his tongue searched the flesh, seeking the place that ached so badly now.

"Hush."

She waited for it now, believing she could control her body since she knew what passion felt like. She was wrong, for his tongue's relentless stroking, slowly then quickly, lightly then with pressure, brought screams so very close to escaping. He paused with his tongue against her but not moving and her hips pressed down in response trying to make him continue. Using only the tip of his wicked tongue, he found it—the center of her arousal and need and he licked the spot and the flesh that surrounded it. Her body tightened and arched against such pleasure.

Clare clenched her jaws against the scream building within her as he used the sharp edges of his teeth on it, even nipping it again and again until it bordered on sensual pain. Then, as her body rocked itself against his mouth, he took it between his lips and suckled it and she exploded from the pleasure. Her body shuddered as she seemed to be weightless, flying, soaring into the air. Clutching the arms of the chair, her eyes focused on him, there between her legs as her throbbing flesh echoed with wave after wave of pleasure.

And he began again.

Grasping her thighs and pressing her legs up towards the chair, he set about removing every bit of the dessert he'd spread there. The only place he did not touch this time was that aching spot that throbbed in time with his strokes. Clare fought against the new rise of pleasure, knowing she would scream. When he plunged deeply inside of her with his tongue, she thought she might have fainted for a moment.

It was different for her, she'd never experienced such an act, but no less pleasurable than every other one of his caresses and touches as he thrust deep. His fingers slid over her slick folds holding her at the brink... of ... something. The unrelenting pacing drove her wilder and wilder with a hunger for more until she could not breathe. The unexpected and shocking feel of his strong thumb pressing against her other tight opening as his mouth then took hold of the aching bud had her gasping. When his fingers slid inside her feminine channel, a torrent of sensations wracked her body with heat and need and desire.

"Scream for me, Clare. Scream my name."

And she did, calling out his name and groaning at the peak of arousal he'd driven her to with mouth and fingers. Touching places she'd never dreamt of in ways she had never imagined. Shaking as she reached satisfaction, she was horrified to hear herself still screaming out his name. He slowed his attentions, easing away from her. His hand remained there between her legs until, with one last lingering stroke, he withdrew it. The scent of arousal filled the area around them, and she swore her screams yet echoed through the large chamber. Iain leaned away and lifted her legs off his shoulders, placing her feet on the floor. How she could even feel the soft caress as his hands slid down her stockings in her overwhelmed and replete state she did not know.

Spineless. Breathless. Shocked to her core. Would she be able to move again?

Would she be able to face him? After what he'd done to her? After what he'd seen and touched? After she had given over her control to him in a way she had never done with J—

Clare moved then, sitting up and tossing her gown down to cover herself. Reaching up, she found her hair a half-loosened mess. Her slippers lay on either side of the man kneeling at her feet, staring at her with an expression of disbelief in his blue eyes. She grabbed the shoes, pushed up and away from him. Standing, perhaps too quickly, she wobbled a bit but the need to escape— escape him, his touch, his all-too-knowing gaze and the need he kindled within her—overwhelmed any hesitation or unbalance. Ignoring whatever he said, she rushed towards the retiring room, needing just to straighten her clothing and appearance before getting out of this place.

"My lady," he said softly. He was close behind her now and she moved faster towards the other room. "I will send the maid to you and have your coach summoned."

Clare slammed the door behind her and collapsed against it, partly to keep him out and to keep herself upright when she wanted to melt and disappear. She stumbled over to one of the small couches and fell onto it. Sobs bubbled up from someplace deep within her and she pressed her hand over her mouth to muffle the sound.

How had she done this? How had she fallen for his temptation even knowing his plan? This was nothing to him but a play in his game of conquest. What did he hope to gain by this seduction? To destroy her sense of control and propriety by exposing her faults? To show her how shallow her love for Jonathan had been since he could lure her into passion with so little effort?

The maid entered silently and offered her help. Clare needed assistance at gathering her hair back into the arrangement that her maid Archer had created this evening. The young woman here seemed to have a talent for it and had Clare looking almost untouched when she'd finished.

Feeling rather shaken, Clare spent some time seeing to her personal needs before going back to the retiring room. The maid awaited her.

"I apologize for not asking your name," Clare said.

"I am Suisan, my lady." The maid curtsied. "There is a footman outside to escort ye to yer carriage, my lady." As Suisan went to answer the knock, Clare reached for her reticule to find a coin for the maid's assistance only to realize she'd lost track of it at the dining table. Unwilling to return to his suite, she was going to ask the footman to retrieve it when the door opened, and the same footman who'd brought her here earlier held it out to her.

"My lady," he said with a bow. "Your reticule and your cloak." He helped her on with her cloak and she found several coins in her purse and handed the maid and the footman each one.

"My thanks for your assistance," she said, unable to meet either one's eyes. There was simply no way that they had not heard her screams and not known what was going on in the other chamber.

"There is a private entrance this way. Your coach awaits outside." The footman stepped back and indicated their direction away from the main staircase and lobby. Away from other people who would see her and wonder her purpose.

Her departure was quick and smooth, and she saw no one else on her way down a private stairway to a discreet door leading to the street. Clare turned back to thank the footman and saw the outline of a man at the top of the stairs. Though too far to see his features, she recognized the shape of the man's body and knew that Iain watched her leave.

A short time later she arrived back at her house, and she prayed that Samantha was not at home or, if at home, that she had already retired for the evening. Apparently the fates were against her, for Samantha stood in the foyer as Clare entered. Poogan intercepted her with a few messages left for her before bidding her good night.

Empty in so many ways, Clare did not have the strength to explain or even dissemble with Samantha.

How could she answer the inevitable questions when she did not know the answers herself? How could she face her cousin after what had happened between her and Iain?

There was only one explanation—she was as lack witted as some had claimed her to be. A woman who meddled in business when she should not. When she should mind her place and her manner and her words.

Once Poogan walked down the corridor to the back stairs, Clare let out a breath and faced her friend.

"Did he hurt you, Clare?" Samantha asked. Taking Clare's still-trembling hands in hers, she pulled her close. "Did he?"

"Stunned. Surprised. Overwhelmed. But not hurt," she whispered. Samantha nodded and wrapped her arm under Clare's.

"Come. I will call for a bath and then you must get a good night's sleep. Everything looks better after a good night's sleep," she said.

As much as she wanted to believe Samantha's words, Clare suspected it would take more than sleep to set right her life and her heart.

That man had invaded her life and torn everything she'd worked for—an orderly life, a sense of purpose, a journey towards fulfilling the last dreams she shared with Jonathan—into pieces that blew away on Edinburgh's winds.

All of that while giving her the most exciting physical experience of her life.

While never seeking his own pleasure. She stumbled and was glad of Samantha's arm holding hers.

Oh, she'd felt the evidence of his own arousal and not once, not for a moment of the whole encounter, did he seek his own release. He had centered his desire on her, touching and tasting her in shocking and exciting ways. Clare would never look upon dessert or cream in the same way again.

No, now more than before, Clare understood that a night's rest would not happen this evening. Her body still ached from his attentions and felt more alive and alert than it had in a long, long time.

How could she sleep when such an ache had been created and when all she wanted was… more?

ELEVEN

Twelve days. Almost a fortnight.

Nigh on two weeks had passed since that night without a word from her. Or even a sighting of her outside her house.

Nearly two weeks since he'd touched her and kissed her and tasted her. Since he'd lost his wits and his control and had feasted on her flesh like a savage without regard for her sensibilities.

But that was what he was—a beast strolling around society in a gent's clothing. Hiding his depravities from the world and making a fortune as he did it. Using his nefarious and morally questionable skills and talents to get what he wanted because… he wanted it. He'd not expected to face someone like her in this contest of power and wealth and she'd become more than an opponent to him.

A strongminded good woman with a purpose in life that was not about *her* needs or *her* wants. Bloody hell, she ran an orphanage! A tremor shook him as he approached the line he could not cross in thought or deed, so he did not.

Even seeking out the physical punishment and exhaustion that the fights gave him did not help his unceasing arousal. And no amount of seeking his own satisfaction with his hand rid him of the inconvenient and hardened reminder that he had not buried himself in Lady Clare's tight passage as he'd wanted to that night. In spite of the lovely Tess's ever-present willingness to help with that matter, Iain could not bring himself to seek out the relief that her talented mouth or skillful hands offered.

Something else, something he thought might be regret tickled his conscience. Oh, not at the experience of pleasuring her, he would do that again in a second, or even taking her hard and deep as he'd wanted to do. Nay, what he did regret was that he'd shocked and frightened her so badly she'd disappeared. He had enjoyed more than just their passionate encounters—he enjoyed their discussions and found her intelligence and courage refreshing, for she confronted him in a way no one had before.

Iain stared out the window of his office, watching as a ship moved slowly to the dock. He put his office on the upper floor of this building for exactly this view. The whole of Leith Harbor spread out before him and the sight of it and his ships pleased him. Between his fleet here and in Glasgow, his rivalled any on the seas. Pride and pleasure filled him.

He'd reached this level of success by having the determination to fulfill his ruthless ambition from that moment in the gutters of Glasgow's slums. And by following his well-laid plans no matter his opponent or competitor.

His mouth watered as the image of her open to his sight and the sound of her screaming out his name as her hips arched, pressing her flesh against his mouth came to mind.

Pulling himself back from the same bloody reaction he had every time he thought of her, Iain downed the last of the whisky in the glass on his desk and sat to examine the reports once more. She had, his sources said, not left her house or gone to the orphanage since that day. Mrs. Hunter kept to her usual schedule of shopping, visiting, helping at Clare's school and so on. Her solicitors and secretary arrived and remained for several hours each day. Her household servants came and went. Life went on without a sign of Lady Clare Logan. A knock drew his attention, and he called out, allowing them to enter.

"Sir," Ned said as he nodded his head. "Ben and Mr. Cairns are waiting outside. Are you ready to see them?" Since he did not object, Ned opened the door to the two and invited them within. Once they were seated, Ned took his usual place next to Iain's desk to make notes of anything that needed to be followed up or tracked down.

"Well? Where is she?"

"We are working on it," Cairns said. Iain said nothing. "She may have left the house the night… in question."

"What of your sources there?" Cairns had mentioned having a servant in Lady Clare's household on his payroll.

"If the lady indeed left that night, it might explain the silence from my source," Cairns said quietly. Iain knew the man was more dangerous as he grew quieter. "I have not been able to locate *her* either." A lady's maid would travel with her, so Cairns' undisclosed source might be the one person closest to Clare. In spite of his frequent use of such spies, he was oddly ill-at-ease over this revelation.

"Our latest offer?" He had ceased interfering with her permit approvals, but that had not stopped him from pursuing the property—his need for that had not changed.

"Refused." Ben placed a letter on his desk.

"The other offer?" Iain looked at Ben. Just because he'd given up one path to pressuring her to accept his offer did not mean he'd given up. They'd arranged for another of his companies, one—like the hotel—that could not be traced back to him, to make an offer on the same property to see her reaction.

"They received the offer, and it is *under consideration*," Ben answered again. "It was sent a week ago."

"Any indication that the lady had seen it?"

"None," Ben said.

Iain closed his eyes, wondering how he had completely fucked up something that should have been signed and sealed months ago. If the staggering amount he'd offered hadn't done it, his reputation and power should have. Anyone with a man of business or a solicitor would know of his acumen and practices. Rubbing his eyes, he shook his head at no one in particular.

All he'd wanted was a chance to find out why she refused such a lucrative deal. That had been his plan. Then he began to think with his ballocks instead of his mind and things went to hell—in a spectacular way. But to hell nonetheless.

"Iain?" Ben's voice pierced his silent thoughts, and he opened his eyes. "What happened between you?"

"It does not concern you," he snapped, slamming his hands on the desk and scattering the papers into the air and onto the floor.

"I beg to differ with ye," Ben said. "Our quarry has run to ground. Negotiations have ceased. All conventional methods that have been successful in the past have failed." The only man he considered somewhat a friend leaned on his fists over the desk. A bold move since Ben knew the brutality in Iain's blood and his capabilities of using whatever weapon he could find. "Ye hiv tied our fucking hands in doing yer fucking business. So, I ask ye again, *Iain*—what happened between the lady and ye that night?"

Iain emptied the room with a nod as Ben remained leaning over him. If his Scots accent was breaking through the cultured speaking voice he usually maintained, Ben was furious. Ben did not get angry—not this angry—often, so Iain needed to pay heed to it.

"Did ye molest her?" Still the Scottish sounds.

"I. Do. Not. Force. Women." Iain pushed the words out through his clenched jaws. He had very few rules by which he lived, but that, that, was one of them.

"Fine!" Ben yelled. "So, did ye *seduce* her then?"

Iain glanced away from his friend's knowing question. Ben had the ability of ferreting out Iain's escape, admitting the truth of a matter when he did not wish to. It had become a game between them—if Ben did not choose the specific and correct word to describe Iain's transgressions, Iain could deny it. It was juvenile and stupid, but a game they played when Iain was not in a mood to discuss some matters.

Yet, Ben had been integral in his success since Iain's rise in Glasgow's competitive, nay cutthroat, environment, and he owed him at least some explanation.

"I tried to."

The three words echoed out between them and then the only sound was Ben's furious breathing, followed by the foulest words they'd learned in the stews of Glasgow.

Words never forgotten and always first out in situations like this one, especially between men, between friends and between those raised in the forgotten and avoided places as they'd been.

"Why did ye do such a thing? Ye ken, ye ken how important she is to this deal. To our expansion plans."

"I want her, Ben. I want her."

"That's what Tess is for. Seek her out. She'll ease your urges and not expect more."

"I want more than that. She makes me want to take her in every way possible—against the wall, on the floor, bent over my desk, screaming out my name until she cannot. I want her naked and writhing under me and I want her fully clothed with her skirts tossed up over her head. I want to argue with her and to prove her wrong. To make her beg." Iain was panting by the time he finished. He poured a large serving of whisky and downed it in one mouthful.

Ben landed hard in the chair behind him. Wiping his hand over his face, his friend shook his head.

"You have it bad for this one. I have never seen you this way." Resting his elbows on his knees, Ben leaned forward. "She *is* a widow, Iain. And can do as she pleases, within the limits of discretion."

Iain smiled at that—almost like giving him permission.

"But, for fuck's sake, every man and woman who was here during that meeting kens what you were doing out there." He nodded in the direction of the small chamber. "And if word gets back to her father, there will be hell to pay for embarrassing him with his daughter."

"I know that." That was the problem after all—even knowing all the problems his lust for her could create, he was losing control over his urges when it was about her.

"These properties are the cornerstone of our expansion, Freddie." Iain growled at the reminder of their past. "This is the final step in controlling the majority of shipping in and out of this port. An untold fortune awaits us. You cannot allow a weakness for the lady to end this." Ben stood then and walked to the door. Turning back, Iain recognized the grim determination on the man's face having seen it many times in the decades they'd known each other. "I will not let you fuck this up for us."

"I will handle this, *Bertie*," Iain said before the now-called Ben could leave. Tit for tat and all.

"You *will*." Ben shook off the vestiges of his past and stood straighter, regaining his composure before twisting the knob. "Just marry the damned woman. You get her body and her wealth."

Ben pulled the door shut so hard that it shook on its frame, which was good because it drowned out Iain's reply.

Marry her? What an absurd suggestion.

Clare waited for the footman to lower the steps and then she left the coach. On her return to town, they'd stopped at her house to allow Archer to get started on unpacking her luggage. That reason should suffice, but the other was that Clare wanted no company while she visited with Caro.

And Caro would brook no excuses for her not arriving as expected. In exchange for her sister's quick assistance *that* night, Clare had promised a more complete explanation than the tearful, humiliated one she'd given. After believing that she could face any challenge since she had handled so many in her life, Clare discovered that she was actually a coward.

And she'd fled.

Fled him. Fled what he'd done to her. How he'd made her feel. The doubts he'd exposed. Fears and desires and needs she'd masked for so long.

After leaving letters with instructions for Duncan and her solicitors, along with one for Mrs. Dunbar at the school, she'd packed quickly and made an escape. Caro had suggested Nairn's small cottage on a loch not far from Edinburgh as the perfect place for a brief respite. *After* a night's rest, that was.

It took several hours to reach it and Clare thought she may have held her breath the whole way, worrying that someone was following them. Clare had visited the cottage before and she found it as it was always left— stocked, comfortable and ready to inhabit. A caretaker lived on the property as did a housekeeper, so Archer's worry she would be in charge of cooking and cleaning were eased upon their arrival.

The cottage, though Nairn's definition of cottage and hers were quite different, consisted of two floors, four bedchambers, kitchen, dining room and a lovely parlor that looked out over the loch at sunset. And it was there, either reading in front of that window or walking along the loch's edge that she spent each afternoon and evening over the next ten days.

Now, walking up the front steps to Caro's door, Clare might be ready to explain herself to her sister.

The admissions she would make would not be easy. Though the critical ones were not directly related to Iain, his actions, *their* actions, had triggered an examination of her deepest fears. An uncomfortable one at that. Yet, understanding what she truly wanted made her life's path clearer.

In many ways though, Iain Buchanan had awakened more than just her body with his clever caresses and scandalous mouth. With his maneuvering and machinations, he'd reminded her of what she had ignored for so long—her need to be connected to her family. A mistake made in the stubbornness of those first years with Jonathan, even her very decision to marry him, had rippled down to separate her from any chance with her parents.

Not that her father had made it easier or even possible. Once his expansive pride was pricked, he'd refused to accept any attempts to reconcile, indeed any attempts to even be in her presence. If she'd done things differently, they may have had a chance of a truce instead of an all-out confrontation. If Jonathan had only…

"My lady," Nairn's footman greeted her as he opened the door. "Lady Nairn awaits you in the—"

"Foyer. Lady Nairn is in the foyer waiting for you," Caro said from over his shoulder. "Thank you, I will see to her now." Once the footman moved away, Caro grabbed her and pulled her close. "You look better, Clare. The fresh air of the loch has brought color to your cheeks."

Clare did not get a word into the conversation for several minutes, until ensconced in her sister's smaller, private parlor with a cup of tea in her hand. Caro could carry on conversations with others by her own efforts which, now to think on it, tended to ease the way through uneasy topics or entrances. Finally, Clare held up her hand, gaining Caro's attention and getting her to pause long enough to take a breath.

"I am well, Sister." Clare placed the cup down on the table and nodded. "The cottage was the perfect place for me."

"Refreshed? Resigned? Resolved?" Caro's gaze was filled with worry.

"As you and Samantha have rightly said, I have been existing and going on as I did before Jonathan passed away. I never truly considered where I am going or how to live after him."

"And *that* man? Is whatever he did the reason behind this self-examination?"

The heat of a blush filled her cheeks as the memory of him, kneeling between her legs, licking her…

"Now you must tell me!" Caro said as she moved to sit next to Clare. Touching her cheek, her sister laughed. "You are nigh to red with this blush." She touched the back of her hand to Clare's cheek. "And almost feverish at whatever you were thinking on just then."

Clare had never discussed the intimacies of married life with her sister. Though Caro and Nairn's passion in public was well-known and well-remarked upon by many, she had no idea of what went on between them in the bedchamber. Oh, she suspected much but knew little. Glancing at her sister's expectant expression, Clare tried to explain it without many details.

"Things with Jonathan were… comfortable. Pleasant and loving." She could not meet her sister's gaze at the disclosure. "I enjoyed our… relations."

"And Sir Iain? Was it uncomfortable? Did he hurt you?" Caro's voice took on a menacing tone. "If he did—"

"He did not hurt me, Caro! I mean we did not do *that*." Her face must be red as a ripe raspberry in June.

"Oh." Caro sat back and a deep frown appeared. "What did he do then? If he did not bed you?"

"Other… *attentions*. With such passion and fervor that I lost myself." She used her hand to fan her hot face, having neither her reticule nor her favorite fan with her, and dabbed her forehead with the napkin.

"Well then." Caro's gaze narrowed. "Did you object or wish to?" Before Clare could speak, Caro patted her hand. "Being overtaken by passion can be overwhelming if you have not experienced it before, Clare." Clare nodded. She had been shocked by what he did and how she felt. And how had she not raised a sound or gesture to stop him. "But it can be marvelous and splendid and something that does indeed take your breath away."

From the way Caro spoke just then and when she grabbed at Clare's napkin to dab her own brow, Clare understood that her sister enjoyed that kind of passion in her marriage. And until that moment when Iain had leaned down and tasted her most private place, when he kissed and used his tongue to send her careening to some kind of bliss, Clare had never felt before or had any idea such a thing could happen. Not that way.

It had never happened to her before.

The man she'd loved had never given her what the man she… detested? opposed? desired? feared? had—he had made her feel desired and euphoric and lost to pleasure.

The tears escaped without her realizing it. Caro dabbed at them and gave the napkin to her when her efforts did not control them. After Caro left for a few moments, a lovely handkerchief replaced the napkin. As someone who rarely shed a tear in the worst of her grief, this last week had proven a surprise.

And yet, Clare felt more in control of herself and understood she needed to make a few changes in her life. She could not let one absolutely breathtaking yet absolutely not-to-be repeated, sensual experience turn her head or soften her heart to Sir Iain Buchanan or his outrageous offers or behaviors. Wiping away the last of her tears, she cleared her throat and stood. Though she had not sorted out everything, she had made one decision.

She could not do this—continue to oversee the businesses she'd inherited, manage the orphanage and other charities—on her own. Other businessmen had friends and colleagues and even trading clubs or societies, but women like her were excluded based only on their sex and not the extent of their holdings. Clare needed help.

She needed family. She cleared her throat again.

"I need your help with Father."

At first, she thought Caro was going to argue or even refuse, but when her eyes lit with an almost-unholy fire of interest, Clare understood. Her sister would do whatever Clare needed. She just prayed she would not regret it.

Twelve

Iain had girded his loins with, hopefully, an adequate amount of spirits before approaching the entrance of the Assembly Rooms on Princes Street. He could handle only a finite number of these society soirees and not lose every layer of gentlemanly control he'd learned.

Tonight's event was the one he suspected would break him and send him screaming like a *ban sith* down the center of the New Town. Though he'd entered the sumptuous building, the hundreds of candles burning in many chandeliers over his head, the crush of the crowd, the heat and smells of the undulating throng of attendees threatened to force him back out onto the street. And that was even before anyone approached or spoke to him.

And it hadn't been the fawning of the mamas with their trailing eligible daughters or wards that made him want to beat a hasty retreat—those were to be expected. It wasn't even the watered-down punch in place of a quality whisky or port or brandy or… a decent anything. Nay, neither of those did it. The situation that had done it was an invitation he received from one of the little lordlings, as he called the sons of nobles who had nothing to do, no meaning in their lives while having enough funds to keep them idle and worthless.

One of them asked him to join in a secret society open only to nobles and other select gentlemen, a polite way of referring to those who were unspeakably wealthy as he was. In their cups from a prior engagement, they were easily manipulated into spilling the information about what made this society so secret. Apparently, the men gathered to drink, watched as naked women exposed their assets, all while the men all wanked their own *members*. And drank from glasses molded into the shape of their cocks!

He spewed the mouthful of punch he'd just taken in at the description that each little lordling tried to expand for his benefit. These pompous little twits thought he would be interested in showing his prick to others in the name of being included in some exclusive club. He'd rather concentrate on fucking real women and ignore the antics of small and stupid men.

"You look like you could use this," Nairn said as he walked up to Iain. He held out a flask and filled a clean glass with amber liquid.

"Bloody hell, Nairn. I owe you for this." Iain swallowed the whisky. When it hit his gut, he sighed. "I do not ken why the leaders of society and Edinburgh allow only swill to be served when there is such an abundance of spirits available."

"As a bachelor you might not understand the true power of women to make our lives miserable at times," Nairn said, filling his glass again. Lady Clare Logan came to mind immediately and Iain drank to avoid saying anything. "Ah, I see you do understand that particular fact."

He could have been friends with a man like Nairn if he accepted friends among his business associates. Or any friends at all. Friends could be problematic when money and investing was involved. And when a man hid his past and lived in two worlds, he could not trust that a collision of those worlds would not happen. Nairn held up the flask, but Iain waved him off.

"My thanks for that." Nairn secured the flask inside his coat pocket, sipping his drink rather than gulping it as Iain did. "Would you care to join me for a real drink?"

"Now?" Nairn asked.

"The marchioness is here, of course. Pardon me for trying to drag you away."

"My wife has released me for the evening," he said. "In spite of what you may have heard, we do not spend every waking moment in each other's pockets." Nairn laughed, acknowledging what he had indeed learned about the couple. "I have done my duty and Lady Nairn is out there with her sister." He nodded to the main ballroom from where they stood in the entrance to one of the side rooms used for cards.

"Lady Clare is here?" He met Nairn's gaze and knew the man was aware of his growing involvement with his sister-by-marriage. "But the earl—"

"Is here as well. A grand attempt to patch things up."

Iain had received word that the lady had returned, but this new development was shocking. "Is that wise?"

"They both wish their estrangement to cease. This seemed a good next step."

A murmuring began on the other side of the ballroom. A growing but hushed wave of whispers flowed along the crowd, and Iain watched and listened as it got closer. Tall as he was, he could see couples lining up for the next dance. He caught sight of the earl and then saw Clare across from him.

This was a Lady Clare he'd not seen before.

This was Lady Clare, the earl's eldest daughter.

This was the Lady Clare who was part of society with its feathers and silks and bobs and bits.

With its rules and its insiders and outsiders.

From the look of it, her being warmly welcomed by her father and included in the dances, Lady Clare Logan was an insider once more.

As the strains of the dance began and Lady Clare accepted her father's hand, Iain could not help but consider what this all meant. A sense of foreboding filled him—about his need for those blocks of Leith properties and about the earl's newly-returning influence on his daughter.

Another worry was how they had not known this was happening. Had Cairns lost his source in her household or had the woman not reported this crucial change to him? He slipped through those standing along the side of the dance floor to find a spot where he could better observe their interactions. Once there, he got his first look at the lady.

Was this the true woman behind the one he'd met? Her smile was guileless and lit her face and eyes. She… sparkled, both from the joy on her face and from the jewels around her neck, on her ears and even strewn artfully through her intricately arranged hair. This time, a few loosened tendrils outlined her face and rested on the back of her graceful neck.

And he wanted to immediately pull out every single pin holding her unruly curls and let them fall. He almost had *that* night. His hands clenched tightly at the memory of sliding his hands into her hair and holding her while he…

"Lady Clare looks different than she has in some time," Nairn said from behind him. Oh, hell, Iain had walked away from the marquess as soon as he'd seen her across the crowded room. "It's good to see her happy."

Iain watched as the lady and the earl moved effortlessly into the progression of the dance, a country reel, with the line of other couples. He noticed they engaged in conversation each time they moved together and while awaiting their turn in some of the figures. Heath even introduced her to several other men during the dance. Some were the little kind of lords—younger men, unattached men, men looking for wives. One who looked familiar was older but not as old as her father. Closer to Iain's…

"Bloody hell!" he whispered. The chuckle over his shoulder revealed he'd cursed louder than he'd thought.

He was not the only one noticing and studying Lady Clare. Glancing around, Iain saw the stares and interested gazes as a number of more men centered on her. In spite of her social exile, those in need of a fortune knew her standing and of her wealth. Some even openly leered when she passed nearer to them in her movements of the dance.

How could they not?

The gown she wore—the fanciest he'd ever seen on her—gave every appearance of being transparent as she spun around. Trim ankles he'd touched appeared as the hem of the layers of it were lifted by the currents she made in the air. The top filmy layer of the gown was the color of her creamy skin and iridescent, as dozens of crystal beads sprinkled over it reflected the lights above and around them. Though it flowed freely around her hips and breasts, the underlayer was more fit to her curves, tucked snugly under those breasts and then tumbling smoothly over her hips and thighs. That one was the color of a pale pink blush, as if white wine had been touched with the hint of red.

His mouth watered as he realized it was very close to the same color of her flesh on which he'd feasted. She happened to glance over and caught his eyes at that exact moment. If it had not been part of the dance that placed her in her partner's hold, she would have fallen, for her stumble was noticeable. Almost as she had the night they had dinner at Nairn's house when she ended up in his arms.

He could not move or look away as the dance continued for several minutes more. Then, the second the music ended, she and her father were surrounded by a gaggle of supplicants, all asking for a dance or to be introduced. Her reconciliation and return to society was a success.

"I think you need that drink now, Buchanan." Nairn tugged his arm until Iain faced him. "I will call for my coach. Caro was planning to accompany Clare home anyway."

Iain needed that escape more now than he had earlier. The air grew thick with the odor of burning candles and the crowd pushed towards the dancing. "No coach, my lord. Let us walk. I know a place."

"I'm certain you do."

Iain took one last look at Clare and her beauty struck him as did her joy at this moment of triumph.

But it was not Clare he worried about for long. As the crowd closed around her, Iain could still see her father as he studied those approaching. And the expression on the earl's face sent a chill down Iain's spine.

He escorted the marquess down the street to the Royal Waterloo where a private parlor awaited him. Only after their first brandy, the one he'd liked so much the first time he'd had it, did he finally understand what bothered him so much about the earl's expression.

It was that of a man counting his winnings during a game of chance rather than skill. Counting them as though he even now knew the outcome. Counting them as if they were his already.

In this case, the gold he was counting was his daughter's and not his.

And Iain suspected that his own pursuit of the Leith properties had taken a step backwards with this development.

Three brandies later, he was more convinced that James Murray, Marquess of Nairn, had a sensible, knowledgeable head on his shoulders in spite of the romantic drama that had brought his wife to him.

Two more glasses of the fine brandy and Iain wished he could ask the man's advice about Lady Clare though he had no intention of losing control of himself as Nairn had. But a man with the advantages of noble birth, inherited wealth and a good title could get away with such things while a grasping schemer like Iain could not.

After their last drink, when Iain entered his own coach to go back to his townhouse, one thing was clear to him above everything else—he needed to get his deal with Lady Clare done before the other vultures descended into their situation. She may have walked into an alliance more dangerous to everything she'd managed to accomplish since her husband's death than one with him. For if he knew one thing, he understood predators.

He was one. The Earl of Heath was another.

Not accustomed to lazing about in bed for hours past dawn, Clare considered doing exactly that the next morning.

Though she danced only with her father, the rest of the ball had been like the ones she remembered from her first events in society. Different from the way things were done in London, Edinburgh *society* was not limited to one certain time on the calendar or to a *season*. Due to the numbers of families involved, it was smaller and more intimate. Holders of titles in both countries participated in both, depending on wealth and position, depending on the locations of their houses and estates and their need to show off, be introduced to important people or even acquire a wife. Those lords in Scotland who held seats in Parliament needed to be in London when they were summoned to a session or when an issue interested them.

As Archer arranged her hair for the day and peppered her with questions about the ball, Clare was actually considering the consequences she would now face. Her father had accepted her request very quickly and that meant one thing—he would reveal his true price of the reconciliation soon. The thing she'd learned as a young girl was that everything her father did was a transaction.

Clare was looking forward to the quiet in the small parlor she used for her meals by the time she made her way down to it. Her morning coffee, the only time of day she drank the brew, was hot and dark and sweet. Sipping it, she glanced through the morning newspaper along with several popular broadsheets to see what was news this day. If she was seeking any mention of her presence at the ball last evening, well, she could not deny it if asked.

"Page three," Samantha said. "Second column from the center, halfway down the page. 'Lady C. makes her reappearance at the Michelmas Ball with her long-estranged father at her side'." She tossed the newspaper on the table in front of Clare. "That is what you were searching for?"

There was silence as Samantha selected her breakfast from the platters on the sideboard. Clare chose not to have elaborate meals, especially in the morning, so a selection of hot foods—eggs, rashers of bacon, some sausages—and some breads and muffins and scones were placed for them to serve themselves. Once seated, Samantha looked at the two pots sitting on the table.

"Your coffee smells divine," she said. Clare reached for the smaller pot at her side to offer it but was waved off. "I love the aroma. I even love the taste as long as there's sufficient sugar and cream in it. But, alas, coffee does not love me back."

"So, you remain with tea."

Clare took Samantha's cup and filled it from the teapot on her side of the table. Again, an adaptation by her household to her morning habits, the teapot—too heavy to lift when its iron ingot was in place and when filled—could be reached from her place. Tipping the silver pot, the dark amber liquid let off a small cloud of steam as it reached the edge.

She could have counted down the number of seconds she had until Samantha spoke her mind. Clare had another seven to nine seconds of quiet. She'd managed two sips of her coffee before her friend began.

"You have reconciled with the earl?"

"We are on speaking terms once more. That is all." Clare said.

Samantha was silent for so long, slowly drinking her tea and staring out the window, that Clare wondered if she'd made an error in expecting the woman's objections to be voiced. And then…

"What will it cost you, Clare? Can you pay his price?"

She had asked herself that question so many times since she first considered doing this. Her intentions, what she needed, was some support, not complete domination, by her father. He may have aspirations of controlling her fortune and her future, but she'd made that break from him years before. And that would not change.

"I made it clear that I was not returning home. That I will maintain my household and my businesses and my separate life."

"So what is it worth to him? What will he gain from this? From you?" Samantha stood and walked to the sideboard. Picking up a few different pieces of toast and putting them back, switching her choices over and over until she finally just tossed them all back and faced Clare. "It took you so long to be at peace—first while Jonathan was alive and then in the more than two years since he passed. And you finally have that. You are an extraordinary woman, a woman in business, a woman helping the unfortunates. And you would give that all up? For what?"

Clare began to rise from her seat when Samantha shook her head.

"Has he made his first demand?"

"Samantha, I—"

"He will want you to marry his choice this time."

"I am not marrying again." Clare spoke the words

softly. "That is one line I cannot cross, and my father understands that."

"Clare," Samantha said, kneeling down next to her chair and taking her hand. "That will not stop him from dangling you as bait to draw in all sorts of offers. Especially ones that will benefit him whether you accept the man or not."

"Sam, if nothing else, I do know him. And I know how he acts." Clare swallowed, forcing some memories of her father's past actions from her thoughts now. "But, I need family."

"Then make one of your own!" Samantha said sharply. She stood and walked away, then whirled back to face her. "Choose your own husband. Choose someone strong. Make a family that does not expect your capitulation!"

Iain Buchanan—tall, dark and dangerous—strode into her mind just as he'd strode into her life. Boldly. Sexually. With his impertinent humor and clever mouth. She shivered at the thought of him in her bed, claiming his marital rights. Claiming… her.

"Aye, like him. He would stand up to your father. Counsel you in business issues."

"The man I marry will control all my properties and goods, Sam. Something I am not interested in giving over to anyone."

"Unless your marriage contract says otherwise."

"Sir Iain Buchanan would not barter away the rights he would have as my husband." Clare laughed aloud—a harsh one—not born in humor. "Not considering his relentless pursuit of them."

"Clare, give him what he wants and keep the rest. You can still—"

"I cannot."

Clare walked to the sideboard, moving plates and bowls around, trying to ease her misgivings.

"Cannot or will not, Clare?" Sam appeared at her side. "Women have so little leverage, but you are blessed with more than enough to protect what you want."

"You do not understand," Clare said, her throat tightening with tears and guilt.

"I do not. You are holding onto those particular buildings with no rational explanation. You, even Sir Iain, own many other blocks that could fit your purposes." Samantha stood back. "So, nay, I do not understand. But I never had a love like the one you shared with Jonathan."

"And I owe it to Jonathan to complete his last project." Clare dashed away the tears. "Our last project, Sam. It will be his legacy."

"I did not mean to ruin your triumphant return to the bosom of your family and to society's ranks. I am going over to the school now. Will I see you there later?"

"I will."

Samantha left the room and Clare refreshed her cup of coffee.

Her friend had given voice to the heart of the matter. It was the same question that her secretary and her man of business and her solicitors had asked but in softer, subtler ways. And as Iain had asked in his brash manner. And there was no way to explain to them because she was still mired in guilt over it. That it was less about her love for her late husband than it was her deep guilt over her feelings about him just before he'd died. eventual regrets for having married him.

Clare could not tell anyone the truth of it—that she

and Jonathan had realized they both regretted their marriage. Being held up as some kind of courageous woman by Iain for breaking from her family, being admired by many for her bravery in following her heart and being respected for her work with the poor and unfortunates were all parts of the ongoing lie she lived.

For no matter what others believed, Clare was a coward. A fool who had made bad decisions worse and who, even now when she knew she wanted to do things right, did not have the courage to admit it.

Thirteen

"This just arrived for you, my lady." The footman held out the tray and Clare knew the sender immediately. "The earl's footman is waiting for your answer just outside."

It had taken her father only hours to begin exactly what she'd warned him not to do—find suitors for her hand. Breaking the wafer and opening the letter, Clare read his succinct invitation. He had arranged a gathering this evening, at his townhouse, she could bring a companion or plan to remain overnight.

There was little chance of Samantha coming along, as opposed to Clare's reconnection with her father as she was. Caro had an engagement this evening with her husband, so they would not attend. In a way, that was better.

"Thank you, William. Tell the man I will not be long." David sat nearby and watched her after William left. She shook her head. "I will write it."

She would not refuse her father, but neither would she allow him to pressure her into a marriage she did not want. He could invite whomever he wished, and she would speak with them, be polite, if not friendly, depending on the man and then simply go home. Though last night had been a late one, she would leave there at a decent time.

Writing her reply, she nodded to David. He stood and took the missive to her father's footman in the foyer.

As the day passed, she worked with Mrs. Dunbar and was alarmed that several more children had stopped attending in the most recent weeks. While her attentions had been turned exclusively to her own concerns. She asked to have Chalmers check into the matter once more. They'd lost a child here and there, but over the last few months, it had escalated. It was reaching such a number that it was possibly a matter for the police's attention now.

Hours later, as she arrived at her father's townhouse, she was no closer to discovering why so many children were not coming to the school.

"I did not expect to see you here, Sir Iain."

Of all the possible men to be in attendance, his presence shocked her. Her father had only considered those men with hereditary titles when he'd begun seeking a husband for her the first time. He'd not been interested in money over titles at that time.

"Clearly your father values my opinions, Lady Clare."

"Opinion on what matters? I thought this was a social evening." His blue eyes flashed at her, and she realized this was the first time they'd spoken since…

"Do you want the polite answer, or should we have some measure of honesty between us, my lady?" Again *that* voice, with just enough of a pleading undertone, sent *that* chill down her spine.

"Can I trust you to be honest?" she asked.

"I have never lied to you, Clare." His voice had dropped so that her name was uttered as a hoarse whisper only she could hear. As he'd issued his sensual commands. As he'd touched her and more. "I may not offer the truth, but I never deny it."

Clare lost her breath for a moment. Her stays felt too tightly tied. She sipped her wine before meeting his gaze. He meant it. He would tell her the truth. She might not like it. She might disagree with it. So… .

"Tell me."

"Your father wanted my opinion about your prospective husbands. Whether they are as financially sound as they present or if there is gossip about unwise investments, et cetera, et cetera."

She would never change her father. He would do what he wanted and needed to do to attain his goals. And those goals were simple—whatever made him wealthier, more powerful or more influential.

"And will you give him such advice?"

"Since it would help me to have the prestigious Earl of Heath on my side, I believe I will."

"Even if I have no plans to marry?" she asked. "Because I do not."

He laughed then, loud enough to draw notice but she could not resist laughing with him. Iain handed off his drink to a waiting footman and wiped his eyes. Clare wanted to kiss him. She wanted to feel his laughter against her mouth and to tussle his neatly-combed hair. Samantha's voice echoed in her thoughts.

There is some leniency when it comes to relationships.

Leniency. As a widow, if discreet, she could…

"If I were to offer to pay you for your advice?" He

stopped laughing so fast, he nearly choked on his own spittle.

Clare noticed that too many of those gathered in her father's impressive drawing room were staring now. Her parents both studied her, exchanging glances between them. Clare understood that antagonizing them was never a good thing. With a nod of her head, she walked away and approached her mother's friend who was with a young man who must be her son.

When she finally had the chance to glance back, Iain stared back at her.

He came here because he was curious—a plain and simple explanation of his reaction to the earl's unexpected invitation. He'd remained, at first, because he could not believe the man's explanation—he'd finally gotten his daughter back in his sphere of influence and wanted Iain's advice. But he remained now because of Clare's words—she would pay him for his advice.

Regardless of knowing how bad an idea it was to do such a thing, the way she stared at his mouth when she asked him convinced him that he would lose a fortunate opportunity if he left now. And probably the best fuck of his life. Somehow, he knew she would not offer the contested property and in this moment, after watching her from his shadowed alcove, he really did not care.

He had sold information to the highest bidder before and benefitted greatly in such transactions. He even sold information to several interested parties at once to his even greater profit. His flexible scruples allowed him a wide swath of choices in his life and accepting her offer, whatever it was, would not create any dilemma for him at all.

The lady had made her way around the drawing room, stopping and chatting with each of her father's prospective choices, all in the smooth, graceful manner expected of someone raised in this life. He could see each man stand a little straighter, grow a little taller, under her attention. Though she managed to get a laugh out of most of them, she seemed to know which of the men were of a more serious nature and adapted her manner to them.

He'd been the recipient of her glances and words, and more, and he recognized the way it felt. How the heat rose in his blood. How his body hardened at the thought of touching her again. How his predator nature stretched inside him, demanding he take her and make her only his.

Just at that moment, as he was fighting the very real urge within him that would see him stride across this luxurious chamber, take hold of her and lead or drag her to the nearest bedchamber, Clare glanced over and met and held his gaze.

The slightest tilt of her head towards the hallway gave him the message she wanted.

Follow her.

Tipping his glass up and swallowing the last bit of brandy, he did exactly that. Iain waited a few moments after she'd excused herself and then he made his way along the same corridor. She paused and opened a door and entered the chamber there. A few paces and he stood before it. A glance around for any witnesses, and he entered.

It was a small closet not unlike the one at his offices where he'd dragged her to continue kissing her. Clare stood in the center, watching him as he tugged the door closed and locked it behind him.

"You have information."

"I do," he said, taking a step towards her. He couldn't help the smile that lifted one side of his mouth as she backed one step away. He liked her against the wall.

"And you are willing to share it with me? To assist my efforts in remaining unwed?"

"Do you see no benefits of marrying now?"

"The benefits of marriage are sorely less for a woman than a man, Sir Iain. Especially a woman of means who must lose everything to a husband." Her lower lip slid out in a show of belligerence even as she crossed her arms over her chest.

He laughed then and mimicked her stance.

"But, Clare, you were married. I know you found joy in it. I have heard about that as much as I have about Nairn and your sister." A strange, empty expression lay on her face for the length it took for his heart to beat and then disappeared.

"Certainly, I did. Like all good marriages, it had its moments." That reply reeked of a long-used lie and covered up some truth she was unwilling or unable to share. He suspected it involved the same reason that left her clutching onto what Logan had left her. But something more than just that. He took a step closer and relaxed his hands.

"You should know that although Elphinstone's title is old and respected, his son is gambling and whor—" He paused. "Spending his fortune on the entertainments of men."

"What about the Earl of Cathcart? Even I have heard some rumors about his... ahem... second household."

"Do ladies truly speak of such things?"

"Aye, we do. But, in this case, the information was brought to me by Chalmers."

"What must he have told you of me if he knew that about Cathcart?" He'd not planned to say that aloud.

"He warned me that you are ruthless, manipulating, dangerous if crossed, a brilliant businessman, and… ."

"And?" He was curious now. Even if she'd not been told of his manipulations, she had seen them for herself. How much did Chalmers discover about his background? His previous life? He took the next to last step that would reach her. Did she realize she was one small step from the wall?

"That, although you have not yet married, you have not suffered from a lack of attention, shall we say, from the feminine gender."

Bloody hell, did she know about—

"'A discreet string of lovers' were Chalmers' words."

Iain must either put a stop to Mr. Chalmers' investigations or hire the man himself to defuse his attention. He felt her regard and the heat in his face. Bloody hell, he was—

"Is that a blush, Sir Iain? I would not believe it possible but for seeing it myself," the lady teased.

He did not wish her to think he had an indiscriminate number of women warming his bed. Firstly, because it was not true and secondly, because he was never indiscriminate. Worst of all, he did not want her to think she would be one of many when she would be the first in so many ways.

"Certainly not a string, my lady," he said, closing the now-small distance between them. "But, aye, always discreet." He leaned into her, his foot sliding between hers to trap her against him. "I do not believe your Chalmers could give you any of their names or details?" Her head barely shook her reply. Their breaths intermingled in the inches between their faces.

"Your price then, Sir Iain?" she asked. Her voice was low and breathy. Did she think he would ask for lands when he could have…

"You." He kissed her hard and quick. "Discreetly, of course." She clutched his arms.

"Me?" she asked, tilting her head up to meet his gaze.

The movement only served to expose her long, graceful neck to him. He leaned down and suckled his way from the feminine line of her jaw along her neck and farther. Her breasts were heaving when his mouth reached the edge of her bodice.

"You. I wish to do pleasurable things to you. With you." He reached under the edge of the decorated fabric and lifted her breast out of the gown. Laving it first, he then sucked the tip into his mouth. His tongue teased the nipple to a tight bud before he bit it. She gasped and arched against him at the same time. "Pleasurable, impolite and even unspeakable things."

His aim accomplished, he tugged the bodice up and eased her breast back into its place, stroking the tip with his thumb once, then twice more, as he did. He could smell her arousal and his cock throbbed for it. Once her gown was adjusted, he whispered once more.

"Discreetly."

Iain stepped back and he was inordinately pleased to see the glaze of excitement in her eyes. Though his cock did not agree, the best thing he could do in this moment, at this opportunity, was to leave her. He turned and walked to the door.

"Once."

"Once? One time, my lady? Or one night? One day?"

From the way her brows gathered, he knew she'd not thought of the possibilities. Facing her, he knew the truth even if she would not admit it. It could never be just once between them. But, if they did this, there would be no misunderstanding.

"One of each, my lady," he said, turning the knob behind his back. "And of my choosing."

Looking at her flushed face and her body that trembled with need and desire from just a kiss and a caress, he would gamble his fortune comfortably that she would return to his bed many, many times.

Day. Night.

Morning. Evening.

Bed. Floor. Chair.

Wall.

"How will—"

"I will send you the reports, on those I mentioned and the others your father discussed. And an invitation," he explained, his body betraying his own arousal now. His blood ran hot and runnels of sweat trickled down his back at the thought of her in his hands. "If you open the envelope, then you accept the invitation. If you change your mind or think better of accepting my offer, return them both to me."

He left quickly then, not his smoothest retreat but he needed to get away before he did something very indiscreet. Grabbing a glass of… something from the servant standing by the door as he entered the drawing room, Iain approached the earl.

"A good night's work then, my lord?" he asked as he

downed the contents of the glass. Whisky. A very good, very smooth one.

"Promising." The earl summoned the servant with the tray. "Did my daughter give you any indication of favoring any of them?" the earl asked. "I saw you talking to her."

"Actually, my lord, the lady expressed in all candor that she has no wish to remarry." He studied Heath's face as he spoke.

"She was a headstrong, stubborn thing, always believing she knew better than me. She will come around to my thinking."

"Will she?" Iain was goading the man, plain and simple, but he wanted to have a fuller understanding of the earl and his plans since they were connected, and might oppose, his own.

"My daughter exposed her weakness by approaching me for a reconciliation. It's easier to break someone's resolve when they have given you free rein."

Something dark and foreboding swirled deep inside Iain at the threat implicit in the earl's words. Break her? Oh, aye, she had approached her father in some emotional if not foolish attempt to reconnect with him. Women did emotional things all the time, but he could think of not a single other woman who was as strong and intelligent and practical and.… .

He liked her. He truly liked her.

And he disliked being part of her father's plan to change her. Worse, the desire to protect her was getting stronger with each encounter or memory or thought of the lady and that was highly inconvenient. Iain had conducted his business in a straight-line strategy of his overall plan—see, want, plan, get, move on to next.

Lady Clare was changing that process to: see, want, plan, pursue, have, need, want, get, keep.

And that was dangerous in so many ways. Like this one when he was considering delaying getting the agreed-to information to the earl to slow down his plans for Clare. So knowing the danger in wanting her more than any other woman, Iain would…

"I think you should hold off, my lord," he said, his brain stunned at what his mouth had uttered. "But I will send over the information as soon as my man compiles it."

A hush fell over the chamber as Lady Clare entered. Was it his imagination or were her lips swollen from just his one kiss? Gazing at the exposed skin of her neck and the tops of her breasts as they pushed against the cloth of her gown, Iain saw the exact spot that he would mark with his teeth when he took her.

When she turned to accept a glass of wine from a little lordling, he decided he would mark her shoulder where it met the muscles of her neck. He would take her hard and fast from behind and bite that spot making her scream as he slid his fingers around to pleasure between her legs. One hand wrapped in her loosened hair, one thrust deep in the heated folds, his mouth and teeth on that sensitive spot, and his cock buried to the hilt in her channel—exactly where he wanted to be.

The glass in his hand stood no chance against his tightened fist and it cracked into pieces in his hand.

"Buchanan?"

The earl's butler was there before anyone could call him. Scooping up the broken crystal and taking the rest from his hand, the man removed all the bits as though it was a usual thing. Somehow Iain had not cut his hand badly. He tugged a handkerchief from his coat pocket and wrapped it around his palm.

"All is well," he said, nodding his respects to the earl and making his escape.

He was disgusted with his lack of control over her. He knew how to deal with obsessions—give in to them and they controlled you. Got you killed. The other was to find a way to get them out of your system. Or dissipate their power over you. The lady was one he wanted to work out of his system—one time, one night and one day.

Lucky for him, he had one other good hand and once he was in his carriage, he used it to ease the raging need for her. It was only as he entered his house that he realized he'd never even considered going to Tess as he usually did for such relief.

He had the envelope delivered into her hands at her house the next morning and then waited all day for it to be returned unopened. Every sweep of the clock's second hand seemed to take a year but, finally, he was ready to leave the office and nothing had arrived from her.

The first part—once—would happen in two hours.

FOURTEEN

Pleasurable things.
  Impolite things.
  Unspeakable things.
  To her. With her.

Those words haunted her as she'd held the envelope in her hands. Unopened, it held such promise and such danger. Did she need to know what her father would know? Would it be worth the personal cost of getting it from *him*?

The strange thing about this was that Clare did not for a moment believe she was in danger. And he'd been quite clear about what he expected from her. A transaction to benefit both of them. If she walked away with knowledge that made her position and leverage stronger with her father and his plans, all the better.

If her curiosity about the man and the pleasure he promised was satisfied, that could not be a bad thing. If he'd spoken the truth to her and would not lie, she would ask him one question before anything happened—if his answer was unsatisfactory, she would leave.

Did he plan to use this encounter against her?

If not, then she would accept his offer.

Clare followed his instructions and arrived at the

private entrance of the hotel. In a dark gown, covered by a long cloak with a veiled hat, no one would notice or recognize her. A footman, a different one than the previous visit, opened the door as she climbed down from the carriage and waited as she walked past him. Then, leading the way, he guided her up the stairs, into the hallway and towards the door leading to the owner's suite.

The retiring room was empty, and the footman led her to the next chamber. Then he backed out, closing the door behind himself. Clare searched around the room and found it also empty. Lifting the veil up and over her bonnet, she walked to the blazing fire burning in the hearth near the sitting area and allowed the heat from it to warm her.

Well, not warm so much as calm her. As she extended her gloved hands towards the flames, she saw them trembling in spite of the warmth.

"May I help you with your cloak, my lady?"

Iain stood just a short distance away from her and she'd never heard his approach. The flames threw shadows on his body and face as he moved closer and reached for the ties of her cloak. As he took hold of the laces, she placed her hands on his to stop him.

"Will you use this as leverage against me?"

Shock froze his features. He released the ties and dropped his hands.

"Nay, Clare."

She stared at him, trying to discern if it was the truth.

"You are a widow beholden to no one and able to do as you please within the bounds of discretion, of course," he said, not looking away. A wicked smile threatened but he controlled it. "I am unmarried, above the age of consent and free to engage in… activities with anyone I please. So, will you engage in activities of a private nature with me, Clare?"

He waited, not moving and barely breathing, for her reply. Her body reacted, her blood heated and the place between her legs ached and throbbed. She believed his words.

"Pleasurable things?" she whispered, tugging the laces loose. He reached over then and lifted the cloak away, tossing it on a chair.

"And impolite, too. Aye."

He pulled on the ribbons holding her bonnet and veil in place and soon that followed the cloak. A tug or two on each glove removed them.

"Unspeakable things," he promised in a deep voice that turned her insides to molten lava. "Take down your hair." The command made her breasts swell and their tips tighten.

"Your choice?" she asked.

"Mine," he growled.

His hands fisted and relaxed over and over, and she reached up to pull the pins holding her hair in Archer's arrangement. With the last one removed, it fell around her and she shook her head a bit to loosen it. The growl this time had no form or words, but the sound of it made her body shudder with need.

Only then, waiting for him to lunge, did she see his own state of deshabille, for he wore a black silk banyan and trousers. No shirt. No neckcloth. No waistcoat. The black hair on his muscular chest was open to her view and Clare could not take her eyes from the rippling muscles of his stomach or his male nipples. His skin was darker, as though exposed to the sun for long periods of time. She reached out to test those beckoning curls and masculine form, but before she could, he took her hands in one of his and guided them inside the robe and lower still.

And splayed them over his hardened flesh.

She gasped loudly and he drew her face to his and took advantage of her open mouth. He kissed her over and over and over until she felt her legs wobble unsteadily from such attentions. As overwhelming as his kisses were, Clare wanted his mouth on her breasts, as he had done in the closet at her father's. She arched, her breasts pressing against the edge of her gown, but hidden by the silk fichu tucked around her neck and shoulders.

Within moments he'd pulled the silken cover off and tossed it aside. His nimble fingers untied the laces at the back of her gown even as he pressed himself against her hands. Curling her fingers around his length, she rubbed over the fabric of his trousers. Her dress gaped, exposing her breasts and short corset to his sight.

"My choice," he said, staring at her until she nodded. "But you will tell me if it is too much." He gave her power over his basest needs and urges.

Faster than she'd thought possible, he slid his fingers into her hair and wrapped the length of it around one of his hands. Then turned her body, encircling her waist with his other arm, walked them over to the large dining table and leaned her over.

"Put your hands on the table. Hold the edge."

The next thing she knew, the cooler air in this part of the room crept up her legs as he gathered the length of her gown and tossed it up past her hips. His hand pressed between her legs and spread them apart. She bucked back, leaning on her elbows as he found the places that had enraged her passion before—the folds, the bud, and the channel that led inside her body. Her hair fell like a curtain around her shoulders and face, the length of it lay in a mass of curls on the table's surface. Her body tightened and tightened, and she could feel the release so close she groaned.

And he stopped. His hot breaths against her back pleased her—he was aroused, rampant from the feel of his flesh against her. The tension in her body eased.

"The bed?" she asked. The door to the bedchamber stood open. The bedclothes had been drawn down, readied for them.

"The table will do just fine," he said. She had only ever…

His one hand, with two clever fingers cleaving her flesh from the front, pressed against the most sensitive of places. Her hips rose higher, and she felt his other hand release the falls of his trousers and then… then…

He thrust inside her and she screamed. So full, so deep she lost her breath. Slowly he eased back until she was almost empty. His hips arched and he plunged into her again. His flesh filled her, and he repeated the slow withdrawal and almost-brutal thrust over and over until she could feel the walls of her channel begin to throb around his length.

But no, he would not allow a simple release. He reached his free hand up and grabbed the length of her hair, twisting it once more around his hand until he tugged her head back, forcing her to rise back onto her hands. He covered her as a stallion did to a mare and whispered wicked things as he squeezed his fingers together.

"I will fill every part of you, Clare," he said against her ear, pulling her hair tightly. "I will fuck you here, on the floor, against that wall." He turned her head towards the wall. "Maybe the bed. Clothed. Naked." He thrust deep with each word he growled. "I may even tie you to the bed and fill your mouth with this," he pressed deeper for a moment, then rubbed that bud between her legs, "as I take your quim with my tongue."

She lost her control then. Waves of pleasure flowed through her body, and she was swept into bliss with every thrust and every tug on her hair. But then he leaned over and bit her! He bit the skin where her neck met her shoulder and the pleasure-pain of it sent her soaring as the tension within let go. Clare screamed his name and lost herself.

How much time had passed by the time she became aware again, she had no idea. The ticking of the clock sounded loud in the silence of the large room. A pop from the fire. Then his breath against her ear.

Though covered by him, she was somehow not crushed by his weight. She shifted her legs and felt him still within her. Her flesh ached now, from the size of him, the strength of his thrusts and the fact that she had not done this in a long time.

"Stay here," he whispered. "Give me a moment."

"I cannot move." His laugh in reply as he walked into the bedchamber made her smile.

Turning her head freely, she rested it on the table as her legs buckled, leaving her lying there on her belly. She could not find the strength to even toss her skirts down. Empty and emptied, that's what she was now. The strength of every muscle had been stolen by the power of her release and she could not rise, even from this embarrassing position.

Iain carried the basin he'd had prepared in from the bedchamber and stopped. Bloody hell, what had he done?

Clare lay sprawled on the table, her gown bunched at her waist, her lovely legs covered in silk stockings but bare to his gaze, and her hair in a pool around her. He wanted to feel sorry for having taken her that way, but he could not find it in him. Neither had suffered and both had experienced a shocking satisfaction.

On the dining room table.

He shook his head as he placed the basin and towels next to her. Dipping the cloth into the steaming water, he rubbed some of the soap into it then moved behind her.

"Clare," he said, not wanting to startle her. He placed the soapy cloth against the folds of flesh between her legs and allowed the heat to soothe the place that must feel quite uncomfortable now.

Dear God, she had been so tight. Tighter than he'd ever imagined she would be. He'd planted himself fully into her with one thrust and her scream as he did was part pleasure, but close to pain. He'd wanted to overwhelm her, to fill her, to take her, but never did he want to hurt her. After her reaction to his mouth on her, he should have realized she would not be one for rougher play.

When the heat in the cloth dissipated, he repeated it a few more times before using the towel to dry her. She did not move during his ministrations and, after adjusting her gown into place, he found she was asleep.

He almost laughed aloud but did not want to disturb her for a few minutes. He gathered up her cloak, bonnet and veil, fichu and gloves and placed them over the chair. Then he poured two rather good portions of that brandy from downstairs and put them on the table in front of the couch.

"Clare," he said, touching her arm. "My lady," he said a bit louder as he slid his arm under her and lifted her off the table.

Catching the rest of her, he scooped her into his arms and carried her to the couch. A few minutes later, he'd settled her on his lap, in his embrace and just enjoyed listening to her breathe. In her sleep she looked even younger and more vulnerable than usual. She looked much like the young maid he'd thought her to be on that first encounter.

He leaned forward and grabbed one of the glasses. The brandy went down smoothly and soon his heartbeat had calmed. Iain had convinced himself she would never carry through with it. She was a lady, he a mercenary businessman and so far below her on the steps of the ladder of polite society—the knighthood aside—that she should have run in the other direction.

Clearly, he'd been wrong about her again.

Iain slid his fingers in her hair and twisted a length of it around them. Like the softest silk, wrapping his fist in it while fucking her from behind had fulfilled his fantasy. His cock stirred a bit, but it would take even him longer to recover from this act of sheer satisfaction.

Besides that, this was their *once*. And, being honest with himself, if they did nothing else, he would walk away perfectly happy. She had reacted to his commands in a way he never expected. He liked control in sex and Clare responded to it by accepting it, obeying him and being aroused as hell by it.

The way her body wept at his vulgar words, uttered while taking her to the thin border where pleasure meets pain just confirmed that there could be so much more pleasure between them. And, with her agreement to give him one day and one night, he could show her many paths to pleasure.

Clare roused a short while later, opening her eyes slowly and glancing around before she met his gaze. Would she be embarrassed by what they'd done, by what she'd allowed him to do to her? Would she decide not to return?

When she realized her position, she slid off his lap to sit next to him. He leaned up and got the other brandy for her. Taking it from him, she sipped it without looking at him.

"Are you hungry? Should I call down for a meal?"

"Will we stay here for the night?"

"Night?"

"Do you not expect me to stay the night? And the day?"

"This was our once."

"Oh dear." She drank the rest of the brandy in one gulp. "If this was once, I did not think I will survive a night with you."

His masculine pride swelled at her words. In spite of knowing now that she was so inexperienced in bedplay that she overestimated his abilities or what had happened between them, he was pleased.

"You are good for my pride, Lady Clare. Very good for it." He reached over and placed his hand on her leg. It felt incredibly intimate to touch her so, inexplicable since he had just been inside her body. "Tell me the truth now—did I hurt you? I'm afraid I let my despicable lust run free once I got you in my clutches."

She laughed at his remark, and he drank in the sound of it.

"I am fine," she said softly, a blush rising in her cheeks.

He lifted his hand and rubbed the back of it against her face. "I had hoped for better than simply fine. And you never answered my question about a meal."

"I am hungry," she said. Turning to face him, they each maintained a polite façade. "And you did not answer mine."

"I did. This was not the night I have planned for us." He stood and retrieved the brandy, filling his glass and adding to hers. "So, we can enjoy a nice dinner now that we have… " There were a number of ways to express what they'd done—none of them suitable for an overwhelmed lady. "Now that our business is out of the way."

"Aye. Our transaction," Clare whispered back.

Iain went to the bellpull and summoned a footman. As he passed the dining table, an unusual but unmistakable wave of regret pierced him. Staring at the place where he'd literally had his way with Clare, something bothered him. Which then bothered him because he did not suffer regrets in his life. He glanced back at the lady who sat calmly on his couch sipping her brandy after he'd practically ravaged her.

She was an enigma. And a wonder. No one else in his life had surprised him as many times as she had. No one challenged him as she did. No one made him laugh like her.

The lady stood and nodded to the retiring room. As she closed the door behind her, he realized he had two regrets about the Lady Clare Logan.

The first was that this was all a transaction, a quid-pro-quo, for them. Oh, he lived his life by paying his way and charging for his services, so he understood it was the norm for him. But he hadn't wanted this to be the bargain they reached.

The second regret was that it could not continue once the bargain was done. Though wealth and power and his minor courtesy title could be considered equal to her wealth and ancient title by some, making some longer claim on her would bring a different kind of attention to him. The family lines in family bibles or old neighbors or vicars to vouch for a family's history were lacking for him and he could never prove his identity.

For the first time in his ill-gotten life, he wished it was not so. That he was… worthy of a woman like her. As he stared at the closed door and then down at his blood-stained hands and felt his black heart beat, he knew he could never be. All these years he'd been quite content, happy, satisfied even, with the life he'd carved out with sheer ambition, effort and work.

When, if, he married, it would be the daughter of some business associate who needed him more than common sense could negate. Iain would get her with child and install her in a lovely, expensive country estate with servants aplenty and carry on making more money, acquiring more businesses, and running the ones he owned.

The soft knock at the door interrupted his maudlin musings and he was glad of it.

Several waiters entered, set the smaller table which they moved at his direction to the center of the room and presented their meal. As he expected, Clare did not return while they were in the room. And when she did, he knew it was better if all they had between them were transactions.

Fifteen

Clare stood at the window, watching the boys run in the enclosed space. The sun had unexpectedly broken through the mist and rain and Peter quickly released them from their studies. One could never depend on either the timing or duration of sunshine in Edinburgh and the teacher wisely accepted its appearance as a sign for a short recess from their slates and books.

In spite of their circumstances, these lads were full of the joyful exuberance of their age. Not yet encumbered by the worries of life, they could run, kick the ball and tussle at a moment's notice. They took advantage of the opportunities presented to them when they appeared and did not look back.

As she let the curtains drop back into place, Clare knew she was doing exactly that with Iain. Once paid for his services and once he gave up on his pursuit of the properties, he would go back to his empire, and she would remain here.

Though she planned changes in her life, there was much to do first. A knock on the small parlor's door drew her back to the demands of the day. She'd taken a pause for tea and noticed that the hands of the clock had moved more than an hour more since she'd entered. It had already happened four times in the three days since…

"My lady, Mr. Chalmers is here."

"Show him in here, please, William." Before he turned away, she added, "And please bring the good whisky and glasses."

James Chalmers was not a tea drinker. And, she probably would want something stronger when he made his report. Something sinister was happening on the streets of Leith and it involved her school. Chalmers strode in and accepted the seat she offered, waiting for her to sit before he did. She allowed him a drink of the whisky William brought and poured before she asked.

"What have you found?"

"Well, my lady, nothing is easy when you are trying to get working people and those who survive on the streets to talk."

"I understand. Fear binds their tongues."

"Aye, my lady. But I wanted you to know that I discovered that a gang under the control of a particularly nasty fellow—" He stopped and reached inside his coat pocket for the small notebook she'd seen him scribbling in often. He flipped some pages back then forward until he found what he was looking for. "A man called Dougal Dubh heads up a crew of thugs for hire and is somehow involved."

The name did not sound familiar, but the methods did. Living in squalor meant a dangerous existence and men like this Dougal Dubh exploited the weaknesses of those unable to defend themselves.

"What do you think is happening, Mr. Chalmers? Should you call in the police?" she asked. Clare knew the answer to her second question before he spoke. Police in the worst areas of Edinburgh and Leith were paid more to look away than to pursue crime in those places. They faced powerful criminals who were organized and better funded, and most times they simply could not overcome the forces against them.

"I have several men assigned to this, my lady. Once I know more, we can decide what to do." She stood, as did he.

"I wait on your report."

Chalmers left and Clare went back to the work that lay untouched on her desk. No matter what happened in her life, she was going to appoint managers for the companies she owned and center her attention only on the school and orphanage. She needed a life and even if she refused her father's machinations, at some point she suspected she would want the companionship that a marriage could offer her.

But she would do that the way she wanted.

A memory of Iain flashed through her thoughts—several memories. Iain carrying her up the stairs after she twisted her ankle. Iain storming into her office, making his demands. Iain taking her on the hard surface of the table. And Iain chatting with her while they ate dinner after that unbelievable act of passion.

The meal was surprising in how mundane and usual it was. She'd known the food would be superb, and it was, but the conversation was exciting. They spoke of business and his properties all over Scotland. They talked about the places he'd visited and places she wanted to visit. And when they ran out of topics, they jumped from one to another to another—sometimes serious, sometimes jesting and light-hearted, other times debating opinions.

The purpose of the evening had been payment for

services rendered but the result had been so much more than that.

And yet, the envelope sitting unopened in front of her belied the purpose for her.

It was hours later, after a meal at noon, that the next invitation arrived. Her body reacted before she even realized what she held in her hands, heating and tightening. She made the comment about not surviving if their evening had been the *once,* and thinking about a day with him or a night in his bed made her know the truth of that casual comment.

Tomorrow morning. The dock across from my office. Bring clothing for an overnight trip.

No other clues to his intention or destination or plans.

Clare shivered in frank anticipation.

Worse, she was completely worthless for the rest of the day and evening, taking supper on a tray in her chambers so she could avoid Samantha's knowing gaze.

The day dawned bright—a good thing considering her lack of sleep—and a short time after leaving her house the coach pulled up at the dock across from Buchanan & Sons in Leith. A man she'd met before stood waiting as she climbed out.

"Mr. Pemberton?"

"Aye, my lady," he said, greeting her with a bow. "If you will come this way." Iain's secretary directed another man to take her bag and they headed down a long wooden dock to a ramp that led onto a sailing ship.

Even living and working in coastal harbor towns like Edinburgh and Leith and even having companies that moved goods by ship, Clare had never been on one and had no knowledge of how they worked. This one was not the largest she'd seen or the largest in this harbor. It had three masts and lots of square sails. More than that, she did not know the details. As she walked along it towards the ramp, she was impressed by it in spite of her ignorance.

"Lady Clare," an older man, tall and bearded with bright green eyes and gray flecks in the dark brown of his hair, said in greeting at the ramp. "I am Captain Charles Ramsey."

"Captain Ramsey." She nodded.

"Sir Iain has asked me to welcome you aboard." He held out his arm to her. "May I escort you? The ramp gets quite steep near the top."

She accepted his help and was glad of it by the time they reached the deck of the ship. Turning around as she caught her breath, the view of Leith and up to Edinburgh was completely different than any she'd seen before, and it fascinated her.

"Wait until you see if from offshore." Clare turned to find Iain watching her. "Thank you, Captain. We are ready to depart now."

"Aye, sir," Captain Ramsey said. "My lady, I hope you enjoy the day."

"Welcome to my latest acquisition, my lady," Iain said. "I thought you might like to accompany me while we take her out for a few hours."

Shocked into silence. Stupefied. He had surprised her in a way she could never have dreamt of.

"From the expression on your face, I am concerned that you don't like being on ships?" Iain stepped closer and studied her face. "Does it make you ill?" He turned and called out to the captain.

"Iain, nay," she said. Reaching out to him, she tugged his hand. "I am surprised, that is all."

"Do you get seasick then?" He covered her hand with his.

"I have never been on the sea to know such a thing," she admitted. He laughed loudly then and called out to Ramsey that all was well.

"'Tis a good day to be at sea, Clare. Smooth seas, blue skies, winds to fill the sails. Come, let's go forward and watch as we leave the harbor."

He grabbed her hand, not in a formal hold, but a friendly one and they walked forward to the front of the ship and stood along the railing. Iain stood behind her, surrounded her with his arms and kept her steady as the ship began to move.

"Here we go," he leaned against the side of her bonnet and whispered in her ear.

With his strong body behind her, she felt no fear, just a sense of exhilaration she'd not experienced in a long time. The gentle winds blowing in her face relieved some tension. When she relaxed against him, he leaned into her.

"Once we clear the harbor, the winds will be stronger," he said. Pointing out into the water, she followed his arm to where he indicated. "We leave the shelter there."

"Where are we going?" she asked, turning her head towards him so he could hear her. The captain and a number of others were shouting out orders and running across the deck creating a cacophony that was hard to hear over.

"Down the coast a few hours, then back in the morning," he said. She shivered and he leaned closer. It was heat that made her tremble, not cold. "The captain is testing out new sails and new crew."

Because they headed into the firth from the harbor, the island of Inchkeith lay ahead of them and the city of Edinburgh lay behind them, and Iain turned them for a better view. The medieval castle high on Castle Rock was impressive even more at a distance than close up. She could trace the steeples of the High Street down towards Holyrood Palace. The terraces and New Town sloped northward from the base of the castle.

There were a few minutes of roughness when the ship left the safety of the harbor, but soon, they were gliding smoothly over the sea, out into the North Sea and then south. Iain spoke often, pointing out places and interesting things to see along the coast. Clare marveled at the different perspective from the sea.

It grew windier as they reached the sea and the ship rose and fell on the waves. She laughed at the motion which forced her to adjust her stance and shift her legs to keep her balance. They indeed rode the waves for some time, away from the firth and south along the coast. Several landmarks she'd seen or visited on land gave her context for their location—Bass Rock and the ruins of Tantallon Castle were familiar to her.

"Are you well?" he asked as he shifted behind her.

She answered, but could not help but tease him. "No *mal de mer* at all, Iain." He was so close that his laugh rumbled through her.

"Good news, for the captain has invited us to share his meal." Iain turned away for a moment, then stepped back from her. "If you would like to take refuge from the winds for a bit, or if you are hungry…?"

He held out his arm to her and she clutched it tightly, using it to support her steps as they walked along the deck. And he continued explaining the workings of a barque, its masts, its sails, its cargo and so on until they reached a set of wooden stairs leading below.

"You know much about this ship."

"Hold on here and I'll guide you down."

He stepped down onto the first step and patted his shoulders. Seeing no railings to grasp, she did as he said and followed him down step by step. He timed their movements to the rise of the ship in the water, so they were firmly on a step when the ship dropped. Like a man used to walking on such a vessel.

They made their way to the back of the ship and entered a large cabin that had windows across the width of it. It was divided into two main areas—one clearly for sleeping and the other for working and eating. Iain left her holding onto the back of a chair placed at the side of a square table as he went back outside to speak to someone.

The bed, for she could not help but stare at it, was larger than she expected within the tighter confines of a ship. Pillows and cushions strewn across it promised comfort and its placement in the cabin gave anyone in it a view out the four large windows looking out from the back of the ship. The table and desk, along with the privacy screen and storage chest were unremarkable and functional, but the other fixtures and furnishings were interesting.

Especially the shelves and shelves of books that lined one whole wall.

Designed to hold the books in place against the ship's movements, the shelves were packed tightly and each one had a rope strung across it that kept the books from falling. Once she felt in control and balanced, Clare walked along the shelves and read some of the titles.

Although many, all collected on one shelf, dealt with ships and sailing and maps, the others were a mix of novels, mysteries, poetry, histories, and such.

"See any you like?" Iain asked, as he closed the door and walked behind her.

"The captain has quite an eclectic taste in reading materials," she murmured as she slid her finger across each book as she read the titles to herself.

"Aye, he does."

She heard the humor in his voice and turned to face him. His blue gaze twinkled, and that damned corner of his mouth lifted just enough that she almost swooned knowing what his wicked smile looked like. And how his mouth felt on her.

"This is your cabin? You are the captain?" He nodded. "And Captain Ramsey?"

"Captain Ramsey takes the command most of the time, but aye, I am the owner and captain when I take the ship out."

"You did seem to know so much about the workings of a ship. Is that how you started in the company? As captain."

He took her hand and led her to the windows. The bottom ledge of the windows had been fashioned into a long bench and covered by a cushion, making it a lovely place to sit and observe the sea. She did and untied the ribbons holding—almost—her bonnet in place. The winds were getting the better of it, so she removed it.

"I started as a worker on the docks and in the warehouses and progressed up until I was a sailor on Mr. Buchanan's ships. Eventually, I captained a ship." His explanation fit what Chalmers had reported to her. He was adopted by Mr. Ulysses Buchanan at some time before he turned twenty and became the wealthy man's only heir.

"And now you own the entire enterprise," she finished. "And still captain your ships?" He sat next to her.

"Nay, I work too much to do it."

"I am impressed, Sir Iain," she said, reverting to his title. "Not many business owners of your renown know enough about their companies to run them, let alone participate in them."

"Those of us who built them do. But those who inherit… Forgive me, my lady, I mean no insult."

"None taken. I am a bit of both, I think. And a bit different as well. I did inherit, but I work now with a number of the companies I inherited and did before…" She smiled at him. "And unlike those properties that are entailed and follow the title, mine do not—"

"Unless you marry."

"Hence my resistance to that institution."

"I understand. Remember, I am helping your efforts to stay out of that trap."

The envelope. The payment for his services.

She shivered as the recollection of his voice claiming her as the price echoed in her thoughts. His gaze was a knowing one—he knew she was remembering what they'd done.

Pleasurable things.

Impolite things.

Unspeakable things.

Immobilized at the rush of heat inside her, Clare could only stare at his mouth, wanting it on her breasts. The knock on the cabin door prevented her from doing something foolish, like begging him to take her here, now.

Captain Ramsey entered and directed a few men as they brought in platters of food and pitchers. Once everything was in place, he invited them to the table.

Clare laughed so much during their meal that tears fell. Ramsey and Iain were longtime friends from all that was said, and they discussed, argued, bantered, jested back and forth for the next hour… or two. The food was well-cooked, deliciously seasoned and filling. When invited to join them in a glass of port at the end of the meal, she did, feeling no shame about drinking with the two men.

After that, Clare accompanied the captain back up on deck and waited for Iain to arrive. The one who climbed the steps to the deck and stood before her was a different Iain, almost as though he had become someone else. He'd removed his coat, waistcoat and neckcloth before leaving the cabin and even changed into different shoes—well-worn flat leather ones. His trousers were exchanged for canvas breeches, tied at the knee, and instead of his fine lawn shirt, he wore a lesser quality cambric one.

Iain Buchanan, the elegant knight and owner of this ship, had been left below deck and Iain Buchanan, the sailor and menial worker, had presented himself for duty. A few of the sailors called out taunts, but Ramsey waved them off.

"To the sails!" he ordered, and more than a dozen men raced to the ropes and began climbing.

Including Iain.

"Come this way to the quarterdeck, my lady," he offered his arm since the ship was bobbing about quite a bit now. "He cannot show off if you cannot see him."

Clare was touched by that. Iain had already showed

off in bringing her to a ship he owned, but this was a more personal way of trying to impress her. A more primitive way even.

The captain guided her up several steps to a deck in the back of the ship that was raised above the main deck. It was a better view of the ship and the sea and the land off in the distance. Clare gasped at the sight of men climbing up and up like the monkeys she'd seen climbing in a zoo.

And Iain was in the midst of them, yelling out insults as he sure-footedly took to the heights of the mast in a race to reach the top. From a distance he blended in with the other sailors and she lost sight of him for a moment.

"He's there, my lady," Ramsey said, lifting his hand to point to the set of sails nearest her. "Oh ho! And he's losing."

Shielding her eyes with her hand, she found him and saw the other smaller sailor passing him as though he was not moving.

"Blackwood is one of our best," Ramsey said. "And Iain is out of practice from sitting behind a desk."

When the other man reached the top, all the men shouted his name, even Iain who laughed at the insults called out to him, too. She expected that they would climb right back down but they did not.

"There is some work to be done up there, checking and tightening and so forth. It may take some time." The captain walked to the stairs. "If you would excuse me, I do have to get to my own duties."

"May I stay here?"

"Certainly, but keep hold on the railing just in case—" The sea chose to throw a large wave at the ship, large enough to make it tilt as it rose, and she grabbed hold before she toppled over. "That. Just in case of that."

A sailor approached him, and he turned away. She leaned her head back and watched as the crew carried out their tasks. Good natured, though vulgar, chatter went on; the men worked quickly, moving across the beams and up and down on the masts. Clare held her breath every time she caught sight of Iain.

This was not the Iain she knew. Oh, Chalmers had said he'd worked on ships and he'd shared some of his knowledge of them, but she did not realize the extent of his experience. Now, she'd seen him as a businessman, at a society ball and as a common sailor. Nay, not common. She lost track of time and everything as she studied his every movement.

"My lady?" She blinked and turned to find a young man there.

"Aye?"

"The captain suggested you might be more comfortable in the cabin since the work will continue for some time." Not certain which of the captains had made the suggestion, she thought it a good one regardless.

Clare followed him back to the cabin and found it warmed by the sun streaming in the windows. She stood enjoying the view for a while, but the motion of the ship was very relaxing. Deciding that reading might help pass the time, Clare selected a novel from the top shelf and sat on the bench along the windows.

The rocking, the lift and the fall of the waves, and the movement through the water lulled her to sleep before she knew it was happening.

SIXTEEN

Iain had not enjoyed himself this much in… in…

Well, never.

Between spending hours with Clare and seeing her experiencing the sea for the first time and then working like he had not in years, he was exhilarated and exhausted at the same time. Even now after washing and stretching his arms and rolling his shoulders, he ached worse than he did after a fight.

But the moment he opened the door to the cabin and found her asleep, curled up on the seat in front of the windows, any sense of tiredness fled. In a matter of seconds, his body came alive with need and desire for her.

Iain crossed the cabin and stood within inches of her, just watching her face in the calmness of sleep. Her bodice rose and lowered as did the rosy skin of her breasts with each slow deep breath. Her hands were tucked under her cheek and she lay on her side. Her knees were drawn up, pulling some of the length of her gown with them and due to her movements, her ankles lay exposed to him.

Bloody hell! He owned a fucking brothel and could see women in every stage of dress and undress and a damned silken-clad ankle was arousing him.

Iain sat on the bed and shook his head. Never had he thought that a gentle, kind, intelligent, and somehow practical and generous daughter-of-an-earl would upend his life as she had. He'd somehow expected that a brash, big-breasted, blond-haired wench would have caught his eye and he'd have been quite happy ensconced in her bed, enjoying her talents. He'd been happy with Tess for years, though he had not visited her bed since the day he'd met Lady Clare Logan.

Noticing the small book on the table at the bedside, one he read on each voyage on the ship, Iain settled back against the headboard. From the looks of it, Clare was deeply asleep and would be for a while, so he shoved some pillows behind him and read while waiting for her to wake.

The quick inhale of a breath followed by sounds of her shifting came sometime later and he thought she might wake. He'd lit some lamps around the cabin and had a lantern on the table once the sun set and waited for her to open her lovely green eyes. From her wary glances at him since her arrival, he could tell that she had expected him to pounce when their day or night came, but their *once* had released all the rage to have her and so he waited. The rage had eased, though not the need or the want. Iain suspected that watching her surprise over his choice of this day's plans would be pleasure in another form—and it had been.

Her smile. Her wide-eyed surprise and appreciation for the views from the ship of the city and places she'd only seen from land. The blush that the sea air and winds brought to her cheeks. The way she gave herself over to him while standing at the railing, leaning into him for support.

He'd also surprised her by revealing more about himself and his past. Most men of business who fought to build their way up leave behind the less seemly connections—and he certainly did that for many of his—but he'd never been able to get the sea out of his blood. Those early years when he was on a ship were some of the best times of his life. Breathing air unspoiled by the smoke of wood and coal burning was like heaven to him.

Oh, it was hard work—some of the hardest he'd ever done—but he had learned about himself, his ambitions, his goals and his determination to have what he wanted. He'd learned of cruelty there, but having survived nigh-to-dying already, Iain also learned how to live through it.

"Iain?" Her whisper sent shards of need through him. "What time is it?" She pushed herself up on her elbows and looked around, staring the longest at the night sky out of the windows behind her. Some of her hair had come loose and tumbled over her shoulders. "Oh." Her expression as she faced him was inscrutable.

"You looked so peaceful that I could not bear to wake you."

"I think the excitement of the morning exhausted me," she said, sliding her feet to the floor and smoothing her gown over her legs. He could not see her ankles now. "We are not moving?"

"Nay. We are anchored just off Berwick-on-Tweed." He slid off the bed and approached her. "Captain Ramsey and most of the crew have sought the comforts of the town and will not return until the morning."

"Oh." Again that one word with too many meanings for his liking. Not when he could not read her face. Was she anxious? Or fearful? Apprehensive about the coming night between them?

Or had she changed her mind?

He had never expected her to carry through with this agreement, her body in exchange for his information. From the fiery lust that sparked to life between them, he'd half thought she would have come to him on her own. But that inkling of hope was doused when she did not return the envelope.

"Have you changed your mind then?" He stepped back. "Would you like me to go?"

"Nay."

They stood staring at each other for moments that seem to stretch on for hours. He was waiting. Waiting for her to move. To welcome him. To want him.

All it took in the end was for her to lift her hand and hold it out to him.

Iain took it and tugged her towards him, slowly, his need to touch her and taste her growing with every second. But this time, this time, he wanted to savor her and not rush through to satisfy his rampant desire. Raising her hand to his mouth, he kissed each fingertip and then kissed a line along her arm, pushing the fabric of her sleeve up.

When he could reach no more of her skin, he moved around behind and kissed along the back of her neck until he found the very spot he'd wanted to mark from the night when they made their agreement. Her head fell back against his shoulder, and he suckled the tender spot at the base of her throat. She shuddered under his mouth and let out gasps in time with every stroke of his tongue and as the edges of his teeth worried against the delicate skin caught between them.

Lady Clare Logan would wear his mark on her skin and know he had done it. A tremor shook his body and his cock hardened more.

As her body fell back against his, catching his very hard flesh between her hips and his, he caressed his way up her—his hands gliding over her belly and cupping her breasts. Her nipples had already tightened into buds, so he rubbed his thumbs across them, making them swell and her moan and press into his grasp. Tempted as he was to make short work of her clothes and repeat the rushed way he had her that first time, he would not.

"Please," she whispered.

"What do you want, Clare?" He knew she liked his kisses on her breasts. He liked kissing them and her. She reached back and slid her hand in his hair and pulled him down.

"Your mouth on me, Iain. Now. I can wait no longer." His cock reacted to that—every word, the strong tone of it, her voice caused his erection to strengthen.

"As you wish, my lady." Iain released her and untied the laces on the back of her dress. Once it was loosened enough, he pushed it off her shoulders and down until her breasts were open to his sight.

Now he could use his tongue to trace her collarbones and he did, tasting the saltiness left on her skin by the wind whipping up from the waves. She'd not worn one of those fichu scarves with this dress, so there'd been nothing to protect her skin from the spray. By the time he was in front of her, she was clutching onto the loose, long shirt he wore over breeches.

He'd not taken the time to dress in his usual daywear for he'd not wanted to wake her by searching through the chest for clean ones. Between his still-damp hair, unkempt and loose around his neck, the open shirt and casual breeches, he was not suitable for company. But as she grabbed hold of the shirt, he did not care. Iain eased down in front of her onto his knees, holding onto her hips as he did, and untied the short stays she preferred. The soft whoosh of the garments dropping to the floor filled the space around them.

Iain pulled her closer and took one breast in his mouth as she'd asked. This time, he met her gaze and she watched as he licked and suckled it, her eyes widening every time he drew it into his mouth and used his teeth on the tip. When he eased back, she slid her hands into his hair and held him there.

"More."

Her head fell back and she gasped as he gave her what she wanted. One and then the other until her knees buckled and she fell against him. He slid his arms around her to hold her steady and did not cease until she cried out, arching against his mouth and thrusting her hips against him until she collapsed.

Iain just remained in that position, holding her tightly until she came back to herself. Deciding to carry her to the bed, Iain was stopped by her hands on his shoulders. Clare reached past his shoulders and gathered the length of his shirt in her hands. Then she pulled on it. Iain raised his arms to allow her to remove it. His naked skin against her softness threatened his control.

He stood, sliding his skin over hers, relishing the feel of her breasts as he regained his feet. Then he lifted her out of the puddle of clothing at her feet and carried her to the bed. She settled with her head on a pillow as he reached for the laces holding the breeches up and him in. He thought she might be holding her breath and then realized she'd not seen him naked or even seen his cock before.

Iain made certain he was not in the shadows as he tugged the laces then eased the waistband down past his hips. At first the head of his erection held them in place, so he reached inside the breeches and freed himself. Her eyes grew wider and his randy laddie basked in appreciation. He grasped it in his hand, stroking once, twice and then thrice, encouraging him to his full length and girth. Stepping out of his breeches, he climbed onto the bed. Clare dropped her legs, all the while her hungry gaze remained on his flesh.

"Bed me." He could not help the smile when he realized she was giving him orders.

Easing her open wider, he knelt between her legs. Iain slid his hands beneath her and he tilted her hips to better accept him. Grasping himself in his fist, he rubbed the thick knob along her cleft, sliding along the wetness from her arousal and orgasm and positioned himself at her opening.

Her tight opening.

He leaned down on his elbows, placing his arms next to her on the bed. "Tell me," he whispered against her lips. "Say it as I would."

"I cannot." She blushed anew and a glance down showed it beginning in the mounds of her breasts, up her neck and into her cheeks.

"Say it." He laughed against her mouth. "Just to me."

From the pause, he thought she mightn't be able to bring herself to utter the foul word, but when she smiled and kissed him hard and quick, he thought she truly might.

"*Prende moi.*"

She'd fooled him, substituting French for gutter words. He laughed at how softly she spoke, as though there was anyone else nearby who could hear her. When he did not move at her command, she thrust her hips up, pushing him inside. *"Prende moi maintenant*, Iain," she demanded now. He did not need to speak the language to understand what she wanted.

"As you command, my lady."
And he did.

The night was all he could have wanted and more.

In between bouts of love play, he taught her more words that sailors used and she taught him more of the very naughtiest French words. They learned more than words through that night.

Sensitive places in curves and along muscles. In deeper places and with hands and mouths.

He pleasured her until she screamed, and she touched him until he begged. Over and over, in the dark and quiet of the night as the gentle movements of the ship soothed their restless bodies and souls.

He took her slowly once more that night before she ordered hard and fast. His hunger for her increased each time until he realized the very dangerous truth—he would want her for the rest of his life.

Her lightness for his dark.
Her smile to test his frown.
Her softness to cushion his hardness.

Now, lying next to her as the first rays of the sun broke the horizon, Iain knew he must bring the night, their shared and soul-shattering passion, and any possibility of it happening again, to a clear and definitive end.

He was losing the sharp edge of his strategy of getting

her lands and he needed it back. He needed that relentless pursuit that drove him and fulfilled his ambitions and plans.

They must go back to a business relationship or to just doing business if she would relent and sell him the lands. It was the only way forward.

"I can hear you thinking." Clare shifted at his side, rubbing her cheek against his chest. "Will you tell me?"

Would he tell her? Of his dilemma? Of the first time in his life that he would regret something? Nay.

"I was thinking of how very stupidly arrogant I was to believe I could climb the sails and not suffer for it," he said.

Sliding his arm out from under her, he dropped his legs off the bed and then stood. His shoulders were on fire, the burn moving through them with every movement. When he bent down to pick up his breeches, he groaned as more of his body protested his bravado yesterday. "I think I should have limited myself to a short time."

He noticed the silence and turned back to find her staring at his morning randy lad. Which was as it always was in the morning. Ready. Moreso with her in his bed.

"Some parts of you seem to be working without difficulty."

"Our conversations in the dark of night seemed to have emboldened you in the light of day, my lady." Iain cursed himself for engaging so with her. He must stop now. "But, I fear that the day is upon us and the crew will return, as we must, to Leith." He turned away for a moment and pulled his breeches on. When he looked at her over his shoulder.

The disappointment in her gaze intrigued him.

He could not let him stop him.

"I am afraid there is no maid to help you dress on the ship." He grabbed up his shirt and put that on over his head.

Clare sat up and the bedcovers slid down to her waist. They'd slept naked against each other for the last hours of the night. It had not been enough. However, it must be.

"Other than the laces on the back of the dress, I can do it myself."

They spent a short while in silence as hot water was delivered and they washed and dressed, Clare between the screen and he in the cabin. From the boisterous laughter and voices outside, Iain knew the crew was back and his time with Clare was growing short. A meal and Captain Ramsey arrived and though enjoyable, the mood was muted.

Ramsey went back to his duties and the ship set sail back to the harbor at Leith. The man had said he was pleased with the new crew members' performances and the new equipment so the ship would be put into the Buchanan fleet within weeks. And that pleased Iain, for as he acquired companies and accounts, he needed the ships to transport goods.

They'd grown since he'd managed to get the huge contract with the Government to transport food and supplies to the continent to support the efforts to defeat The Corsican. When his efforts helped, and the king awarded him his knighthood, his business soared. And so did his need and ambition for more.

"May I ask you a question?" Iain had been in his thoughts and he'd not realized it. Clare still sat across the table from him, sipping her tea.

"Certainly." He suddenly had the urge to get the whisky from the cabinet and drink a very large glass of it. Or to sew his lips shut so he could not utter words that threatened.

"What made you do it? Offer me this deal?" she asked. Her gaze took on that sharp and intelligent look and he knew that the shrewd Lady Clare faced him now. It was time to bring this to a close.

"Other than the obvious one?" She blushed. She *blushed* even after everything, every act, they'd done. "I did it so that you might look kindly on my offer when you sell."

"I am not selling those properties, Iain. I'm not certain why I must continue to insist on repeating this."

"You are deluding yourself, Clare." He stood and walked to the windows, staring out at the sea.

"I am?"

"Aye, sadly in this case, all your knowledge and business savvy and good practices will not help you resist the forces against you." He sat back down across from her.

"More than my father?" Concern lay across her lovely face now. Good.

"Your father is the most immediate. The most obvious. When you considered your reconnection to him, for whatever reasons you had, you did not see how it would enhance the larger ones." He'd seen it. Hell, he'd been part of it, he knew that.

She shook her head. Then she slid her hand slowly on the surface of the table. He'd gambled all his life and learned to read people and their *reveals*. She'd controlled it in previous encounters, or he'd been too busy thinking about what he wanted to do to her and with her that he'd not realized it. Now, after the overpowering lust had been somewhat satisfied, he could notice it.

She was worried.

Good.

"Between his pressure and now sponsorship of you in society once more, and that of your business partners and even your competitors, and your social world, you are fighting against mighty forces that set out, from the moment of your birth, to tie you to a husband in marriage and take away your control."

"And my properties." Clare paused and then began to say something and stopped herself. She was going through each argument in her thoughts and discarding them as she saw the futility of them. She truly was brilliant, but he'd learned early and often that the most intelligent person did not always win the battle.

Because Clare quite simply could neither conceive of the greedy, malicious underbelly of business nor understand how widespread it was, she could never fight it.

But you do. She would be the perfect—

He ruthlessly pushed that doubt aside. This needed to end.

"So, if I may give you a bit of advice?" He waited on her nod. "Sell everything. Set them up the way you wish them to be and sell them with stipulations in place."

"But the school and the orph—"

"You were a noble lady. You *are* one. Ladies contribute, they do not run orphanages." Her eyes flashed with fury, turning the green depths of them to the color of lightning in the summer sky. "I know you wish to argue that but consider your future. A wealthy noble husband does not begrudge his noble wife a large account for supporting such worthy causes. One stipulated in your marriage settlements." He leaned forward resting his elbows on the table. "Control what you can, Lady Clare. Sell while you can."

She pushed back from the table so quickly the chair wobbled on its back legs. He'd never seen her this angry.

"How convenient that you would suggest that!" She glared at him and all he could do was take in how magnificent she was even in her fury. "Why should my dreams and plans lose to your ambitions and schemes?"

There it was—the emotional part of this problem.

"Tell me, Clare," he said, lowering his own voice. "Why do you fight for these properties so hard? I know you have sold other parcels, other companies even. Why these?"

The look in her eyes at his question could only be described as bleak. For a moment, he hated that he'd asked her and what he was about to tell her.

Then do not tell her.

"These were the last plans I made with Jonathan and… they were important to him—a personal matter. I'd never seen him want, nay need, to carry out a project like this one." She'd stopped herself from adding something else just then. Now, she dashed a tear away and looked at him. Scorn filled her gaze. "You have only ambition and greed moving you through life. As far as I can tell, that is what you live for."

"If this was so important to him, Clare, then why did he agree to sell the property to me."

The sound of her indrawn breath filled the cabin. Her hands clenched into fists and she shook her head.

"He did not!" she whispered furiously. "This is low even for you, Iain."

"I have not lied to you. I would not."

"And you have proof of that?" She backed away from the table, putting distance between them, clasping her hand tightly.

"A gentleman's agreement," he said. "We had not formalized it yet when he—"

"Died." Empty. Her voice was empty. "Leaving it all to me."

"Aye."

"So all this time, you believed you had the right to it."

"I do."

Clare walked to the door and opened it. Staring back at him with those empty eyes. Something was wrong in this. She had not fought him in his assertion at all. Rather, it had rattled her at some deeper level, one that she did not even realize or mayhap what it was.

"I will be on deck."

"Clare—"

"I paid your price. You have had your once, your day and your night. So, it is over."

"Aye." He had done it. Impugn her late husband and she wanted nothing to do with him.

Then, she was gone. He wanted to call her back. To make sure she took her cloak and her gloves. To make her…

Stay.

Iain wanted to break something. To punch someone. To fight the growing rage within him.

But he was the one he wanted to punish the most.

And he could not do it here.

Iain gathered her belongings together with her cloak and gloves and gave them to one of the crew to take to her. And sent a request to Ramsey to see to her on the voyage to Leith.

Then he pulled out his leather satchel and went to work.

Hours later, he stood in the shadows and watched her leave his ship.

Leave his life. Without looking back.

For no matter what happened when she discovered he was right about her husband, about his plans to sell the property she now defended with all of her efforts, she would want nothing to do with him.

Can you blame her?

Seventeen

Life, her life, would go back to what it was before the storm that was Sir Iain Buchanan had entered and blown it all to bits. Clare repeated that to herself, over and over, day after day, for the next weeks, believing she could make it so by pure force of will.

Though she attended a dinner or two with her sister, she avoided her father and turned down his invitations. They still saw each other at her sister's and he tried to make introductions to those he thought she should marry, but he must have sensed a change in her, for he did not press too hard. Even if he did not understand it.

And she would not speak of it.

The nights were the worst for her.

For, damn the man, he had shown her what pleasures existed in the dark of the night. That beds or tables or the wall even could be places of passion and relief. That pleasure could be fast and hard, or slow and filled with begging. Even now, after he'd shown her that he was nothing more than a man pursuing his own ambitions at the cost of hers, she wanted him.

Worse than the physical need was the rest of it.

She liked him. He was quick-witted and intelligent and could converse on any number of topics. He'd traveled widely, read widely, and had had experiences she could only dream about.

He made her laugh. He made her sigh. He made her scream.

He made her want to love again.

Damn him. And damn her for falling for it.

Well, she would take control of her life and her wits and carry on as she'd planned.

"My lady?"

Clare blinked several times and noticed that David stood before her desk. How long he'd been standing there while she'd been going over the same arguments she'd contemplated yesterday and the day before. Her sense of usefulness and competence was destroyed. Her attentions flitted like a butterfly across spring flowers.

"My lady, Mr. Chalmers is here."

"What time is it, David?"

"Nearly eleven of the clock."

Clare turned around and stared at the clock, disbelieving what David had said and discovered she'd lost the entire morning since she'd sat down at her desk.

"Bring him in, please."

Chalmers walked in in his slow, deliberative pace and sat in the chair in front of her after his bow. Did anything ever rattle his reserve?

"I have discovered more about the reason the children are leaving, my lady."

Each day, more children had not attended. Their attendance was down to fewer than a dozen when they'd had as many as five dozen. The new school and residence planned was to expand to older children, those of almost working age, to teach them skills they could use to seek meaningful employment. But, from the numbers now…

"What is going on?"

"I traced the problem back to the area where they live, especially the few blocks nearest the north end of town."

"Problem?"

"The one I mentioned to you before, my lady. Dougal Dubh and his gang make sure no one comes."

"I do not understand? What business is it of theirs?" She understood that conditions could be dismal and dangerous in sections of town where the criminal element ruled.

"Someone made it their business, my lady. Someone was paying them to interfere with anyone who wanted their children to attend."

Something about the way he said it made her skin crawl and her stomach tighten. When she met Chalmers' gaze, she knew the worst of it.

Iain Buchanan was behind it.

"Why?" she whispered, even knowing the answer.

If no children came to the school, she had no reason to expand. No use for the properties. They would become expensive empty buildings, useless. She would have no choice but to sell them. Sell them… to him.

"Do you know it for certain, Mr. Chalmers."

"I have had men following various of them and their leader has reported to Sir Iain's offices several times over the last three weeks." That meant that even while he was *having* her, he was undermining her plans and her resolve. His words made more sense now, meant to encourage her doubts.

"You mentioned this man before?" He nodded. "A nasty fellow?" Another nod. "What do you suggest?"

"I need a bit more time, my lady. To finalize my investigation. Then I can make some recommendations to you about how you might handle this."

"Very well," she said as she stood. "And thank you."

A stabbing pain pierced her as the truth hit her—he was paying men to terrorize children and keep them from an education that could help them in life. She remained upright until Chalmers closed the door behind him. Then she collapsed back onto her chair, barely making it before the tears came.

Both Chalmers and Lamb and even Duncan had warned her of his ruthlessness and determination. That he did what he needed to do to ensure he got what he wanted. Behind the veneer of a gentleman and a man now entitled to move in the highest circles of society, he did so while plying his trade as he wished. Deceiving and forcing his will as needed.

As humiliating as this was for her, she would not allow him to harm or threaten these children who'd done nothing to him except gotten in his way. Because of her. If he was low enough for this, she doubted his claim of never having lied to her. About Jonathan's plans or anything else. Or in the way he did not have to lie unless she asked him a very specific question about a specific possibility.

Lies of omission were still lies.

Iain had promised to stop interfering with her project approvals but had not promised that he would not interfere in other ways. So, while she'd thought one thing, he'd done exactly what he'd wanted. And he'd distracted her in the basest way while doing it.

A memory of his eyes staring into hers as he used his tongue to make her scream entered her thoughts and her body arched immediately remembering those intimate attentions.

She jumped up from the chair and walked to the window that faced the street. Unlatching it, she pushed it open several inches and let the cool mist of the day in. It did help the heated flush, but nothing would stop those memories. Not so long as he was in her life. And probably even after he was gone from it.

Rubbing her temples against the ache that had sprung there, she considered the options available to her to make him stop. And there was only one. Closing the window, she summoned David and asked for the documents on the offers and discussions about the property.

The path was clear for, even if Jonathan had changed his mind and done the unthinkable and accepted his offer without telling her, there was no way that he would ever want children used as pawns in this nefarious game Iain Buchanan was playing. Though she could not bring herself to believe Jonathan would have done that—gone behind her back and against her wishes—it mattered not now.

If giving him what he wanted resolved the threats and danger and gave her students the chance to return without interference, then she would have time to sort through it all and decide what, where and how to accomplish Jonathan's last project.

For no matter the difficulties and recriminations between them at that time, she did not doubt his commitment.

Two days later, her carriage pulled up in front of his offices, and with only one wayward glance to see if the ship was still docked, she entered and politely requested to speak with Sir Iain on an urgent matter. From the flurry of voices and his employees hurrying about, she knew he was not on the premises. But she also understood that they knew she would not come here unless it was important.

"My lady," his secretary greeted her just minutes later. The same man who had escorted her…

"Good afternoon, Ned."

"Was there an appointment I did not ken about with Sir Iain?" He opened the notebook he held and ran his hand over the open page searching, she knew, for one that did not exist.

"Nay." She stood then and approached him. "I must speak with him immediately."

"I can have him at your office—" He stopped and glanced first at the book, then the clock on the wall, his pocket watch and finally at someone over her shoulder.

"I apologize, my lady," his man of business said. For a moment, she saw a strange expression in his eyes, but then it was gone. "Sir Iain is not here, and we do not ken when to expect his return."

"I will wait," she said, taking her seat once more. "A cup of tea would be nice while I do."

The confusion on their faces, unable to believe she would not acquiesce, was rewarding. They could shift and stammer and deceive and be part of his shameful plans all they wanted, but somehow, they folded in the face of politeness.

"My lady, I have no way of—"

"I will wait, Mr. Gilchrist." She reached down into the satchel she'd brought along to hold the papers and such and withdrew a small book. With a smile, she opened the book to the ribbon placeholder and began to read. He walked away muttering under his breath.

She had no idea how long it would take to retrieve him, but now that she was prepared and ready to face him, she had no intentions of leaving without doing so. A lad of eight had shown up today with bruises on his face and it sickened her to think she had the means to end it all. So, she sat and read.

His employees, to a one, were courteous and the requested tea, along with biscuits and even small cakes, arrived quickly. Ned offered her the use of a small office away from the main entrance, but she declined. The view of both the street, the docks and most of the employees who worked in the offices was better from right here. She would see anyone leaving or approaching the premises.

Though she expected him to arrive within an hour at the most, he did not. Ned's consternation grew each time he glanced at the clock. After sitting as long as she comfortably could, she stood and walked to the windows. The day had dawned bright and pleasant, dispelling the fog of the last two days and reminding her of the day they sailed down to…

"Ned, I am going to get some air." He stood immediately and rounded his desk to her side.

"Lady Clare, I can schedule a more convenient time—"

"I'll just be outside, Ned. I am not going away until I speak with him." She'd said it quietly but his eyes flared in alarm. She turned the knob and stepped outside before he could say anything else.

Crossing the street, she approached the entrance to the dock. The ship they'd been on was gone but the harbor was a busy place. Making her way along the wooden dock, she stepped off the main pathway and into one of the unused gangways, Iain had told her they were called, that now led to an empty berth.

It was fascinating to watch all the activity around

her—ships and boats of all sorts and sizes entering and departing, boxes and crates being loaded on and off by hardworking crews of men and more. In spite of using shipping companies, she'd never paid heed to how it all worked. Though she could not admit it, at least standing out here was more comfortable than sitting in that chair inside.

"My lady?" She did not recognize the voice but when she turned, she knew the speaker.

"Mr. Cairns."

"My lady, Sir Iain cannot meet you today," he said. His gaze did not flinch, he did not even blink as he spoke. And he reminded her of Chalmers in his manners. "It is simply not possible." He was not lying or dissembling or delaying. And she knew it.

"Why not?"

It was rude to ask, for the polite thing to do was not embarrass someone trying to beg off. Clare was not feeling polite in the moment. Cairns threw his gaze to the sea before speaking.

"Sir Iain is out there," he finally revealed. "Ned should have told you, but it is not the practice to give out his whereabouts when he is not available."

"At sea?"

"Aye, until the morning." He nodded behind him. "Your coach is waiting." Indeed, her coach, along with Chalmers, waited across the road. "Can I carry that for you?" He looked down at the satchel she'd placed next to her feet.

"No, but thank you," she said, retrieving it.

He stepped back and allowed her to lead. When they crossed the street, Chalmers waved off the footman and opened the door for her.

"I will see that Sir Iain kens you were here to see him, my lady."

"I have no doubt he'll hear all about it, Mr. Cairns." She climbed into the carriage.

"Should he expect you tomorrow or should he call on you, my lady?"

She glanced at Chalmers who'd scowled and growled with every word Mr. Cairns spoke. On a day when she had less to worry about, she would ask Chalmers for an explanation, but now, today, she wanted to be gone.

"Tomorrow noon, Mr. Cairns, if you'd be good enough to tell him to expect me."

"Of course, my lady." This time Chalmers snorted aloud. Leaning closer to the open window of the coach, he spoke. "Shall I tell him what matter you wish to see him about?" An epithet erupted from Chalmers that he did not even try to disguise then.

"None of your business to ask or to ken, Cairns. Now step away or be run the hell over where you stand."

Anyone else would have jumped back several feet at such an order, but Iain's solicitor simply glared at hers and slowly took a half-step away from where he stood. Her coachman would never run someone over, so she did not fear for his safety from that, but whether he was safe from Chalmers was a question she could not answer.

They rode in silence until they'd turned onto her street and approached the townhouse. She had gone alone because she did not wish to discuss this with anyone until after it was done.

"I did not realize how upset you were by my information, my lady. I have some recommendations ready for your review—"

"Thank you, Mr. Chalmers. I am fine."

"Cairns said you have been there for hours. I could have told you—"

"Are you still having him followed?"

"Aye, my lady." From his direct stare, she knew the rest of it without him stating it—he had her followed as well.

She gathered up her reticule and the satchel and waited for her doorman to open it.

"I will finish this myself, Mr. Chalmers."

And she left him without another word.

Wisely, he did not follow her into the house.

"Good afternoon, Clare. Are you in for dinner tonight or do you have plans?" Samantha stood inside the foyer as Clare entered. "I had thought to invite Peter, but if you'd prefer not, I will keep you company."

"I fear I will not be good company this night, Sam," she admitted. "But I am in for the night."

"Should I leave you then?"

"Nay," she said, taking Sam's hand. "Invite your scandalous young man for dinner with us."

In the end, it turned out to be a lovely, quiet dinner among friends and Clare was glad for that. It did seem that all the anxiety and worrying had dissipated once Clare made her decision and plan. Actually, handing over the deed to him would be the easy part now that she'd faced knowing she must.

And, it had been no point of contention for her since she knew that the safety of those she was trying most to help was at the heart of it.

As she lay in bed waiting to sleep, she repeatedly told herself all would be well. That she was better off this way—breaking off ties completely and walking away from this destructive force in her life.

So, if she was completely convinced of the rightness of her plan, why then did her heart plague her with thoughts about what could be between them? Why did images of them on his ship, watching as they sailed south, repeat over and over in her thoughts?

Why did his whispered words of praise and affection remain in her memories? The way he spoke to her as if she mattered? As if they were partners and not competitors and opponents?

As she finally, finally, drifted off to sleep, one thing became very clear to her—in spite of it all and if everything could be changed or fixed or proven untrue, he could be the perfect man for her. Between their companies and the breadth and width of their investments, from the way they enjoyed each other and challenged the other, it could be good between them.

The sad truth of the matter was that nothing could ever work between them and on the morrow it would end.

He would win and she would walk away, and stability would return to her life and safety to those she cared for.

Her life would go on, without him.

Eighteen

Three weeks of bloody hell.

Iain paced along the pavement in front of his office, but it did not give him the ease it usually did.

Clare had left that morning not to be heard from until yesterday's unexpected arrival here, while he was out there. Iain stared across at the harbor's opening to the firth and the sea. She'd left when Cairns explained his whereabouts, but his employees remained in an uproar for hours after his return near dawn this morning.

No one knew what had brought her there or why she would not consent to setting up an appointment. Everyone remarked on her pleasant manners and how she sat politely and waited. So few ladies of quality visited that she made quite the impression doing so on her own, without the contingent of men she'd brought along the first time she'd deigned to step through his door.

Cairns spoke of nothing different or new in his reports on her—she'd attended very few public events and had done most of her work from the office she maintained in her house. Though Mrs. Hunter visited the school and orphanage on an almost daily basis, it seemed Lady Clare avoided it.

At Iain's direction, no other offers had been made on

the embattled properties. He'd spoken the truth when he'd revealed that it had been her late husband's idea to sell them to him. Hell, Jonathan Logan had been the one to approach Iain about the possibility. It had been just after a council planning meeting about expansion coming to the harbor and town and Logan expressed the interest. Their men had made a few exploratory bids and such, for Iain very much wanted that land, and he had shaken hands with Logan just three weeks after he'd first expressed interest. And the man was dead before Iain could sign a contract for it.

Three weeks later.

Glancing up at the sound of the wheels of a coach rattling over the cobblestones, he saw it was not Clare's. Instead it was a large cart and not a coach at all. The driver tilted his head as he passed, for most knew him here on the docks. He was not like the posh owners who ruled from their luxurious country houses or estates—he lived up in Edinburgh and worked here every day when he was not traveling.

Three weeks.

Clare showing up, demanding to speak to him.

Three weeks.

Iain could not explain where the thought came from, but a wild possibility pushed into his mind.

Lady Clare… Clare… carrying his child.

He reeled back, only the wall of the building prevented him from falling to the ground. Running his hands through his hair, he wondered if it was possible. He'd withdrawn each time, but they'd fucked so many times that spilling inside of her was absolutely a possibility.

Then the image of a pregnant Clare filled his mind's

eye and he shuddered. Naked on his bed, fuller, larger breasts that overfilled his hand's grasp and a fully-rounded belly. Incredibly arousing. Incredibly beautiful. She glowed from the life within her. And she was h—

The carriage pulled up next to him and stopped before he was even aware of its approach. He dropped his hands and stepped a pace away from the door as her footman jumped down to open it. Clare did not look at him as she climbed out and refused to accept his hand when he offered it. She reached the sidewalk and told her coachman to wait for her.

"Lady Clare," he said, trying to get her to meet his gaze and to see if she gave away any hint of what he suspected. "I have a carriage at your disposal, my lady. No need for them to wait."

"Sir Iain," she nodded but did not look at him. "Wait for me," she said once more to the coachman.

"Would you like to go inside?"

He stepped back and waited for her to go as Ned opened the door to the offices.

"I would prefer not," she said, looking across the street at the docks.

"Damn it, Clare," he whispered harshly. "Look at me!" She almost did—her gaze lifted but stopped short of his eyes.

"Come, let us speak where we cannot be overheard."

Without waiting, she walked around the carriage and crossed the street, stopping near the seawall. He waved Ned off and followed. The agitation rolled off her in waves as he watched her choose her position and wait for him. From the clenched hands to the set of her chin, Iain could see how upset she was. He waited, not wanting to upset her more until he could wait no longer.

"Are you carrying my child, Clare?"

That drew her gaze and he saw a flood of emotions in her eyes—shock, fear, uncertainty, longing and finally resignation.

"I… ." She shook her head and stared away. "I cannot."

For a moment, devastating disappointment filled him. Unable and unwilling to dwell on that and all the ramifications, Iain let out the breath he was holding and shrugged.

"'Tis been three weeks and with the sudden demand to speak to me and with what all we did—" He stopped there, fighting the memories of every moment they'd shared from overcoming his control. He'd never wanted to think about having bairns or marrying, not until he had that momentary idea that she might be carrying his child. Then, he wanted it with every fiber of his being. But, all that was for naught. The pragmatism that had saved his life many times rose within him. "If that is not what brings you here—"

"It is not."

"Then what does?"

"I'd been warned of your ruthlessness and single-minded focus when you decided you wanted or needed something. Chalmers paid you no compliments when he told me of your past and the practices you use to impose your will on others."

Bloody Chalmers! How much did he actually know? How much had he told her?

"And?"

"Blackmail. Twisting arms. Threats. I thought I understood how low you would go when I discovered your interference with my approvals."

"I never said I would not use any means at hand, Clare. I am not above bare-knuckled fighting for what I want." His fists closed and opened as he wondered if she knew he used bare knuckles to do exactly that?

Her face went ashen at his words. She wobbled and had to grab hold of the chest-high wall next to her to steady herself. He reached out, but she shrank back so he could not touch her. Worse, her body shook and, for a moment, he thought her ready to retch.

"You must stop," she said in a pleading tone he had last heard in much more pleasurable circumstances. The sound of it now turned his own stomach.

"Do not beg, Clare."

"Do not beg?" she stabbed him with a sharp gaze. "Fine. I will do the only thing you seem to understand. I will make you an offer."

Iain felt like he was in a nightmare. Her anger, nay fury, bubbled within and poured out of her and he had no idea what he'd done. He'd not given up hope of getting the properties but had put a stop to making offers or discussing the matter at all. A cooling off period. In the meantime, he'd conducted his business as was his practice—studying investments, meeting with bankers and company heads, manufacturers and suppliers.

"You must stop hurting the innocent children caught in this fight between us, Iain." He stiffened at her words, shocked by them and without any clue why she would say it.

"Children? Hurting children?"

His world closed around him as his gaze narrowed to the long tunnel of light and his stomach roiled. Knowing, surviving the desolation and violence of the streets, Iain had sworn to never take part in it or allow it when he controlled an area or a building or business. His back stung from the lash, his jaws ached from the punches and his body burned with the indignity of what he'd suffered all those years ago. Memories he did not wish to surface.

But the thoughts and memories that now assailed him reminded him of the horrors for innocents on the streets. He forced out a denial.

"I do not hurt children." She paled at his voice.

"Paying someone to do it makes you no better than the one raising his fists."

The words came out as an angry curse—she was spitting mad. She crossed her arms across her chest and straightened before him. Iain rose up to his full height and stepped closer to her, leaning in close to make his point.

"I do not hurt children!" he barked at her.

She stumbled a step back and Iain heard the approach of someone behind him. Turning to face the threat, he saw Chalmers running towards them. Following on his heels was Cairns and both men wore the same expression; both broke into a run. Iain saw the fear, the fear of him, in her eyes and hated himself for it.

"Forgive me, Clare," he said, backing up and letting his hands fall to his side. "There is no cause for concern, gentlemen," he called out over his shoulder to the other two.

He watched as Clare nodded at her man. The two waved off others who gathered at the sound of their shouts. When they were alone once more, he let out a long breath.

"Explain your accusation."

She stared at him for several moments as though deciding if he was daft or not before speaking.

"Come now, I know that Cairns is very capable of reporting back to you the success of your efforts. Attendance is down at the school, children are leaving the orphanage and now I have discovered that they are being accosted by your man."

Cairns had told him about fewer children but had not assigned a reason for it. Oh, the community of Leith knew there was a battle in their midst, and some would seek to avoid being caught in the middle of such a thing. Safer not to be in the line of fire. But, he had not ordered such actions.

"I have nothing to do with this, Clare. I would not I—"

The icy glare froze the declaration on his tongue. She did not believe him.

"The ruffian behind it reports to your office, Iain. Some menace called Dougal Dubh. Come now, I may be a woman and too stupid or weak to stand against you, but I cannot bear the pain these children are suffering."

Neither could he.

"I was one of them, Clare. Bloody hell, I grew up on the streets. I fought my way out and would never use my strength against bairns." He was out of breath from the words and the pain of his past.

Only a brief flare of confusion in her green eyes gave him any hope she would hear him. At the same time he realized that he had exposed a deep secret of his past to her with his attempt to deny. No one knew that truth. From her expression and the anger in her body's stance, her belief that he was the cause of it had not changed and he suspected she'd not even truly heard his words.

He needed to speak to Cairns and find out what she was talking about. To get to the truth of the matter.

Without some sort of proof, she would never believe him. Proof which would not exist in a world where records and evidence of that kind landed a man in chains on a ship being transported or at the end of the executioner's rope.

"Fine, my lady. Since you will not believe my words, what is it you want?"

"Stop this and you can have what you've wanted."

It took a very long second for Iain to remember wanting anything but her. He did though and a short burst of euphoria at finally getting what he'd pursued flashed through him.

"You will sell the properties to me?"

"They are yours as soon as you handle this. Stop this man, stop his attacks."

His words would not do any good in the face of her ire, so he nodded to her and then waved Chalmers to them.

"See the lady home safely, Chalmers."

She did not fight or say another word. Chalmers held out his arm to her and she accepted it, which told Iain how upset she was. He held his place even when she tripped and Chalmers had to wrap his arm around her to keep her upright. He made his own way back to his office and by the time he'd climbed the stairs to it, her coach was gone.

Cairns followed him in and stood in silence at the door.

He'd not let on that he knew the man she'd named. Dougal Dubh was almost the king of criminals in Edinburgh. Almost. Known for his cruelty and his absolute adherence to being a paid man—a man willing to do nearly anything for the right price—Dougal Dubh was not a man to be challenged lightly.

Iain had not hired him. He was not even certain this involved him. But he needed to find out and put a stop to it.

Not because Clare demanded it. Not because she dangled the prize he needed before his eyes.

No, he needed to find out because this crossed one of the very few lines he'd drawn for himself in his life. And there was another reason as well. Iain knew he had not ordered or paid for such attacks. So, if he had not, who had?

Hours later, he'd found out little except that Cairns had seen Dougal Dubh near the offices and had reports of the man in the area over the last weeks. That in itself was not unusual since the man worked and made his living in Leith, the docks and anywhere in the city or stews where he could earn a shilling or two. His gang was loyal to him and those he terrorized were too frightened to do anything but follow his orders. A wave of nausea settled in his gut when he thought of those days in his early life.

Unable to find out more about the man's connection to Clare's problem, Iain issued an invitation to Dougal Dubh. And by the time he finished with the man Iain would know the truth.

Iain walked down the stairs, already in simple black breeches, boots, and a loose shirt. The pub and the fights had been closed to keep this a private challenge. Dougal had three of his men with him and Cairns waited in the shadows for the outcome. He must have encountered Dougal at some time. However, Iain could not remember.

What struck him was they were both called the same thing—dubh—for their coloring and if someone suggested that they were possibly brothers, after seeing Dougal, Iain would not have been able to argue.

Tall, muscular, with thick black hair, the man seemed to be about the same age Iain thought he was. Scarred from years on the street, Dougal's nose had been broken before, several times from the way it bent to one side then back to middle. If luck were with Iain, it would have another mark by the time he was finished.

"We have some business between us," Iain said, once they faced off across the open space of the room.

"This is how you welcome a guest, Buchanan?"

He moved and shifted, widening his stance and centering his balance and watching his opponent for signs of weaknesses or openings to attack. His plan was simple—to beat Dougal Dubh until he gave up the name of his contact or friend in Iain's operation. Simple really.

How hard could it be to do something he'd done dozens of times before?

He laughed later when he remembered the question he'd asked himself. Well, after spitting out mouthfuls of blood and wiping sweat and more blood from his eyes. The only thing that had turned the fight in his favor was that he was fighting against the exact same kind of man who had tried to kill him that night so long ago.

One he'd sworn would never prevail over him again.

With his question answered, Iain had Dougal seen to and removed along with his friends, and Iain could now…

His mind drifted for a moment and he blamed it on the several blows he'd taken to his head in the last hour.

First, he would tell Clare, so she would know he'd done as he said he would.

She still will not believe you.

Nay, and he was coming to believe it would be best if she did not. Clare was too smart not to remember what he'd said and to seek out the truth. Though most who knew were long gone, he did not want questions raised that could affect his investments and businesses. Knowing he owned this disreputable place could be looked on as folly or eccentricity, but if the rest about him were known, not even the knighthood could protect his interests.

Rubbing the back of his hand across his bloody face, he was ready to drop. In this weak condition, his conscience might even win a few battles. He nodded to King who bolstered him as they climbed the steps. The sheer exhaustion from returning from working on the ship to Clare's appearance to this was taking hold and he would never make it farther than up the stairs here. As he fell on the bed upstairs, Iain could not remember when he'd slept well.

She would hear you out if you do not take her offer.

He slammed back a mouthful of whisky before he got an answer he did not want. Another and another followed until he was certain there would be silence within him.

He had lived without her before, and he would again once everything was settled.

Keep it all business. All services paid for. Quid pro quo.

Another thought occurred to him but between the pain and the *uisge beatha*, he allowed the dizzying darkness to pull him down. He was comfortable there. Freddie Dubh was better lying in the darkness.

NINETEEN

Chalmers had seen much in his time as a solicitor and even more before that when he smuggled and then when he worked for some of the rougher gangs, smoothing out their legal situations. That part of his life was more like a bad dream that wakes a weeun from their sleep in the middle of the night. Since working his arse off to get educated and establishing himself here in Edinburgh, he'd not seen Cairns in two decades. And since they each resembled their father, no one ever considered they were related.

As he accepted the two envelopes from Lady Clare this morning, he was certain there had never been two more pigheaded while intelligent people than these two. And, somehow both he and his half-brother ended up working for them. They must have offended the fates to end up on opposite sides of this business.

He made his way to Leith, deciding to take the long walk downhill and try to clear his head from everything. It would take more than an hour, but it would settle his nerves before he saw his brother and turned over the deed in his bag to Cairns' employer.

Oh, the deed was bad enough—the spoils of war between the knight and the lady that Sir Iain did not deserve. But the sealed packet bothered him, and he did not know why. Other than his brother's writing on the outside, the lady's name written in Cairns' recognizable script, Chalmers had no idea what was inside. From the size of it, it was multiple pages, very like the reports he prepared for the lady and his other clients. The lady asked for it to be returned to Buchanan and so he took it along.

The sun hid for most of his walk down and Chalmers was glad he'd reached the pub before the rains began. Taking a seat in the shadowed corner, he sent a lad over to Buchanan's offices with word to Cairns. This place was far enough away from the polite world and the pubs they patronized that he used it as a meeting place on those occasions when he needed to meet with people with whom he did not wish to be associated. He'd just finished his first ale and pie when Cairns entered, his gaze immediately seeking out the darker places in the low-ceiled establishment. Cairns told the barmaid to send two more and sat down opposite him.

"This is a bloody mess," Cairns said, removing his hat and shaking off the rain from it. The floor would never mind the water.

"You have no idea," Chalmers said. "The kidney pie is good if you are hungry." The maid dipped low as she placed two mugs of ale between them on the table. Her own lovely wares jiggled and threatened to fall out as she bent over and shifted the mugs.

"A pie for my friend, lass," Chalmers said, tossing a couple of coins to her. "And bring another one and a pint for me."

Her hopeful expression soon gave way to the acceptance that they would be sampling the pub's wares and not hers and she walked off, hips swaying, to get the food. Once she left, Chalmers opened his satchel and took out the two packets. Sliding the deed across the table, he watched Cairns' face as his half-brother realized what it was.

"The lady is going through with it then?" he asked as he pulled the packet to him.

"She is a lady and honors her debts," Chalmers said with a bit of brass in his voice. "Worse, she's a good one and didn't deserve to be caught up in Buchanan's nets." Cairns' brows raised and he cleared his throat. "No offense meant, of course."

"None taken. He's worse than bees with a honeypot when he decides to pursue something. Once he sets his sights on it, it's better to take his money and walk away." Cairns lifted the mug and almost drained it, wiping his mouth with the back of his hand.

"Fair warning would have been nice. You were involved before I knew you were working for him."

Cairns tilted his head in acceptance. "True. But I expected it to be quick and over. For the lady to fold her hand when he made the offers. He didn't shortchange her on the amount he was willing to pay."

"Nay, most generous of many I've seen offered. But then it got personal," Chalmers said. His search of Iain Buchanan's background had uncovered a number of discoveries best left buried. "Tess cannot be happy."

Cairns had tipped the mug up to get the last of it and choked at his mention of the woman Buchanan kept at The Cock's Spur. Good. His brother needed to understand that Chalmers had discovered some of the lesser-known details of his employer's life. It took several hacking coughs before Cairns could breathe once more.

Taking advantage of his brother's surprise, Chalmers lifted the other packet and slid it across the table. The maid returned with the pies and mugs, and it took several minutes to get it all settled before them. He noticed that Cairns was staring at the new envelope with a puzzled glint in his eyes.

"So, what did you send the lady?" Chalmers asked before biting into the pie. He waited to learn if Cairns would ignore the question or lie in answering it.

"Reports Buchanan asked me to send her." Cairns let out a breath before continuing. "Men her father wants her to consider for marriage."

Now he understood why she'd not asked him for such reports—she'd gotten them from Buchanan… and Cairns.

"Anything of interest?" This time Cairns did the delaying tactic of biting into his pie and chewing it slowly.

Cairns shrugged. "Some better than others."

"Financial or otherwise?"

"Whatever I found that might be interesting."

Chalmers leaned over and flipped the packet, showing the still-intact seal on it. "When did you deliver it to her? I never saw it until this morn."

Cairns wiped his mouth, drank the last of his ale and stood. Without a word, he took the packet and nodded.

"My thanks for the meal. The pie was good."

He watched his brother walk out, but Chalmers remained at the table. He could have lifted the seal with no difficulty if she'd given him warning and time enough. That seal had given Cairns pause and Chalmers suspected the reason for it.

Lady Clare had never opened it.

Knowing Buchanan's ways, Chalmers understood that some deal was made. And, from the events of the last month or so, he suspected there had been more than this one. The lady's problem was that she thought that others conducted business as she did rather than as Buchanan did. In the five years he'd been employed by her, more so in the last two years since Jonathan Logan's death, he tried to give her balance. To watch out for the seedier elements and guide her decisions since she was a woman, a lady, in a world that did not believe women should be involved in business and in one where others thought it their due to take advantage of her.

But Buchanan had slipped under his guard while Chalmers thought he was watching. The rogue appealed to the lady and that was a strange development in her life of correct behavior and society upbringing. Neither Logan nor his wife had ever strayed as far as Chalmers could find and the lady had ignored every effort to gain her attention and favor since her husband's death. They were having a rough patch when the man died, he knew that much, but what marriage did not go through one here and there?

Even after the lady's reconciliation with her father, which he'd counseled against, she continued to show no interest in remarrying. Considering what it would mean to her control over her fortune, Chalmers understood her reluctance. She put off every man who approached with relentless kindness and grace but reject them she had.

Then she disappeared with Buchanan overnight on that ship. Oh, he'd known about it and had even followed her that morning. 'Twas not his place to interfere.

Now, it was a mess for even a fool could see that it was personal between them and not business.

Worse, he thought they would be a perfect pair together. For the lady though, he could not see her with him. Oh, she'd married herself a commoner and this one was a knight, a bit of a step up. It was the rest of what Chalmers knew of the man's past that he understood would keep them apart.

He tossed another coin to the buxom maid on his way out.

It would be interesting to see what Buchanan did now that he would get what he wanted.

Or had the man gotten what he thought he wanted only to lose what was the most important thing in his life?

Iain stared at the two packets of documents on his desk—one expected, the other one a shock. She'd promised him the deed if he handled the mess and here it was.

"I can see that is filed," Cairns offered with a nod to the deed.

"Nay." Iain covered the large envelope with his hand. "First make certain Ben is gone and without other problems. Between you and Mr. Brown, I'd like all of the business he handled reviewed before we move ahead."

Once Iain had gained the identity of the person ordering Dougal Dubh's attacks, he'd fired Ben, giving him a generous amount of money to keep him happy for a long time. Bertie had not even looked surprised by Iain's discovery, almost as though he was waiting for it to happen after their blow up. It would take some time to be certain that he had no other personal endeavors going on alongside his actual assignments, but it was a necessity. Iain would not file any deeds or contracts until they had all been looked over.

Once more he would move forward, trying to ignore the stabbing pain in his gut from the one man he'd considered a friend. A man who understood Iain's drive and his hunger because it was like his own. A man who thought Iain's desire for the widow threatened all they'd planned and had lost faith in their plan. A deep sense of sadness filled Iain, one that his pragmatism usually beat out of him, at the loss of one who'd stood so closely by him.

"And the other one?" Cairns asked. The man knew what was in it, for he'd prepared it himself.

"Unopened?"

"Given to me as it is, sir."

"She never opened it." Iain leaned back in his chair.

She'd never opened it, the reports he'd promised in exchange for her, her favors, her time… her body. Yet, she had followed his instructions, even his sensual orders, first at the hotel and then on his ship and denied him nothing.

Gave him everything he'd dreamt of and wanted, now thinking back to those hours in her company. She did not parse out bits. She threw herself into their time together fully, with curiosity and enthusiasm. No reservation or regret.

He accepted what she gave because it was their deal. Until that last morning when he had some niggling concern about keeping it as just business, so he could walk away unencumbered by regret or want for more. And Clare had agreed when he reminded her of the arrangement.

Had she already decided that she would not use what

he'd sent her? Had she other reasons for their liaison, ones she did not tell him?

Why would someone like her allow someone like him to have her without some guarantee of protection or… more than that? If anyone saw them or discovered their trysts, she would face the humiliation of it, not him. If she became—

I cannot.

Two words filled with absolute yearning and cold desolation as a response to his question. Had she truly come to his bed for the pleasure he offered in exchange for nothing more than his help in avoiding suitors? And then left it just as easily?

"Anything else, sir?" Cairns asked.

"Nay. Just see to Ben's files." Cairns had reached the door when Iain spoke. "Cairns, put this in your files." He handed the reports back to the man who'd created them. "We might have use for them."

Cairns took them and left with a nod. Leaving Iain with the deed he'd been after for… years.

With the war over and the seas open once more, ships would once more rule the waters. Though he'd been lucky not to lose any vessels to Napoleon's naval forces, he'd been biding his time and waiting for the time to expand his fleet and take on more business. The new offices would be a centralized location for representatives of all his companies in one place—increasing productivity and improving planning. Iain had begun in advance trying to acquire the site but now with the war finishing, now with the property in hand, he could make his move.

So why did just looking at an envelope holding a piece of paper make his stomach sour and the need to retch even stronger? And why did his head fill with a piercing pain? Why did this victory not feel like a victory?

Iain knew the answer. If she had actually asked him for the truth instead of making a devil's bargain for the outcome she needed, he could have told her the truth and together they could have done something about it. If she had only not behaved as he did in making black and white decisions, he could have… they could have…

Clare had treated him as he treated her—a business arrangement. She had not crossed the line he'd drawn in the dirt—he had. He had wanted more than business. He'd wanted her to be there with him for himself and it looked like he had gotten what he wanted and walked away. The deed in his hand was another proof of his failure with her.

With the one woman who had made him fall in love.

And bloody hell, but he did not like it!

TWENTY

Clare smiled at Caro's attempts to be gentle but firm with her. Her sister's true gift was giving orders and expecting any and everyone in the vicinity to jump to fulfill them. This change in Caro's strategy, for that's what it was, was soothing and frightening all at once.

"I am glad you decided to join us," Caro said. "I have missed having your company at these dreadfully boring dinners."

"If you took a small interest in Nairn's—"

"I am interested in Nairn, Clare. At least the interesting bits of Nairn," Caro said, lowering her voice. "I have been wanting to see this house since it was finished last year," she confided.

Clare could not help but laugh aloud. Her sister had been at her side these last weeks, silently supporting her. At times, Clare would swear she could hear Caro's teeth grinding in frustration as she held herself back from asking all manner of questions.

She had given a broad sketch of what had happened between her and Iain—there had been an attraction, a moment or two of infatuation, a business deal and now they were done. Caro knew it involved her now-cancelled plans to open a large location for her school and so she designed her explanation to elicit this change and clearly it had worked. Oh, Caro was biding her time and would pounce when she thought the time was right.

Nairn's large carriage came to a stop before a huge townhouse on the very fashionable, in-demand St. Andrew's Square. Twice as wide as any of the others that ringed the perimeter of the square, it was built from the same butter-colored sandstone used in most of the other townhouses but, being newer, the color had not yet descended into what residents called 'the symphony of greys' from the soot and ash of the city.

This one had six windows across, with a large entrance in the middle of the first floor. Light poured from the windows, illuminating the entire area and making the outside lanterns unnecessary. Footmen and attendants swarmed, opening doors, helping them down, escorting up the double staircase and into a foyer that Clare could not help but stare at in awe.

The height of understated luxury, the décor was in muted tones rather than the garish golds she would have expected from the owner of such a magnificent home. She'd known that some large townhouses here in New Town were large enough to have ballrooms that could hold one hundred people and now staring up at the staircase leading up to a second and grander floor, Clare knew this was one of them.

"Who owns this house?" she asked Caro in a whisper. "I thought it was one of his partners in that investment scheme in the west?"

"Nairn said the owner has just been raised to the peerage. A hereditary title of earl from the king for his substantial investments in both canals and industry in the west." There was a faint echo of displeasure in her sister's tone, but then Caro had never fallen from the elite ranks that held that bloodlines—the longer the better—as Clare had.

The Caledonia Canal had been under development for years now, perpetually underfunded, undermanned, undersupplied and just behind schedule. Nairn, along with several others, had been organizing funding for the huge project meant to help unemployment in those living in the Highlands after the last Jacobite Rising. In the last years of the war against Napoleon, ships and supplies were always in danger and the reliance on canals had grown.

Nairn and even her father had been original subscribers on the Forth and Clyde Canal, the other western canal system, and Jonathan had invested as well. Passenger and transport of goods during the war had earned a good return for investors. Clearly the king and government wanted to reward someone who'd been a steadfast supporter of the projects. A strange thought teased at her as she realized that—

"My lord, the Earl of Ardgour," the butler droned out from the doorway that led to a large drawing room behind him.

Clare noticed the expression on Caro's and Nairn's faces just before their host entered. She did not need to turn around to know who the new Earl of Ardgour was. Caro watched her closely now and Clare could see her concern. Even Nairn who was familiar with showing his emotions to his wife, only stared as Iain joined them in the foyer.

"Welcome, Nairn, my lady," he said to the others first. When he turned his attention to her, Clare was torn apart. Her body reacted, even weeks and weeks after they'd had any contact at all. It had taken all of a few encounters and one night to train her to want his touch. Worse, she could not look away.

He wore formal apparel for dining in society and she could not help but stare at him. He still favored black, but now his waistcoat was an exquisite pale blue, embroidered with gold and white and deep blue thread in patterns of… She stopped herself as she took the first step to get closer to see what was decorating his waistcoat. No matter what they were, they matched the shades in his eyes.

"Lady Clare, welcome to Ardgour House."

"Thank you, my lord," she said as she curtsied to him. If he was now a peer, he was due the courtesy. "This is new?"

"The house? Nay, just the name of it. The title, aye." He shrugged. "I received notice from the Prince Regent of my elevation, but luckily my title will not include that troublesome summons to Parliament. So, as I understand it, I am not to be too *gauche* and inform everyone of my new title yet. I am keeping it among… friends for now."

She could not help it—his attempt at a French pronunciation made her laugh. The memory of him trying to twist his tongue to repeat the naughty French words flitted in her thoughts.

Clare glanced around him and found her sister and brother-by-marriage staring at them, and so concerned that Caro did not bother to put on her polite face. The expression she wore now was the one Clare had seen on her sister's face when she'd fallen off her horse and lay senseless on the ground at age nine.

"Forgive them," he said. "I asked them to bring you to dinner."

"Because you knew I would refuse an invitation from you?"

His self-deprecating smile surprised her—it was a far cry from the usual supremely confident one he wore. "I suspected you would."

"You have lived here all this time?" Clare's legs were shaking so much she needed to sit. At her first step towards the chair nearest her in the drawing room, he nodded to the nearest footman.

"I have. There was just no opportunity to invite you here."

The footman returned and offered her a glass on his tray. "For you, my lady," he said, waiting for her to take it.

A glance at Iain told her he'd arranged for it. Taking the glass, she looked at the deep amber color before sipping it. The brandy from their dinner at the hotel. It matched the color scheme in the furnishings and decorations around them. If it seemed obvious that he knew what she liked to drink, he covered it well by sending the footman over with glasses for Nairn and Caro.

"A brandy I found if you do not mind having it before our meal," he explained. "Nairn has tried it." They walked over towards Clare and joined them in the seating area that broke the huge area into manageable smaller arrangements.

Clare took another sip of the excellent brandy and wondered what was happening here. She should be angry to have been duped into coming here. She should be furious to see him at all, let alone now that he had been honored, again, by the king. And yet, the break between them had been a clean one, made gentler when the huge payment was deposited in her bank for his purchase of the properties. Rather than paying her the amount first offered, as she expected, he'd paid her the last one—the one that was most advantageous to her. When he'd done that rather than refuse the deed, at first Clare railed at his probable involvement after all. He'd warned her time and time again he would do what was necessary to get what he wanted.

Tempted at one moment of weakness or another in the last weeks to return it, she instead began plans for building a new location. Inconvenient? Aye, but the additional monies he'd paid would fund the difference in costs.

She wanted to believe it was to soothe his conscience, but when it came to business, she did not think he had one. It was her conscience that was the problem here— for she'd known since the day after she'd sent the deed to him that a gentleman's agreement between him and Jonathan had existed after all.

The slip of paper on which a few scribbled lines confirmed his claim had fallen out of a larger portfolio. She'd been examining a collection of notes and documents from the time his first offer arrived through the latest one and the paper was easier to lose than to find. Written in Jonathan's hand, it outlined the basic agreement between the two of them. The date was from before his death, during the time of dissention in their marriage when she'd faced doubts and regrets about her choice to turn away from her family and marry him. She knew he'd been excluding her from many discussions and had truly never realized this was exactly as Iain had insisted—a gentleman's agreement and more.

Duncan offered his resignation when she showed it to

him. He had filed the paper away when Jonathan had died, remembering now the initial discussions of it with Jonathan. In the face of ensuing events, and in the face of her absolute refusal to consider selling to Iain, he had put it in the files and never mentioned it to her.

That little piece of paper forced her to accept that the perfect marriage in her memories, even the relationship she had with Jonathan about business matters, was not the one they had in truth. Knowing that truth had not been an easy matter to deal with. But it had freed her from some of the regrets and doubts of the past.

It had not, however, helped her sort out the complicated mess of feelings involving the man seated next to her. Iain had shown her such joys and adventures and teased her with possibilities and then schemed to get what he wanted. Endangered children for it.

I was one of them, Clare. Bloody hell, I grew up on the streets. I fought my way out and would never use my strength against bairns.

She could see him as he'd spoken those words to her—not the relaxed, recently-ennobled man but the one whose gaze flashed as he denied his involvement. She'd been so intent on stopping his plan that she had not even realized he'd said this.

Desperate. Disgusted by her accusation. Giving up trying to explain when she'd insisted. She'd not wanted to believe that the man who had introduced her to pleasure and had shown a lighter, gentler part of himself could be the villain she thought him to be. However, the message he'd sent through his man Cairns and the gradual return of her students to her school and even more attending did not lie—he'd fixed it once she'd made her offer.

I grew up on the streets. I fought my way out and would never use my strength against bairns.

"Lady Clare?"

Her name drew her thoughts back from their flight of memories and she realized, from the silence in the chamber, he must have said it more than once. Caro's mouth tightened as she tried to give Clare some message, but Clare had been too deep in thought to know what it was. She lifted the forgotten glass to her mouth and sipped it.

"Is it not a very good brandy, Caro?"

"Mmmmmm," was her sister's only response.

"I imagine Lady Clare is still recovering from the shock at being lured here without knowing it is my house."

"I am more surprised by the title, Buchan—" Nairn stopped and nodded. "Ardgour." He lifted the brandy in salute. "Congratulations on the title." After they'd all raised their glasses, he asked his true question. "So, tell us how this happened. I know it's unseemly to ask, but I fear I am curious."

"A real dilemma for you, eh?" Iain laughed. "Considering the extent of our involvement in recent months, I do not mind overmuch. But," he said, then paused.

"My lord, dinner is served."

"Thank you, Puggles."

Clare looked at the butler to see if Iain was teasing him in some way, but the man's blank face suggested otherwise. He turned in the doorway and waited for them to proceed. When Iain stood, she expected he would offer his arm to Caro's as the ranking woman. Instead he leaned forward and offered it to her.

"I am taking a page from Nairn's book and setting my own rules in my own house."

She could not refuse him, no matter the questions that bubbled up from within about what had happened. It was an intimate dinner, clearly meant as a first approach, for his own reasons, and the only one who would be embarrassed would be her.

"Puggles is the happiest one in the household over the new title. His pompous behavior will not be reined in now," he whispered once they'd passed by him on their way into the dining room.

She laughed at it and yet she knew that servants could be more concerned with the prestige and standing of their household than the lord or lady who held the title. And though butlers could be pretentious, she knew that Archer—and any self-respecting lady's maid—would be far worse.

True to his word, Clare was seated at his side which worried her a bit. She was still not sure of his aim, other than to impress her. Or impress Nairn, who continued his easy manner with Iain. Now, she supposed, he was an equal of a sort. Equal in status with her father. That made her want to laugh. Certainly more than a tolerable knight, he was a peer and a sinfully wealthy one at that. How others in the peerage would take to an earl who was unashamed of his wealth and his relentless pursuit of it and deeply and personally involved in trade, she could not predict.

"I did not see your man at the planning council meeting in Leith, Lady Clare." He waited as the footman ladled some of the soup into his bowl.

"You were at the meeting?" she asked.

The footman served her next and before he could

answer, Puggles announced the course… in English! After he'd moved back to the edge of the room, Iain nodded at her.

"Your house your rules, my lord?" He nodded as she noticed Nairn's and Caro's inquisitive glances. "How long do you think it will be tolerated?"

"Well, at least until I learn some French," he said. He took a mouthful of the red wine before he asked again. "So you did not send someone to take part in the discussions?"

The silence was noticeable as Nairn and Caro looked around at everything in the room except her. They knew it was not a topic she wished to discuss.

"I did not."

"They are talking about developing trade schools to train young men and women in employable skills."

Her throat tightened and tears threatened as she heard her dream being spoken of yet without her being involved. She refused to fall apart now. Refused to be baited when he had much to answer for yet.

"My lord, may we speak of other topics? I fear Lady Nairn will fall asleep by the second course if we indulge in such matters as business and education." There. All her years of training in manners and polite behavior did come back to her when needed.

"I do not mind—" Caro began to speak, and Clare shook her head.

"Does this house have a garden, my lord?" she asked, diverting the conversation. And she just stared at him until she saw the moment he capitulated.

"It does, Lady Clare." Placing his spoon in the empty bowl, he waited for the footman to remove it. "Perhaps I can entice you to return in the daytime to see it. Puggles has employed three gardeners and promises it will be the jewel of Edinburgh for the spring blooms."

He was humoring her, at least she thought so until he declared war with his next bit of conversation.

"Have you heard, Lady Nairn, of the new style of service that is sweeping France and is gaining ground even in the great houses of London?"

Caro looked as though she been caught between two hunters, each aiming their bows at the other. Her gaze shifted from Clare to Iain and back, unable to decide if she should jump in or take cover. "I have heard of it, my lord, but am not familiar enough to comment on it."

A smile teased the edges of his mouth. A mouth and lips she knew well, and she had to shake herself free of the bewitchment that threatened if she continued to stare at him.

"Lady Nairn, it is called dining *a la Russe* and it is said that it will replace *service à la française* society dinners forever."

All Clare could do was laugh at his antics, for they were directed at her and planned as thoroughly as Wellington's campaigns.

"Peace, my lord." She held her hand up between them. "Peace." Caro and Nairn gaped in open curiosity at the exchange between Clare and Iain. She had so much to explain to them and she wanted the truth from him. What had his words meant when he claimed his innocence? "All is well, Caro."

"Will you receive me on the morrow and allow me to explain?" he asked her, a seriousness shone from his blue eyes she'd not seen before.

"I think you should, Clare," Nairn said softly. Caro reached over and covered her husband's hand. "I suspect there is more to this than you might be aware." Iain looked surprised by both Nairn's speaking up and by whatever it seemed that Nairn was aware of.

"I could—" Caro started.

"Nay. Thank you, but nay," Clare replied. "Fine, Lord Ardgour, you may call on me."

The rest of the meal concluded with no further French pronunciations and a semblance of polite conversation with Nairn playing the moderator to keep things going. And her brother-by-marriage somehow managed to keep her sister from asking all manner of questions on the ride home after dinner.

In the morning, she had David empty her day of any appointments, though lately she had had very few, and she waited for his arrival at noon as he'd said.

After telling Samantha about the visitor who would arrive in a few hours, she'd left almost immediately afterwards, claiming errands that needed to be run. The wink she'd given Clare as she departed the house reassured her of Samantha's ongoing support. She'd been a huge help with the school over the last several months and even though Clare understood there was an additional reason for her increasing presence there, she appreciated her friend's efforts. Clare had begun considering asking Samantha to take over the school as a full-time commitment from her.

Then, just a few minutes prior to noon, there was a knock at the door and she heard him enter at Poogan's invitation. Standing as the door to her office opened, she took in a slow breath, trying to calm her heart that always raced whenever he was near.

TWENTY-ONE

In all of his life, Iain had never been nervous when walking into a meeting or gathering of any kind. Not facing kings—of England or of the criminal element, and not facing friend or foe. But walking into Clare's office, understanding the importance of every word he would say, made his insides threaten to rebel.

His mouth went dry, his hands began to sweat inside the fine leather gloves he wore, and his clothes felt too tight and too hot with each step he took. Iain always prepared for a meeting or when they were acquiring businesses or properties by reading everything, every report, every paper, every bit of gossip collected until he could repeat it from memory.

He'd done that for the meeting where he'd laid out Buchanan & Son's offer. Meticulous preparation always helped. Always swayed the disputes in his favor. Always.

Until he'd forced his way into her life and met someone who would not be moved by the strength of his arguments or offer. Someone who stood firm for her dreams in the face of his greed and ambition.

So, what could he say?

He'd spent the whole of the night walking the docks,

pacing, and searching for the words, the reasons, to convince her of his absolutely mad idea. But there were no reports for him, no sheets of paper with carefully prepared information that would make her believe him.

And all that he could think about, all he could rely on were the memories they had made. As her butler opened the door to allow him entrance, he only hoped it would be enough.

"My lord, come in please," she said, greeting him in the same voice filled with grace and calm she used to greet any visitor. Only when she held out her hand to him and he felt the slight tremble when he took hold of it did he have any hope. In spite of the need in him to touch her, he bowed over her hand as he'd seen others do and stepped back.

"My lady, thank you for seeing me." She nodded over his shoulder, and he heard the door close.

"Would you prefer to sit here or in the more comfortable chairs there?"

They could go on like this for hours and it would get him nowhere. So, he did something he'd sworn never to do.

"Bloody hell, Clare, I cannot keep this up." She startled at his words and possibly at the way he yelled them. "I have never done this before—I swore I would not."

"Do what?" she asked. She did sit down then, at her desk, and he gained some comfort when her fingers slid along the edge of the wooden surface. She was nervous, too.

"Explain myself." He let out a breath, needing to look away from her and yet unable to. "Until I met you, I never even considered it."

Clare looked at him and nodded.

"I spent the first fifteen or sixteen years of my life in the stews of Glasgow," he began. "I have no idea of when I was born or who my parents were. By the time I was aware of myself, I worked for the worst of the worst, but he kept me fed mostly and out of the rain." He gazed off, staring out the window as memories he'd held back flowed freely. "I did what he told me to do, when he told me to. You didn't refuse Albert Sanders' orders and live to tell."

"Why do I think you did refuse?" she asked quietly.

He smiled and met her eyes. "Because that part of me hasn't changed at all." He nodded. "Aye, when I was about fifteen or so, he drew a line in the muck and I would not cross it."

"A child?" So she had heard his words.

"Aye. A man had crossed Sanders and the only thing he had left in the world was a wee lass. He told me to—" Her indrawn breath stopped him. Pain filled her lovely green eyes. "I… avoided carrying out his orders the first time and there was hell to pay." The beating rendered him useless for more than a week. Once he'd recovered *enough* to do the deed, Sanders returned. "He gave me a second chance to make it right." The soft hitching breaths told him without looking that she was crying. "When I did not, he had his strongman finish me."

"Oh dear God!" She wiped the tears away with the back of her hand.

"Dinna greet, Clare. Dinna greet for me," he whispered, hearing the accent of his youth sneak into his words. That second beating was the worst of it, for he'd taken control of his life and his fate that day.

"I had a friend or two tucked here and there who

helped me, saved my life, after Sanders left me bleeding in the gutter."

"And you survived."

He held out his hands and shrugged. "Better than ever."

"How?" At least she'd stopped crying. He could deal with her anger but not those tears.

"Doing whatever I needed to do, Clare. Do not make a hero of me, for these hands are marked with the blood of those who stood against me." He knew that would destroy any chance of him in her eyes, so he walked to the window and tugged the drapery aside.

"Is that when you learned to sail?"

"Sail? Aye. And I was sent to the western islands and worked in a kelp factory processing seaweed when the wars stopped its production on the continent. Worked my way up in old Buchanan's business until I took it over, making my first fortune on that."

"First fortune?"

"Kelp processing led to a bigger fleet. A shipyard to build our own then we began in the shipping business. From there, canals and factories. More ships. Using my ships and companies to supply the war efforts for the king." It felt strange and exhilarating to explain half of his life in such a concise way to someone. He'd never laid out the connections before and he could sense her curiosity and almost hear the questions stacking themselves in a pile in her thoughts.

"The canals that won you your title?" she asked.

"Well, the king offered me an earldom first but I did not want the burden of that title. I only wanted what would open doors into the places where wealth and power lived and a knighthood *for services rendered on behalf of the kingdom* did just fine."

She laughed then and shook her head at him. "You turned down an earldom. Only you would do something so—"

"Stupid?" Her laughter rushed over him, soothing his shattered nerves. "Nay, once money was made, the title—even just a knighthood—became irrelevant, really. All those bluebloods, too good to lower themselves to trade, all the while they cannot resist a profit for their coffers."

"Now your blood is blue."

"I doubt that a sword tapped on my shoulders and a piece of parchment from the king will do that."

He walked back and went to the mahogany cabinet in the corner near her desk. The extremely well-stocked cabinet. He chose a whisky and poured them both a large portion in the crystal glasses on the shelf. Handing her one, he nodded and drank deeply from it. Sitting before her, he leaned against the back of the chair. He waited because he knew she would ask—

"What was your name?"

"I was called Freddie. Freddie Dubh," he said.

"Dubh? Like that man Dougal?" She drank now, at the reminder of the terrorized children.

"For our coloring. Black hair both of us." He slid forward, resting his elbows on the desk and running his hands through his hair. "Clare, I had nothing to do with him."

"Chalmers found—"

"Chalmers was right. He was coming to my office. But I had nothing to do with it. My solicitor thought he could help my goals by scaring you off. If no children came to the school, you would have no reason to remain and to enlarge your facilities or expand into the ones I wanted."

"Mr. Gilchrist?"

"We go back to very early days in Iain Buchanan's empire as you called it. Being a solicitor is not his first career." And it would not be the one Bertie would return to now that they had parted ways. "Once Dougal and I understood one another and he told me who was paying him, I put an end to it all."

"I... ." She started and stopped a few times before putting the words together. "I did not believe you."

"When I thought on it, why would you?" She shook her head. "Nay, I had deceived you, I had interfered, and I had lied to you in a number of ways in spite of swearing I had not. I let you believe you meant nothing to me other than an offer made and terms accepted."

He walked around to her and tugged her to her feet. When she did not resist, he thought there might be the smallest chance for them. If she was not frightened off by the past he'd shared with her, there may just be a chance.

"Each time I told myself I did not want more than your body, it was your kindness, your intelligence, and your frank curiosity that intrigued me and called to me. Every time I pursued what I wanted, you were in my way. You were my obstacle—teasing me with all that you are, Clare. Taunting me with everything I had never had. With all that is too good for the likes of me."

"Is that why you accepted the title?" He could see her turning what she'd heard over in her mind.

"Aye, I thought the title would make things easier for you if you did accept me. I know how you struggled during your marriage, living outside the world you'd been raised in and away from most of your family and friends. And I know you loved Logan without a title. I know I can never compete with the love you had for him. I can never be your first, but I want to be your last, Clare."

Iain leaned down and kissed her. Not the possessive kind, but just a kiss to reacquaint them. Her stricken expression, her usually lively green eyes fading to an empty stare, made him lean back. Then, she burst into tears and pushed out of his embrace. Though he enjoyed the way she could still surprise him, this was startling.

When she rushed out of her office leaving him standing there gaping like a fool, it took him several moments to gather his wits and go after her. By the time he followed, she'd left a trail of servants looking much as he did—dazed and confused. He reached the street and stood on the landing of the steps for a better view of the square, the streets leading into it and the houses all around. She was gone.

Do not make a hero of me.

He'd confessed his past to her, even about the violence of his life and worse. A hero? Nay. A man who'd survived the most hellacious of lives to rise from it, using his own ambition as the force to do so. He'd outlived and outmaneuvered stronger, richer, more dangerous men than himself and he still walked the earth alive.

When most men she knew faced decisions about the cut of their clothing or their choice of beef or lamb at dinner, Iain, Freddie, had grown up making decisions that could prove fatal every day of his young life. She thought of every lad in the school and understood some of what they faced, and what threatened them in the worst areas of the cities and towns. But how many of them had the drive of young Freddie Dubh and would survive to reach adulthood?

Hero? Nay, he was not. But now that he had revealed his past to her, Clare knew that he was brave and resourceful and accomplished and though his morals were somewhat questionable, he had them and lived by them. She could not condone the crimes he'd committed along the way, but she would not damn him either. For he had more courage and integrity than she ever would.

He lived by his convictions, his beliefs, while she masqueraded as the virtuous widow who yet mourned her beloved husband. A woman who stood up to the powerful men in her life and made her own way. A woman who chose love over class and position. A woman so frightened to live her life that she hid behind deals and contracts instead of claiming what she wanted.

Clare knew Iain thought he'd lose her when he revealed the sordid details of his past. Well, Clare would lose him when he learned her truth.

A man like Iain Buchanan needed a strong woman at his side who was as bold as he was. As brave as he was— walking in a world not his and flourishing in spite of it.

But Lady Clare Napier Logan was not that woman.

She returned a while later and got her cloak and reticule and had Poogan call for a hack. Over his objections to traveling about the city in such a vehicle when her perfectly fine carriage could be readied quickly, Clare climbed into the nondescript coach and went to the one place she needed to see to break from her past.

TWENTY-TWO

The key was always with her. Whether at the school or at home or even when she was out, it was a reminder to her of promises made and promises broken. Now though, she understood it was the obstacle to the rest of her life. The hack dropped her in the alley between the two large warehouses where a smaller, less obvious door would allow her entrance.

With the key in her pocket.

Unless Iain or his man had had the locks changed. She smiled when the key turned and the door opened.

Hearing nothing that would indicate men were working inside, she stepped within and closed the door behind her. Even though she walked quietly towards the center of the huge building, her strides echoed in the cavernous space. Clare glanced around, remembering the changes, the renovations, that were planned to change this one empty place into a place of training, education and safety for as many young men, and young women in the other building, as they could fit.

Walking around the perimeter, she could hear their discussions as each person gave their opinions on what was necessary. Of how they could raise enough funds to support it as an ongoing project after she paid for the initial development. Peter and Georgina planning what the classrooms would need and how many teachers they would hire if they could. The tradesmen and women who would train the students in skills that would get the jobs giving their ideas of how and when that part of the plan would happen. The architects stammering over her constant demands for improvement of the plans. The solicitors patiently explaining how each change would delay the approvals, never realizing that someone else was actually doing that.

As she walked along, lost in the past, Clare noticed that the building had been cleaned out. No piles of trash or unused slats or other construction materials. There was no sign of any construction yet, but having heard Iain's plans and knowing how long he'd waited for these Clare knew it would begin sooner rather than later. The scratch of boots on the rough floor made her turn.

"I thought you might be here." Iain stood in the shadows near the door she'd entered. "You kept the key." He nodded at her hand. Clare still carried the key in her hand.

"Aye."

He took a few paces bringing him close to her. She held out the key to him and dropped it in his hand when he lifted his hand in front of him.

"I wondered if you'd resorted to a strategically twisted hair pin or two." He came closer.

"Do they actually work?"

"Aye, if one has learned how to do it." He glanced around the structure, and she noticed he was dressed just as he had been the day he stormed into her life—all in black now. No walking stick this time. No hat.

"And you know how?" Clare knew the answer

without him saying it. The glint in his eyes and the lift of that corner of his mouth told her he did and that he was good at it. She took in an uneven breath and knew she must leave. Leave this place. Leave him. The question was out before she could stop it. "When do you start…?"

"The preliminary work, the planning reports and the surveys have been done and submitted."

"Ah. The planning council meeting you mentioned."

She took one more look around and turned to leave. In a way it was better that her temple to Jonathan's memory and his legacy would not be here. Clare would build a school in his memory, but now it was more about her need to break from the lies she'd lived than to keep his, their, sainted memory.

"A lesser man might have been alarmed when the woman he loves runs, literally runs, from his declaration to her."

"Iain."

"Clare."

"Maybe if you told me what happened between you and the sainted Jonathan Logan, I would understand." She stared at his bold question. "All I have heard from everyone who knows you, from the reports Cairns… from reports and even gossip, speak of your devotion to each other, your absolute love for each other. That you gave up your world to be with him and the two of you had a marriage unlike anything in polite society."

All the lies she'd lived so easily exposed in his words. Oh, she knew Cairns gathered whatever information he could before Iain began his approach. Chalmers had done it for her, but apparently Iain protected his secrets with more vigor than she had. The stakes were so much higher for him, of course.

And yet, she could not say the words that would insult Jonathan. They had loved. They had done wonderful things to help the less fortunate. They had…

"None of this, none of my fight to keep these properties was actually done for him," she said. "I did it because of my guilt and failure." He looked askew at her, confusion in his eyes. "I told myself that he offered me everything I dreamt about as a lass—a man who valued my opinion, who loved me and wanted me as an equal partner in his life and in his business and charitable pursuits."

"And he did not?"

"It was all such a romantic dream, but nay, he wanted a well-bred wife who would know her place and take it. After the excitement of standing up to my father and feeling so very brave and powerful even, things changed. He changed. Well, if truth be told, I just did not see him—I saw what I wanted."

"Clare, you were young—"

"And foolish and headstrong and unwilling to accept that my marriage and my life was not what I'd left my family and society for. Once I'd thrown my life into a whirlwind of defiance and ultimatums, I could not admit it. And as I demanded he honor our partnership, he—"

"Began asserting his power."

"Aye. And using my money, an inheritance from my mother's mother that he took control of when we married. Oh, I did not mind, we'd planned it together and it was the beginning of our, his, fortune. I just did not expect him to take over all of it. Then the disagreements began. He began shutting me out."

"He made his gentleman's agreement with me." She nodded. "Does Caro know? Or Nairn?"

"I do not think so. Nairn might have known more because… well, Father and even Jonathan may have confided in him at the time." She sighed. "By the time of the accident and his death, we were estranged, even though I could never admit it. All because I was too stubborn to listen or realize I'd made a huge mistake."

"Then he died," he whispered. "And it was all yours."

"Aye. And everyone praised him and our efforts. And his memory and our love."

"So you kept up the charade."

"The work I carried on was not a charade. I want to help the less fortunate." She smiled then. "The plans I made were actually larger endeavors than he would ever agree to. But all to his credit. I could not admit I'd followed him and allowed what I thought was our mutual love to blind me." She shook off her melancholy. "So now you know that I turned my mistake into a shrine for my late husband."

He muttered something that sounded like one of the filthy epithets he'd taught her during that night. Then she realized the worst part was coming for her.

"I know that whatever happened between us was a manipulation, Iain. After you discovered who owned the property you were actually entitled to buy and she refused you, you ingratiated yourself into her family and business associates. You enticed them into helping you without them even knowing. So nothing that has happened between us is real or true."

"You are wrong, Clare. You knew exactly what I was doing."

"I did indeed and could not stay away." He preened for a moment, a purely male reaction to her admission.

"It may have begun as my plan, but it took less time than you think to go awry."

"How long?" she asked. "How long until I was a worthy adversary for you?"

He laughed then and she remembered how it felt to be in his embrace when he did that.

"I believe it took exactly three-and-one-half minutes after I pushed into your school and mistook you for a servant. It was not my last mistake or misjudgment of you, but it was the first one."

"I'm glad of that," she said. And she was. No matter that they would part, she knew he would remember something about her.

"And now?" He began walking towards the main entrance that opened onto the same street as his office, so she walked at his side. A hack would be easier to hail there than in the alley where she'd entered.

"You have what you should have had, and I am moving most of my endeavors back into Edinburgh. Leith harbor will be the new headquarters of the Buchanan & Sons empire. I will establish the school and training center, but just not here."

"Will you be content, Clare?" He faced her and watched her intently.

"I think so. I have accepted that we did good work, and I will continue to." She watched him then. "And I do wonder what a Caribbean island might be like. I think I might travel a bit more."

"I know some ships that travel there regularly and they have cabins for passengers, if you are interested."

As much as she longed for such a voyage, a clean parting was the only way. "I will keep that in mind."

They walked in silence until they reached the large

doors that were wide enough for wagons to come and go through. He reached to lift the bar to open one and stopped, turning to her and leaning against one of the doors.

"You were an obstacle until I fell kicking and screaming in love with you, Clare. What I said at your house, about being the last man for you? I meant that."

Words were hard to say as her eyes burned with tears and her throat tightened at his admission. She needed to get away from him, from the weakness she felt around him.

"I think it's best if we part as friends, Iain. Or at least—" she paused and swallowed several times against the need to cry. "As business associates."

"Do you think you could love me, Clare? In spite of what you know about me? In spite of knowing I will never truly change?"

"It does not matter—"

"Does not matter?" He took her hand and pulled her closer. "Love does not matter to you."

"Love matters. But I have been fooled by love before. I thought I was in love and it turns out I was simply infatuated." She tugged her hand free. "Please let me go. You have what you wanted."

"Do you love me, Clare?"

How could she deny it? She'd known what he was about and had still fallen in love with him. She would just say the words and escape. And move on, without him and all the complications.

"I do love you." She moved to push past him when he took hold of her shoulders and held her there.

"Good. That will make this all easier."

"What?"

"Come outside."

Iain lifted the bar and set it aside. He pushed the door, and it swung open.

He could only smile as she saw everyone waiting for them outside the warehouse. In addition to her staff from the school and his, Lord and Lady Nairn—Nairn and Caro they'd said to call them—and even the prickly but completely loyal Mrs. Hunter and most of those who worked in his office now stood assembled to watch what would either be his defining moment or utter humiliation. When he'd scoffed at Nairn's public antics, Iain had not understood the strength of love and what he would do for that love. Now though, now he did. With the help of most of the people here, he had done as he should have when she'd given up the deed. Cairns walked up and handed him the papers needed to finalize the deal of his life.

For he knew that whether she accepted his proposal or not, this property and the ones around it would allow her to finish what had been her dream. And that it would give her some peace at the guilt she felt about the decisions she'd made. The ones she thought were mistakes of her past. Iain had never felt so good about his ambitions being stymied.

"Clare, this is yours." He handed her the amended deed giving her full ownership to the four blocks behind them. "And these have been approved." The plans she'd made for the warehouses and additional ones that her solicitors and staff had created.

"What is this?" she asked, staring at the pile of papers in her hands.

"Full ownership of the properties and buildings you need to complete your plans."

That she was stunned pleased him. Nairn elbowed him then and Iain did what he'd sworn he would never do. Kneeling before her, he stared into her eyes, and he begged.

"I want to marry you, Clare. Will you marry me?"

Those gathered gasped and held their collective breath, as he did, waiting on her answer. Nairn nudged his shoulder, thankfully, because in his terror she would refuse him again, and in public, he'd forgotten the final contract. Sliding the folded sheet from his coat pocket, he held it out to her.

"What is this?" Opening it, she blinked and blinked.

"I would like this all to be your wedding gift, but if you accept my proposal, it will remain under your full control as part of our marriage contract." He swallowed. "But it is yours no matter what you decide."

He nodded at the very short agreement that would give her everything she already possessed and half of his. His solicitors had nearly fainted at his order to write it so, but luckily Cairns was made of sterner stuff than Brown was and accomplished it.

His stomach churned as he noticed the tears streaming down her cheeks. So, public embarrassment it was. The silence was becoming uncomfortable, and he heard Nairn cough and Caro whispered something.

"I will marry you, Iain."

The cheering happened before the words sank into his terror-ridden mind. Nairn pulled him to his feet and shoved him towards her. Someone threw flower petals, Mrs. Hunter he thought, and people clapped.

He could not stand another moment of not touching

her, so he wrapped his arms around her and kissed her, claiming her as his for the first time. Her cheeks blushed when he lifted his mouth from hers.

"We will do well together, I think."

"Do you not foresee any problems?" she asked in a teasing tone.

"Oh, I foresee many arguments followed by even more bouts of bedplay to make up for them."

"I think I would like that, Iain."

"We did not truly get to *unspeakable* in our previous efforts, but now we will have time for that." His body reacted to the fact that she would be his—every day and every night.

"I would like that as well. *Pleasurable* and *impolite* were quite nice."

"Nice?" he growled. "I do not do nice."

"I fear for society's survival now with such a daring earl among its members," she said as he released her at her sister's demand. "If they were shocked by Nairn's rather tame efforts, imagine what will happen when the new Earl of Ardgour begins misbehaving."

"As long as the new countess is at his side and misbehaving with him, he does not give a rat's arse what they think."

Iain watched as their friends and associates all greeted her warmly and understood why the act of kneeling before her had not been humbling but rather freeing. Nairn must have known his thoughts for he clapped Iain on the back.

"I told you it would work," the marquess said. "When you do it right."

If it ended with Clare being his, it was the right thing to do.

Now, all they needed to do was… he pushed aside all the arrangements and scheduling they would have to do to accomplish a wedding and moved to her side. If he truly was handling this the right way, he might be able to convince her to anticipate their vows with another sea voyage.

In the end, he needed little of his negotiating skills and just needed to point out the ship waiting at the dock with her name on it and she agreed.

In fact, by the time they married four weeks later, he'd enticed her through *pleasurable* and *impolite* and had made good headway into *unspeakable*. He just hoped he was strong enough to survive being the last man Clare would ever love.

EPILOGUE

Ardgour House
Lochaber, Scotland

Clare studied the surface of the loch as she waited. The sun peeked through the thick layer of clouds and skipped its way across Loch Linnhe, illuminating tiny ripples in the water. Although she loved living in the city, this place had become special to her since Iain had been granted his title and the lands attached to it.

There was more to the way the title had been granted but she was not certain if she should believe what he'd said or not. When he'd approached the Prince Regent in an attempt to accept the previous offer of a hereditary earldom, he told her that he'd jested he would take a title with lands attached over any seat in the House of Lords and so the Prince Regent accepted him at his word. Since his title was part of the Scottish peerage, unless named a "Lord of Parliament," he would not be seated. Considering his businesses, their businesses and their marriage, Clare was pleased when he'd refused that offer.

These last three weeks had been their first significant separation since their marriage a year before and she decided quickly that she did not like it. She preferred him close, in their house, in the office… and in her bed.

She missed him. She missed sleeping in his arms. She missed arguing with him over meals and missed making up from those arguments. Shaking her head at that admission, Clare moved from the windows and made her way to the entranceway to the large manor house to wait. Her efficient butler approached but a quick shake of her head sent him off to other duties.

She'd sent Peffers away in an attempt to prevent another embarrassing moment like the one that had happened when Iain had returned from a short visit to Glasgow. Not expecting him back so soon, she'd been in the drawing room that faced the mountains and did not realize he'd returned. One moment she was working on a report and the next, she was lying on the desk's surface with her skirts tossed up and her husband, so impatient that he'd not closed the door behind him, between her legs. Peffers had followed Iain in and by the time either of them noticed, the butler stood shocked and still with his rapidly blinking eyes as the only sign of life.

Clare laughed then, remembering how difficult it had been to face the man for days after that. Though he spoke not a word and gave no hint of what he'd witnessed, Clare knew. And she truly did not wish to repeat the situation, here in Ardgour House or at their house in Edinburgh or in her house that was now Samantha's. The door opening drew her attention back and her breath held in her chest at the sight of him.

He'd not changed before leaving the ship, so he stood before her looking like a pirate—trousers so tight they outlined the muscles of his thighs, a white shirt with the laces hanging and the neckline open exposing the wide expanse of his chest and his black hair hanging loose and windblown. Leather boots that reached his knees encased his lower legs. Her hands itched to touch him, to trace her finger along the muscles and to run her hands through his hair and grab hold and pull him to her.

He had done this to her. He had freed her from inhibitions and limitations and allowed, nay encouraged, her desire for him. And he refused her nothing, whether pleasurable, impolite, or downright unspeakable. No touch, no taste, no act of joining their flesh was forbidden between them. Any request was honored between them. Her body trembled in anticipation of what magic he would weave between them as he closed the door behind him and dropped his bag on the floor.

Each step he took closer sent her blood heating and racing through her. The place between her legs ached. Her mouth went dry and by the time he stood within reach, Clare was so breathless that she could not help but fall into his arms.

"Lady Clare." He wrapped his arms around her, holding her soft curves against his hard angles. "I have missed you." His mouth lowered to hers, he thrust his tongue in, tasting her deeply. Clare raised her hands and slid them into his hair, clutching him and keeping his mouth on hers. He lifted his head and met her gaze. "Are you well?"

His hand slid down to cover her belly as he studied her face. Resting it there, he spread his fingers until they lay over the small but expanding bump. She released his hair and reached down to cover his hand with hers.

"I am well, my love," she whispered. A hint of wonder filled her voice, for this was something she never thought she would experience. Each previous pregnancy had ended by this time, so Iain had convinced her to have a little hope. The slight movement under their hands, like the touch of a fluttering of wings within her, made her smile. "We are well."

He laughed as he bent over and scooped her into his arms. Walking through the entryway to the grand staircase, he did not pause in carrying her up to their private apartments on the second floor. Someone had left the door ajar, and he did not pause as he opened it with his shoulder, swinging her carefully through, and then kicking the door closed.

He tossed her on the bed, taking a bit of care in his handling of her now, and watched as she slid back against the pile of pillows in front of the elaborate carved headboard.

"How were the seas?" she asked. Clare would not get many questions answered before he joined her in their bed, so she asked another. "And your business in Glasgow?"

He tugged the shirt over his head and threw it onto the floor near the foot of the bed. "You should join me in Glasgow next time, love. The building is next to the shipyard and it is magnificent to see." He sat on the bench at the end of the bed and loosened his boots before working them down and off. "The seas were challenging. We ran into a storm coming back from Glasgow as we approached Oban and the loch. The winds were strong enough to blow us out past Mull, but we were able to steer into it and to the calm of the loch."

He was aroused, aye, and still excited by the physical struggle against the storm and their success in bringing their ship through it. Clare understood this about him— she'd learned it when he'd revealed the lower level of

The Cock's Spur and its activities in that month before their wedding.

When she watched him fight, bare-knuckled and barefooted, stripped down to his trousers, she was paralyzed with fear and anxiety seeing this Iain Buchanan, or rather Freddie Dubh in action. The façade torn away, the true man underneath was exposed in all his brutal, ruthless glory. And that was even more frightening.

Then her emotional reaction when he won his fight was a mix of arousal and terror and anger. She'd cried first, then swung at him, slamming her palms against his chest inconsequentially until her hands ached. Iain did not stop her. The passion that overwhelmed her did not seem to surprise him, and he allowed and then encouraged her to express it. And she did—ravaging his mouth until he carried her upstairs to a private chamber where she took the rest of him. It took some time to work the terror and excitement out of her body and soul.

Iain had that same expression in his eyes now as he made his way around the bed and stood staring at her with open desire and what she knew now was love. He let out a ragged breath as he spoke.

"Do you like that gown?" he asked. She could only nod. "Then take it off before I rip it from your body."

Clare decided the gown was expendable and opened her arms to him. And he did exactly as he'd said, the fabric standing no chance against his intentions or his strength.

It took several bouts to calm both of their sensibilities that afternoon. They remained abed, their caresses more soothing then than arousing and this was the time Clare truly enjoyed with him.

"You will be able to travel in the morning?" he asked,

his hand resting on her belly again. When he'd left her morning symptoms were at their worst, so she understood his concern.

"Aye." She traced the outline of his larger hand with a finger. "Most of it has eased."

"So, you can travel by boat?" He lifted his head and leaned up on his elbow. "Or would a coach be better?" She had the feeling if she told him it would be easier to travel by warship back to Edinburgh he would make it happen. He reached up to cup her cheek. "Which would be easier, love?"

"The canals are smooth enough. And I could not miss the opening." The celebration to mark the opening of the new school was at week's end and they needed to make their way back to Leith.

"I would guess that doubled over and heaving would not keep you away," he said, laughing. He sat up next to her and she felt the loss of his touch. "I do not blame you at all." She laughed at his words, for she would be at the opening no matter her condition or the weather. "I will make certain you are there even if I have to carry you to the school and hold you up to stand."

The tears flowed before she knew it, trickling down her cheeks. Iain rubbed his thumbs across her face, wiping some of them away.

"Are these those tears of joy that women always speak about?" He kissed her tenderly. "You are happy, are you not, Clare?"

The vulnerability in his voice surprised her. Though he never showed this to anyone else, he'd revealed his own fears and desires to her. And even his guilt.

"I am very happy, Iain. Thrilled even, considering that my dreams are coming true when I did not think it was possible."

"And… ." He did not finish the words.

"Aye, my love. I am happy in our marriage, too."

He had asked her this before and her answer was the same. After he'd displayed an honesty she had not thought possible and told her details of his life, his businesses and his plans, he had offered her a way out of their unorthodox marriage contract. For a man used to getting his way by use of any means, neither she nor her solicitor could believe it. Nor, from their expressions, could his advisors.

In the four hours of that meeting, he had answered every question and explained the inner workings of his companies to her. And then he'd dismissed all of the others and spoke to her privately. His offer to allow her to walk away, while keeping ownership of the property she'd signed over to him along with the other buildings and land he'd added, had stunned the breath from her. But she did want to marry him, and it had nothing to do with the offered contract and properties. He'd proven himself to her and that mattered not.

Clearly though, he still had doubts.

Those doubts were based on his own way of accomplishing things in his life and manipulation was his strongest tool. He'd used it on her early on, but when he'd laid bare all his enterprises and plans, he'd made that weapon useless against her.

"I am happy, Iain. I was intent on never marrying again. You know that," she said. He nodded. "And though it would be easy to say that I married you to get those properties, as you'd planned to do with me, I can say I married you for love."

Iain leaned down and kissed her.

"So, it was not my indecent wealth?"

"Nay." He kissed her again.

"Or for my illustrious new title?"

"Nay, Iain."

"Nor for the unspeakable sexual pleasures I have introduced you to?" His eyebrows waggled then and she laughed. When unspeakable sexual pleasures were involved, his expression was one of intention and concentration. She did not answer quickly enough, so he possessed her mouth and tasted her deeply. "I knew it was for my body and the pleasure I bring you!"

"Well," she whispered against his lips. "There is that."

His appetite for her was relentless and some hours had passed before they finally left their chamber to eat supper in the smaller dining room. Later, in the dark of night, when they again lay entangled in their bed, Clare told Iain why she loved him.

"Iain, I married you because you have used your ambition to make my dreams come true. And I love you because I mattered enough to you to make that happen when it would have been easier for you to walk away."

He rolled to his side and gathered her close, sliding his arms around her with his hand resting on her belly and the unexpected, impossible bairn growing within her. They fell asleep like this nigh on every night now.

Oh, Clare could have made vague emotional explanations and declarations, but she knew that he had a clearer, black or white, way of looking at life… and love. Explaining it as a transaction, a quid pro quo, made it easier for him to accept what he could only see as a weakness in himself.

But she knew the truth of it—she loved him because he was the first man to see her. And though their first encounters were not the most pleasant, and their confrontations were volatile, he never treated her as anything other than a serious opponent, worthy of respect. That respect and his bold attentions made her believe she could do anything.

And she would love him forever for making her feel that way.

Meet Terri Brisbin

RWA RITA®-nominated, award-winning and *USA Today* best-selling author **Terri Brisbin** is a mom, a wife, grandmom(!) and a dental hygienist who has sold more than 3.5 million copies of her historical and paranormal romance novels and novellas in more than 25 countries and 20 languages. Her current and upcoming historical and paranormal/fantasy romances are published by Harlequin Historicals, Oliver Heber Books and independently, too.

Visit her website for more info about Terri, her works and upcoming events.

Connect with her on
Facebook @TerriBrisbinAuthor
X (Twitter) @Terri_Brisbin
Instagram @TerriBrisbin

TerriBrisbin.com

Author's Note

Dear Readers,

I hope you've enjoyed this story set in Regency Edinburgh and Leith. Many Regency-era fans are quite familiar with the customs of that time period—things like balls and courting and marriages with those prized "special licenses." But many of those customs are only applicable in England and Wales. Though Scotland joined with England and Wales in 1707, they had different laws and educational systems (including their universities), better medicine practices and education and so on. So pretty much everything readers (and fans of *Bridgerton*) know is based on England.

When writing this story, I fell into that situation several times and had to go back and re-research the subjects of Scottish marriage laws, property rights of married women, business law and more. We all know about Gretna Green where couples from England could marry without posting banns, etc. but that applied to ALL of Scotland! So, no special license was required to marry quickly – all you needed was two witnesses and a declaration of the man and woman that they were married! (Yes, those "irregular" marriages could be registered but that's another story!)

Another area of huge differences was the peerage or noble titles. Those in the Scottish peerage had different "rules" than the English ones did. Just having a noble title in Scotland did not give the person the privilege of being summoned or seated in the House of Lords of Parliament. So, though the King of England (or the Prince Regent during that time) granted titles and privileges, Scottish peers needed to be named as a Lord of Parliament for them to serve in Parliament. Then, as now, England controlled Parliament and this was one way the Scots were held to fewer seats.

When it came to granting Iain Buchanan a title with lands, I needed those lands to be in a certain area—close to shipping lanes (and water), a bit away from Glasgow and towards the Hebrides, etc. Working with my maps and books, I discovered Ardgour at the northern end of Loch Linnhe. It was perfect for me, for what I needed and for what Iain required, too. So, Iain was granted the Earldom of Ardgour.

In reality, the area of Ardgour has belonged to the powerful Maclean clan, the Lord of the Isles, whose seat was at Duart Castle on the Isle of Mull. Though the Macleans eventually lost much of their land to the Campbell Earl of Argyll in the late 1700s, Ardgour remained a Maclean holding. Even to this day, the lands of Ardgour are managed by the Macleans of Ardgour. Since there never was an Earl of Ardgour, I created one for my story because once Iain Buchanan knew about the area, he wanted it… and it was impossible to say no to him.

Now, I'm on to researching about the universities of Scotland and professors for book three – THE LADY'S TUTOR and its hero Professor Gill MacIvor. You met him briefly in book one – THE LADY TAKES IT ALL – but he'll be back in the next book.

Happy Reading,

Terri B